What people are saying about …

A HEARTBEAT AWAY

"A transplanted heart comes with a double dose of nightmares for its recipient and is the catalyst for danger, romance, and lives forever changed. Riveting and poignant with breath-catching twists, surgeon Harry Kraus offers masterful storytelling and 'grace from the cutting edge.' A perfectly prescribed read!"

Candace Calvert, author of ECPA best seller *Code Triage* and *Trauma Plan*

"*A Heartbeat Away* is a medical thriller brimming with suspense, mind-blowing twists, romance, and a spiritual message that reaches deep into the soul. Harry Kraus has masterfully crafted another dynamic story. Highly recommended!"

Mark Mynheir, retired homicide detective and author of *The Corruptible*

"An intriguing, fast-paced, compelling story that had me glued to the pages and raises the question, can we pass along the essence of who we are? Can you change someone's eternity from beyond the grave? Fascinating medical questions with a riveting plot. Highly recommended!"

Susan May Warren, award-winning, best-selling author of *You Don't Know Me*

"Harry Kraus knows how to put a reader's heart through the ringer. Fast-paced, suspenseful, and emotional, *A Heartbeat Away* kept me reading late into the night, eager to know where Tori Taylor's new heart would lead her. This one's a keeper!"

"Writing with the authority of a physician, Harry Kraus takes us inside the world of medicine to meet a surgeon who needs a heart transplant … in more ways than one. This is, without a doubt, Dr. Kraus's best novel yet."

"Harry Kraus is as skilled with a pen as he is with a scalpel. *A Heartbeat Away* is a compelling, page-turning story that surprised me at every turn. And it is ultimately a beautiful picture of the depths of the human heart when God is allowed to reside there."

"I don't normally read medical suspense novels. But I read this one. And once I started, I couldn't stop. *A Heartbeat Away* is a great read. It has everything I want in a book. And it's based on a premise I've never heard of and found utterly fascinating. Do yourself a favor, get this book!"

A HEARTBEAT
AWAY

A HEARTBEAT AWAY

a novel

HARRY KRAUS

David C Cook®

transforming lives together

A HEARTBEAT AWAY
Published by David C Cook
4050 Lee Vance View
Colorado Springs, CO 80918 U.S.A.

David C Cook Distribution Canada
55 Woodslee Avenue, Paris, Ontario, Canada N3L 3E5

David C Cook U.K., Kingsway Communications
Eastbourne, East Sussex BN23 6NT, England

The graphic circle C logo is a registered trademark of David C Cook.

This story is a work of fiction. Characters and events are the product of the author's
imagination. Any resemblance to any person, living or dead, is coincidental.

The Scripture quotation in the epigraph is taken from The Holy Bible,
English Standard Version® (ESV®), copyright © 2001 by Crossway, a
publishing ministry of Good News Publishers. Used by permission. All
rights reserved. Other Scripture quotations are taken from the Holy Bible,
New International Version®, NIV®. Copyright © 1973, 2011 by Biblica,
Inc.™ Used by permission of Zondervan. All rights reserved worldwide.
www.zondervan.com; and THE MESSAGE. Copyright © by Eugene H.
Peterson 1993, 2002. Used by permission of NavPress Publishing Group.

LCCN 2012941318
ISBN 978-1-4347-0257-9
eISBN 978-1-4347-0511-2

© 2012 Harry Kraus
Published in association with Natasha Kern Literary Agency,
PO Box 1069, White Salmon, WA 98672.

The Team: Don Pape, Dave Lambert, Amy Konyndyk, Jack Campbell, Karen Athen
Cover Design: Nick Lee
Cover Photos: iStockphoto (couple); Shutterstock (eye); stock.xchng (fire)

Printed in the United States of America
First Edition 2012

1 2 3 4 5 6 7 8 9 10

062912

Dedicated with love to my mom,
Mildred Brunk Kraus
August 26, 1926–May 8, 2011

ACKNOWLEDGMENTS

Special thanks to Mark Mynheir, friend, novelist, and former homicide detective, who assisted me with police matters.

I will give you a new heart, and a new spirit I will
put within you. And I will remove the heart of stone
from your flesh and give you a heart of flesh.

Ezekiel 36:26

1

Between the gods and men.

Are surgeons.

That's the way Victoria "Tori" Anne Taylor, MD, always explained it to the sea of gaping medical-student faces as they prepared to begin their clinical rotations. She would pause for effect after the word *men*, turning one sentence into two and solidifying her own near-godlike status among the students who may have been book smart but didn't know a normal S-2 heart sound from the bass rhythms throbbing through their iPod earbuds.

Tori looked around the busy anesthetia holding area and reviewed the operation, going over every step, imagining each movement as a choreographed symphony of dissection. She'd once heard that the best professional baseball hitters did the same thing as they stood on deck, just before entering the batter's box. They saw the windup, the delivery, and the anticipated trajectory of the fastball, knee-high, just painting the inside corner of the plate. They saw their swing and the bat impacting the ball. Imagination led to success. Hitters who could see what would happen before it happened were the ones the fans adored.

And so it was with oncology surgeon Tori Taylor. Her operations were a thing of beauty, her even rows of sutures lining up like little soldiers on a Civil War battlefield. Predictably, home runs for Dr. Taylor were the norm. And behind her mask, she enjoyed the students' worship.

But today was different.

Today the operation she imagined was not going to be performed *by* her; it was going to be performed *on* her. The mental review of her surgery was her way of coping, a vain attempt, a desperate grasping at something she was loath to give up: control.

Illness had changed everything. No longer was she wearing the stethoscope; it was being gently laid over her sternum. And the eyes that couldn't hide concern were not hers but the eyes of her surgeon. The blade of the scalpel pointed toward her, not away. Up was down. In was out. Black was white, and control was a mirage, a wavering image floating above the minds of lost desert nomads or surgeons who thought they could predict outcomes because of their obsessive grip around everything manageable.

She'd lost control.

And that terrified her.

The face of a nurse appeared over her. Tori had seen this particular nurse a thousand times during her own tenure as a cancer surgeon, but, like all of the others, he was a background person, a nameless helper in orbit around her.

But today was different. She wanted—no, she *needed* to know the nurse's name. She strained to lean forward, gripping the railings of the stretcher, and grunted. She attempted to focus on his name tag. Her voice was as weak as she felt, barely a whisper. "Jeff."

"Don't try to talk now, Dr. Taylor. They should be coming to get you soon. Dr. Parrish is closing on the case in front of you."

That "case" has a name, she thought. Tori closed her eyes, annoyed but understanding. The nurse wasn't allowed to mention a name.

"Don't be afraid," the nurse continued. "Dr. Parrish is the best."

Do I look afraid? I'm not afraid!

Fear, Tori thought, was another needless emotion. She prided herself on operating on a higher plane than those mortals who struggled with the baggage of feelings. Emotions interfered with her ability to make tough decisions. When your enemy was cancer, being touchy-feely paralyzed your ability to cure. *My enemy has no feelings. Cancer attacks without respect to beauty, form, or function. In order to win, a surgeon must match her foe.*

She watched the staff scurry about, activities that Tori would have participated in just a few months ago without thinking. Hanging an IV, walking from bed to bed checking vital signs, pushing a stretcher. These were the mundane and unappreciated acts made possible by a functioning and efficient heart—something she no longer had.

As the staff cast furtive glances in her direction, Tori recognized contempt in some, pity in others. Their eyes sent the message: *Oh, how the mighty have fallen.* She may have stepped on them, reprimanding inefficiency, ineptitude—or worse, laziness—in this field where the stakes were health or illness, life or death. But now the tables were turned. She lay dying, her heart whimpering with each beat.

She heard low murmurings from beyond the curtain. The staff didn't seem to know what to do. It's neither professional nor personally satisfying to gloat over the dying.

Her heart had been ravaged by an evil lover of sorts, a virus that followed a cold-like illness, something Tori had pushed through, taking Tylenol and Sudafed until she just became so *weak*. At first, she'd just thought she had been pushing too hard, working late, performing too many operations in spite of the flu.

Later, she had awakened one night breathless and sat up gasping for air that suddenly seemed too thin to satisfy. She coughed frothy sputum into a Kleenex and stared down at her bare feet. *Where did my ankles go?* Extra fluid had taken up residence in her lungs and formerly shapely legs. Tori picked up her phone and dialed 911, explaining to the rescue squad that she was in acute heart failure. She demanded and received morphine, oxygen, and Lasix. Control.

Her heart-lover had a name: coxsackievirus B. It embraced the muscle layer of her heart with a savage jealousy, inflaming the muscle into submission and weakness. Regular medications improved things a little, chasing bully symptoms off the playground for a few hours, but then they would return and remind her to take the tablets that made life's menial tasks possible.

But medicine could not provide a cure. Only surgery could do that. Only the transplantation of a new heart could cure.

Ironic, Tori thought, *that a surgeon can only be cured with the knife*. Finally, the woman who had not had so much as a childhood tonsillectomy would be submitted to the same controlled violence that she had inflicted on thousands of others.

Another face appeared above her, a female of about fifty-five with short, cropped gray hair and a no-nonsense demeanor. She turned to face a mobile computer monitor. "I'll need you to verify your identification," she said. She lifted Tori's arm and studied her wristband.

"Victoria Anne Taylor," she whispered, rolling her eyes. *Protocol.*

"And what operation are you having today?"

"Heart transplant."

The nurse entered the data, clicking boxes on the computer screen. A moment later, her face appeared again. This time she was holding a small electric hair trimmer. "I have to prepare the operative field."

Tori shook her head. "I don't have any hair on my chest."

"Just routine," the nurse responded, lifting and pushing Tori's gown up under her chin.

The nurse studied Tori's chest for a moment before lowering the gown again, but not before Tori's eyes met those of a passing orderly who seemed to be enjoying a quick peek at Tori's ample anatomy.

Tori shook her head. "You should have pulled the curtain."

"Dr. Taylor," the nurse responded, "you've never cared much about that before." She offered a plastic smile. "It's only business."

Tori winced. She must have slighted this nurse a time or two in the past. Or maybe a hundred times or two. *How petty. A taste of my own medicine.*

The nurse studied Tori's face. "You'll need to be aware of the pain scale," she said. "In recovery, the nurses will want you to rate your pain on a scale of one to ten. One is a slight annoyance. Ten is the worst agony you've ever felt."

"I understand."

"Who will be waiting for word from Dr. Parrish when the operation is over? Parents?"

Tori shook her head and spoke with effort but not emotion. "My parents are dead."

The skin around the nurse's lips tightened, highlighting a series of wrinkles like little spokes radiating from the hub of a wheel. "A friend, perhaps?"

She stayed quiet and shook her head.

"Husband?"

"There is no one."

"Would you like the chaplain to come by before you go into surgery? He can offer prayer—"

"No thanks."

The nurse walked away, but not before noisily pulling the curtain to shield Tori from the clinical traffic.

Tori closed her eyes and adjusted the prongs of the oxygen tubing, seating them more comfortably in her nose. She made an attempt to look at her situation objectively. What exactly should she think about as someone was preparing to lift out her damaged heart?

Her first thought struck her as overly sentimental. *Someone had to die last night. A life cut short so that I can continue mine.*

Whose heart will be beating in my chest? What was her life like? Was she a professional like me?

What will it feel like knowing my heart spent years pumping someone else's blood?

She heard the curtain rings sing against the rod again. *Probably the protocol nurse.* Instead, when she opened her eyes, she saw Jarrod Baker, a radiation oncologist.

Six months ago, the hospital grapevine had proclaimed that Jarrod and Tori were an "item." They had been, in fact, the ultimate medical power couple, gracing the social network, each with his and her own ties to the movers and shakers within the university. Professionally, they matched, their fields a natural complement. He killed cancer with radiation beams; she wielded a scalpel in the same battle.

They'd shared meals and movies, walks in the park, and racquetball. But Jarrod had wanted more from their relationship. For a while, he had pursued her. He did not seem to mind that others spoke of Tori as the "ice princess." For Jarrod, it seemed he had struck gold: benefits without all the emotional baggage.

Tori was only mildly annoyed at his persistence—a number one on the pain scale. For Tori, their relationship was detached convenience. She was expected to date. Jarrod fit the bill.

Was she so used to steeling herself against the baggage of negative emotions that threatened her professional decisions that she'd been unable to unwrap her heart?

But a month ago, Jarrod had stopped calling. As they'd both prided themselves in being above emotion, Tori's illness created the elephant in the room that kept them from moving forward. She didn't ask for empathy, and apparently, he was unprepared to help her face the looming grim reaper.

The hospital grapevine told her he'd moved on. There was an emotional respiratory therapist named Tami who'd just joined the staff. She cried at movies and dotted the *i* in her name with a heart. Sweet.

Tori watched his eyes widen as he assessed her new clinical situation.

"Do I look that bad?"

He shook his head. "No, no," he stuttered. "You look great." He paused, looking at the monitor and not at her. "It's your big day. I heard the residents say a heart was available."

She felt him take her hand. She looked away.

"Tori," he began. "I'm so sorry—"

She silenced him with a squeeze of the hand.

"I should have called." He hesitated, seemingly unable to meet her eyes. "I didn't know what to say."

Ironic, she thought, *a man who deals with death in his clinical practice doesn't know how to deal with personal loss.*

She watched as he rubbed out a few wrinkles on the cotton sheet. "Your guilt doesn't help." She paused. "I would have pushed you away anyhow. It's the way we're wired."

"I'm supposed to be here giving you support."

"I'll be fine."

He nodded. "Yeah, Tori, you always are."

She let the comment pass. She was just too tired.

He shuffled his feet. She could see he wanted to say more. He didn't. Finally, he just gave her hand a squeeze and said, "Your clinic nurse is outside."

That brought a smile to Tori's face. "Thanks for coming by."

He nodded again and slipped away, pulling back the curtain to allow Brittney Simms to enter. Although Tori was demanding of Brittney, the outpatient setting allowed Tori to step down a notch, and her relationship with Brittney was strong, built on years of teamwork.

Brittney smiled and wiped the corner of her eyes with the back of her hand. "Hi, Doc."

"Hey, no cryin' here. This is the best day of my new life."

The nurse pushed a rebellious strand of red hair behind her ear and nodded. "I know." She held out a large envelope. "It's from the patients in the clinic. I've been collecting comments, knowing this day would come."

Tori slipped the card from the envelope. A seascape decorated the cover. Inside, it simply said, "Wishing you a rapid recovery." There were comments from at least thirty patients.

She read over the names. It read like a who's who of patients in major abdominal surgery. Mr. Jones had a Whipple resection, a delicate and detailed removal of the head of the pancreas and the duodenum. Charles Smith had an extended right hepatectomy, a removal of two-thirds of his liver for cancer. Melody Jane had her rectum removed. Paige Withersby had a thyroidectomy.

Brittney smiled. "These patients would be dead without you."

"Don't be melodramatic, Brittney. They'd have found another surgeon."

She shook her head. "Not a better one."

Tori handed back the card. "Keep it for me. I want to read the comments after my surgery."

An orderly appeared, pulling back the curtain. "Showtime," he said.

Tori looked at him and frowned, motioning him closer. When his ear was within a foot of her mouth, Tori exploded in an emphatic whisper. "Don't ever say that again! This isn't a show. This is my life we're talking about."

The orderly, a college-age boy with blond hair and a bad case of acne, backpedaled. "S-sorry. I didn't mean anything by it."

Brittney stepped forward. "Don't worry about it. I've heard her say the same thing."

Tori shook her head. "That was before."

The orderly cleared his throat. "It's time." He transferred her oxygen supply to a portable tank and lifted her IV fluid to a pole attached to the bed. "Let's go."

Brittney brushed back another tear.

"Don't cry," Tori said.

"I'll be praying for you."

Tori nodded. "Thanks."

The distance to the OR must have been less than fifty feet, but it could as well have been fifty miles. Tori reviewed her life, her education, her career, and decided it would be okay to die.

The orderly pushed her past an elderly gentleman pushing a wide cotton floor duster. She reached for the orderly's sleeve. "Stop."

He hesitated as she motioned the older man with the mop to come forward. When their eyes met, she said only two words. "I'm sorry."

He nodded. They'd reached an understanding.

Six months before, Dr. Taylor was leading clinical rounds in the ICU, teaching, probing the residents' knowledge, lecturing on subjects as they came up in discussing the patients' conditions. There must have been a dozen or so following her. Her chief resident, two other surgery residents, two interns, four students, as well as a collection of the ICU nursing staff. Dr. Tori Taylor was in the spotlight. Bright. Smart. And to the resident staff, just short of divine.

They came upon a patient, an elderly man having a gastrointestinal bleed. He'd just had another black stool, the specimen deposited in a bedpan that he'd pushed aside. The specimen was still fresh and the characteristic sour odor unmistakable. Dr. Taylor wanted to continue rounds, but the smell was overpowering. She lifted the bedpan and called to a member of the environmental services staff, an elderly man passing by at just that moment. "Could you take care of this?"

The uniformed man shook his head and wrinkled his nose. "That's not in my job description."

His attitude infuriated the surgeon. "And just what is your job description?"

The man shrugged. "I mop the floors."

Tori Taylor didn't hesitate. She held the bedpan out at arm's length and turned it upside down, plopping the contents onto the floor. "Now it's in your job description."

The incident caused quite a stir. Environmental services demanded an apology. Dr. Taylor refused. Apologies were for the weak. The story was circulated among the surgical house staff, ballooning Dr. Taylor's reputation. She wouldn't take anything from anybody.

Now, seeing that same member of the environmental staff, she had at last offered that apology, as a result of a twinge of a new emotion: guilt. She squinted to read his name. "Darryl." She lifted her hand in a weak wave. She hadn't even known his name.

The orderly edged the stretcher forward toward a set of double swinging doors that led to the operating rooms. "This is as far as I go," he said.

Quickly a team of masked men and women, their outfits complete with scrubs, hats, and shoe covers, surrounded her. She thought she recognized Dr. Parrish, the lead transplant surgeon. He pointed to the portable cardiac monitor. "When did she start that?"

Tori tried to concentrate on the blipping neon line on the monitor, but the rate was too fast. She started to feel faint. Breathing was more and more difficult.

She listened to the urgent voice of her surgeon. "She's in V tach! We need to get this patient on bypass. Now!"

She felt a fluttering in her chest. She knew exactly what her surgeon referred to. Ventricular tachycardia. She lifted her fingers to her neck, doing her own self-assessment. She touched Dr. Parrish's arm. "Don't rush," she said. "I've still got a pulse."

Her comment didn't erase the strain from his face. "I get that, Tori, but I don't need to tell you that this isn't a particularly good sign. Your heart doesn't seem to want to last another hour."

"I'll hang on," she whispered.

Her surgeon didn't respond. Her statement didn't appear to encourage him. The pace of activity around her accelerated.

The ceiling tiles blurred as she was wheeled quickly into an expansive operating suite. She studied the masked figures, guardians of the sterile fields of instruments lying ready for use. Someone pushed a mask over her mouth and nose.

A voice from somewhere else. "Take a deep breath. Pure oxygen."

In the final minutes leading up to her surgery, a flight of images from her past pushed away the noise of preparation. She closed her eyes and tried not to think, but faces of the young men who had pursued her, wanted her, but whom she'd set aside in her professional quest, flitted past, floating on a sea of regret.

I haven't loved.

The thought assaulted her. She opened her eyes, hoping to erase her unwelcome guests.

I should think about all the people I've helped through their hours of need. Think about victories over cancer, parents who will live to see their children graduate, wives who have beaten breast cancers to celebrate anniversaries, and grandfathers who will attend another season of Little League baseball.

But her trophies felt hollow against her own failure to find love.

Someone lifted her blankets. She was cold. Exposed. A nurse began painting her chest with an antiseptic.

I'm still awake!

But nothing changed. Everyone continued as if she hadn't spoken. *Stop! I'm awake.*

Can they even hear me?

She followed a scurry of excitement with her eyes, straining to see around the mask and the hand that squeezed it against her lips. A member of the donor team had entered the room. She caught a glimpse of a woman in scrubs, arms chest high, holding something in a stainless-steel basin.

"Delivery," she said, as if someone had ordered pizza. She held the basin holding the mound of red-brown tissue toward a nurse still guarding the back table.

"Accepting delivery of donor heart."

Another female voice announced the time. "9:05."

Tori managed to twist her head to see. Everything around her seemed to slow. It was only a few seconds, but the weight of the moment focused the event with a clarity Tori had never experienced. In that surreal instant, she envisioned the intersection of two lives filled with emotions, love, pain, and relationships. Two paths converged into one. From birth to the present moment, she imagined her life and the life of her donor as two lines at warp speed, surging toward this one fixed point. With time compressed, the sounds of a lifetime of experience zipped along like an audio file played at fast-forward. *My new heart!* As the two lines intersected to become one, a bright light appeared.

Someone touched her eyelids, forcing them to stay open as a light flashed to check her pupils, and turned her face away from the back table. She felt something cool against her eyes as the anesthesiologist spread a protective ointment across their surface. She tried to blink. She understood what was happening. *Taping my eyes shut for protection.*

She attempted to lift her hand. She wanted them to know.

She met a restraint. *I'm still—*

Tori attempted to scream but made it only to the second word before a blissful coma descended.

2

There is a place of twilight between the coma of anesthesia and the first moments of awareness where the defenses are lowered. Memories bubble to the surface and are freed like carbonation seeking escape from the top of a cold soda. For Tori Taylor, it was a place of terror, a place where thoughts spurred by prior pain fought for recognition through a haze of sedatives and painkillers.

I'm burning. My arm is on fire.

Smoke chokes me. I spit and gasp, falling to my knees to crawl away from the yellow hell in the next room.

I listen as human screams fight to be heard above the roar of flames. I cannot breathe.

The demon man is calling out for help, but I cannot save him, for I have sent him to the hell where he belongs.

"Don't fight, Tori, you're in the ICU. Your surgery is all over."

A blurry image floated above her head. A face, a nurse with a soothing voice. Tori wanted to tell her about the fire, but she could not speak.

The face above hers was female. Young, maybe twenty-five, brown hair cut short, the wash-and-go practical cut of a professional. Green eyes sparkled, gems set in ivory sclera.

Why does she look familiar?

"Tori, don't try to speak. There is a tube in your windpipe."

You can say trachea. I'm a surgeon.

Tori tried to reach for the tube. She needed to pull it out. It seemed to make breathing more difficult. Her hand wouldn't move. Restraints bound her wrists. *I must have tried this before.*

"Don't fight the machine. Breathe with it."

Tori shook her head. She looked over her left shoulder. A monitor revealed the regular blips, a neon-green stripe dancing to a rhythm across the screen. *My new heart.*

"I'm giving you something to ease your mind, to help you breathe with the ventilator."

No, I don't want to dream!

Tori watched the young woman adjusting an IV drip.

She began to float. The fire returned. Thick smoke blurred her vision.

Someone called to her. A man.

An evil man who was burning.

Darkness.

"Take this," she cried. A female face appeared above her. Short hair. Beautiful green eyes. She shoved a paper into Tori's hand. Tori looked at it. In block letters was a number: 316. "Memorize it." She paused. "It's the proof. I want to make that bastard pay."

She heard a scream. Tori concentrated on the number. Of course she could remember. It was only one number.

Blackness. Pain.

A man's voice. He sounded strong. *Dr. Parrish?*

"Is she off pressors?"

The second voice sounded young, a voice she recognized as a resident she helped train. "Only on enough dopamine to tickle her kidneys, not enough to squeeze her heart." Tori watched as the young man pointed toward a pressure readout. 126/80. "She's doing that on her own."

"Excellent." A pause. "Can we get her off this ventilator?"

The resident surgeon, Dr. Joel Thomas, leaned over Tori's face. "Dr. Taylor, can you lift your head for me?"

Tori lifted her head from the pillow but not before she felt a stinging sensation spreading across her chest.

"Good, good. Call respiratory. Let's set up an oxygen mask."

A few minutes later, the resident physician removed the tape securing Tori's endotracheal tube to her cheeks. "Cough," he said. When she obeyed, he pulled out the tube with one swift motion.

As they positioned an oxygen mask over her face, the memory of the horrible dream lingered. Was it only a nightmare?

Dr. Parrish smiled at Tori. "Victoria, you really gave us a scare. It looks like you got a new heart just as your old one gave out." He shook his head. "Timing is everything."

She nodded without speaking. Someone had died so she could live. A few moments later, she managed a whisper. "What day is this?"

"Monday."

"No." She closed her eyes in disbelief. She'd lost three days.

She took inventory. In spite of having a new pump, minor things like shifting around on her hospital bed or lifting her head seemed to exhaust her. The past few months had wreaked havoc on her muscle tone and endurance. Six months ago, she would have enjoyed a six-mile run through the Richmond suburbs. Now, she found herself winded at the thought of taking one step.

With her restraints off, she started her own assessment. She lifted her left arm to see an arterial line exiting her wrist. She felt her upper chest. There she found another IV, something she'd placed many times herself, a central line that led directly into the large vein above her new heart.

She remembered the message and the paper that had been shoved into her hand. She lifted it.

The paper was gone.

Over the next few hours, she drifted in and out of sleep, each time returning to the same horrible dream of fire and pain. When she awoke again, a nurse was standing at the bedside recording something on a keyboard. She recognized the face but didn't know her name.

"Well, Dr. Taylor," the young nurse said, "it's nice to see you awake."

"Something burned my arm. Fire."

The nurse leaned forward, frowning. She quickly looked over Tori's wrist, lifting it from the bed. "Your arm looks fine to me." She ran her fingers over Tori's upper arm. "What's this? A skin graft?"

Tori nodded. "I burned myself on the muffler of a dirt bike when I was very young." She paused, thinking. "I don't even remember it."

The nurse nodded. "Well, you're not burning now."

"I remember a fire. My arm was burning."

The nurse's eyes widened. "Oh, you were on propofol for sedation. Many patients say it burns when it goes in. I'm sure that's all it was."

Tori shook her head but wasn't ready to argue with the nurse. The experience, be it a dream or a memory or simply a distorted hallucination from all the drugs, *seemed* real.

Someone had died in a fire. Someone who meant to do Tori harm.

"Whose heart do I have?"

The nurse, a twentysomething with short hair and green eyes, smiled. "I have no idea. That information is strictly confidential."

"Certainly you heard something." Tori paused. "News of an auto accident perhaps?"

The nurse shook her head.

Tori squinted at the nurse. "You look familiar."

"I've seen you in the ICU."

"You have a tattoo on the back of your left shoulder."

The nurse smiled. "Nope. Not me."

"I seem to remember you having a tattoo. Two little hearts."

"Sorry. Not me."

"You gave me a number. Told me to remember. Three sixteen."

The nurse smiled sweetly, the kind of smile you offer to someone who just spilled his or her lunch tray. "And just when did I do this?"

"You don't remember?"

"No."

Tori took a deep breath. The memory was still fresh.

"What's your name?"

"Dr. Taylor, you've talked with me hundreds of times. Are you feeling okay?"

Tori sighed. "I just had a heart transplant. I'm exhausted." She paused, staring at the nurse. "I'm sorry, I don't know your name."

"Jennifer," she said.

Tori nodded. "Thank you," she whispered.

The nurse stepped back but halted as Tori whispered her name. "Yes?"

She wanted to ask if anyone had visited but knew better than to open herself up to the pain of reality. Instead, she said, "Nothing."

Three days later, Tori Taylor had just completed a walk in the hall with a nurse when Dr. Samuel Evans entered. Dr. Evans chaired the surgery department and had his name on more book chapters than Tori could imagine. If there was ground that seemed hallowed to Tori, it was the area between the door to the chairman's office and his massive mahogany desk. "Well, look who's up," he said.

"Just made my first lap around the nursing station." Tori wiped her forehead with the back of her hand. "Might as well have been a marathon."

"It will get better."

"Give me a few weeks, a month max. I'll be back."

"Take your time." Dr. Evans looked away as the nurse helped Tori back into bed.

The nurse gently spread the sheet over Tori's legs. "Just press the call button if you need anything."

"Honestly," Tori said once her nurse disappeared, "this is driving me crazy. They act like I'm going to break. I need to get out of this place." She sighed. "Seriously, I think I can start again on the first of the month."

"That's only three weeks." He shook his head. "No way."

"I'll prove you wrong." She glared at the chairman, but he turned away.

"I'm putting you on three months administrative leave."

"But I'll go nuts. I—" She stopped when she saw his expression. Beneath his short white hair, his brow was furrowed, his eyes dead. "What aren't you telling me? The Board of Visitors …"

He nodded.

"They want me out?" She huffed, suddenly aware of her utter exhaustion. "You stuck up for me, right? They can't just—"

"Of course I stuck up for you. Getting them to agree to a three-month leave was the best I could negotiate."

"But why now? I'm disabled. This has got to be illegal."

"It's not illegal. They made their decision a few weeks ago. They didn't even know you were sick."

"So you knew and didn't tell me?"

He nodded soberly. "I thought you were going to die. So telling you the board's decision was needless."

She took a deep breath. This was so unfair. She was the best surgeon in the department.

"I'm sorry," he whispered.

"So what's the deal? I get three months off and then what?" She looked at him, her eyes pleading. "Look, Sam, you know me. I need to work. My patients need me."

"Come back after three months. Three months after that, as long as you've behaved, I get to keep you." He traced a line across the floor with the toe of his shoe. "It's conditional."

"On?"

"A few things," he said, acting nonchalant. "I'll need a written apology."

"I already apologized. I saw the janitor on my way to surgery and—"

Dr. Evans held up his hand. "Not to housekeeping. To the nursing supervisor."

"Is this about Mr. Gates?"

"His nurse, yes."

"She missed a dose of a critical medicine. She failed to give a patient with a known history of venous thrombosis a blood thinner. My patient threw a clot that nearly killed him." Tori shook her head. "I spend seven hours doing a liver resection and he pulls through just fine, until he meets Nurse Tearful."

"You called her down in front of the other nurses."

"She almost killed my patient."

"Tori, the nurse's father is on the Board of Visitors. That's the reason for the review. As it turns out, Nurse Stanfield isn't alone in her sentiment. Your file has six other letters of complaints from the nursing staff."

"Half of them were from my resident days. I've mellowed."

He lifted his eyebrows. "Really?"

"I'm harder on myself than I am on the nurses. I demand *and give* perfection."

"You're too young to be a prima donna. Just write a nice letter. Promise to do better."

"I don't do touchy-feely. The incompetent nurses get their feelings hurt and I'm to blame."

"You can't come back to work unless you agree to write a letter."

She folded her arms across her chest.

Dr. Evans walked to the door. "I'm sorry, Tori. That's the way it is." He paused before adding, "There is one more requirement."

She looked at him without speaking.

"You have to agree to counseling. Learn to express your emotions in a positive way."

"I never once raised my voice to those nurses. My emotions weren't out of control."

"It's not a matter of control. You called them idiots." He shook his head. "One of the nurses claimed you said he had a stupidity virus."

"Because he acted stupidly. He clamped off a chest tube to stop the bubbling. When we discovered it on rounds, my patient was in distress from a tension pneumothorax. He'd have died in another ten minutes."

Tori watched as a smile fought with the edge of the chairman's lips. He cleared his throat, and the smile disappeared. "You've got some time to think about it." With that, he turned and left, before she could fire back twenty excuses. He closed the door behind him, leaving Tori alone.

Then, for the first time since she was a little girl, Tori began to cry.

3

Tori quickly wiped her tears with her hand when she realized that someone was pushing the door open again. Her eyes met those of Charlotte Rains, the closest person to a true friend that Tori had.

"Don't you know how to knock?"

Charlotte smiled and placed a bouquet of flowers on a small table by the bed. Daffodils, Charlotte's favorite. "I didn't want to wake you in case you were sleeping." She took a deep breath and folded her arms across her chest.

Tori flinched. *Here it comes.*

"Girl, you should have told me. Imagine my surprise when I arrived back in town and heard the news."

"I didn't want to bother you."

Charlotte huffed and smoothed the front of her blouse. Charlotte was sixty, African-American, and as skin-color-blind as Mother Teresa. She ran a soup kitchen for Richmond's homeless and had taken Tori in during her last year of high school right after Tori's mother died of breast cancer. Though only seventeen, Tori had a posture of self-defense and self-preservation that was clothed in a thick blanket of I-can-take-care-of-myself independence. Nonetheless, she needed a place to stay, and Charlotte had been Tori's mother's choice to help provide a bridge until Tori was old enough to be an independent adult. Tori tolerated Charlotte's bubbly exuberance for life because of one thing: she knew Charlotte's love was as real as the pain Tori had been through in losing her parents.

Charlotte smiled. "I don't know whether to rejoice because you're okay or scold you for thinkin' you had to go and do this alone."

"You were with your family. How long had you been planning that reunion?"

"Two years."

"See, I didn't want you to miss it."

"You're my family too." She reached out and took Tori's hand. It felt good. Tori managed a smile.

"You look great."

"Tell the truth."

"Okay, you look like you just lost your last friend. And don't tell me that the strong and independent Dr. Taylor actually has tears. I'm callin' the paper!"

"Dr. Evans just left. They put me on a three-month administrative leave." Tori dropped Charlotte's hand so she could put finger quotation marks around the last two words.

"That's good. You need time to recover."

"It's not for recovery. It's because a few nurses complained. It seems there is little tolerance for my discipline style."

Charlotte sat and joined her hands so that they could rest on the ever-present black purse on her lap. "I know Dr. Evans. He's just helping you save face. Don't you get it? You'll stay out three months and then come back and everyone will just think you were out because of your health. It's perfect."

Tori shook her head. *Pollyanna.* "It's horrible. I haven't taken a vacation week in more than two years. What am I going to do with three months?"

"Rehab." Charlotte shrugged and looked like she wanted to say more.

"What?"

"Maybe this is the time you need."

"The time I need?" Tori shook her head. "I'm a surgeon. I need to work."

"You need to heal."

"I've got a new heart. It won't take long. I just need a little endurance."

"I wasn't talking about your heart." She paused. "Not your physical one anyway."

Tori didn't respond. She'd shielded her heart for so long, she didn't see the need to start unpacking now. She'd succeeded in a demanding field where many men failed. Emotions just got in the way of making objective clinical decisions. Just because she was taking a break from work didn't mean she had to start crying over every hangnail.

Charlotte let her comment float. After a minute, she stood. "When will they release you?"

"Not sure. I'm supposed to have a biopsy of my transplant tomorrow to check for early rejection."

Charlotte wrinkled her nose. "I'll be back." She paused at the door. "Call me tomorrow. I want to know how things go."

Tori watched her friend leave and felt her throat tighten, closing to keep a sob from escaping. *What's happening to me? A friend leaves me and I find myself fighting back tears. This medicine must be working on my mind.*

A minute later, her door swung open again and a visitor walked in from the bright hallway beyond. This time the silhouette belonged to Jarrod. He flashed a quick smile. Probably the one he let patients see. "Hey."

"Hey," she said softly.

He seemed to be inspecting her appearance. *Ever the clinician.*

From the bed, she decided to see him as his patients did. Professional. Cool. He wasn't rough on the eyes either, his brown hair just beginning to curl and touch the top of his white coat. From her position, he looked tall. This one was strong, strong enough to bear the stories of hundreds of cancer victims. He wasn't exactly warm. In fact, in his demeanor, he'd been detached. Even in their most intimate moments, he'd remained a safe pick, never probing. *Never caring?*

"I didn't come while you were in the ICU. Knew you'd be needing your private time."

How efficient. Like me?

He inspected the flowers, lifting open a little card. *Checking for competition, Jarrod?*

"How are you?" he asked.

"It's weird." She laid her hand across her breast. "This heart was someone else's. I find myself thinking about her."

He let it pass. "Your nurse told me you've been up walking."

She nodded. "Every day a little more." She motioned to him. "Hold my hand."

He squinted at her. They'd never been much for this sort of tenderness. He sat on her bed and took her hand. His was warm. She curled her fingers into his and took a deep breath.

He tried to fill the silence with words. "When will they let you out?"

"Shh. Just be quiet and hold my hand."

"Listen, I—"

"Shh. We can communicate without talking."

He stood up and pulled away. "Where'd *that* come from?"

She smiled. "Don't know." She paused. "Not sure I care. I know it's different for me, but I think I'm okay with a little change."

He wrinkled his nose. "A little?" He smoothed the lapels on his starched white coat. "Look—I'm on rounds. My team is in the hall."

"Boy, aren't you the efficient one, combining a visit to your old girl and rounding at the same time?"

"Tori, it's not like that."

"Isn't it?" She sighed. "Go on."

He looked at her, backing away. It was a look of wonder. Surprise perhaps, the look you give to a child who just quoted Einstein. "Good to see you, Tori. I'll check on you tomorrow."

She nodded, but inside felt her heart leap to follow him. She wanted more than the polite conversation of strangers. She wanted to tell him things she'd never shared. She knew it was new territory, but she wanted to share her *feelings*. She wanted him to know about the nightmares, her fears, and about the number.

She'd felt something else when he held her hand. She'd been giving him strength, a tender touch of unspoken communication. *Love.*

4

"Wow, you were incredible out there. Where'd you learn to play like that?"

Christian Mitchell looked up into the prettiest green eyes and smiled back. "Africa. I played a lot of street ball growing up."

The girl pushed blonde bangs away from her face and held out her hand. "I'm Emily. Emily Greene."

He nodded. Everyone knew Emily.

"I heard your family was from Africa. Your dad was a doctor or something, right?"

"Something," he said, echoing her words. "A surgeon."

"You live on the Cassady farm, right?"

He nodded, unsure why this popular beauty would want to talk to him.

"They're letting us stay there while my parents are on furlough."

She wrinkled her nose. "Furlough?"

He didn't want to use the *m* word with her. As soon as he said "missionary," most of his new acquaintances found a reason to move on. "My parents work for a service agency in Africa. When we get time off in America, they call it furlough."

"Nice." She wiped her brow. "I'm a mess. We just finished volleyball practice."

She looked anything but a mess to Christian. He wasn't sure what to say, so he just looked out over the soccer field and tried to keep his mind off Emily's short shorts.

"Got wheels?"

"No. My mom's picking me up."

"I can give you a lift. Our place backs up to yours."

"You have the strawberry farm?"

"It's my dad's."

His throat felt suddenly dry. She wanted to give him a ride? "Uh, sure."

He followed her to her car with the distinct thought that his social status at Shore High was about to make an upward turn.

A minute later, they were in her BMW convertible with the wind in their hair. They approached a curve, and Emily ignored the sign posting a reduced speed limit. Christian's knuckles whitened as he gripped the door and braced himself against the dash.

Emily glanced at him. "Don't worry." She laughed. "I'm an organ donor. I signed up on the back of my license."

The BMW magically tracked around the corner.

Christian relaxed.

A little.

Emily slowed and turned into the gravel lane leading up to the Cassady farmhouse. "You looked a little freaked out back there." She hesitated. "I was only joking."

He shook his head and wiped beads of sweat from his forehead. He inhaled deeply, bringing in the scent of honeysuckle. He forced a laugh. "This car is amazing."

The bedroom is on fire, flames blocking the doorway. How appropriate—the room that had become a hell is now an inferno.

Calls for help. Forgiveness. So sorry.

Too late for that.

I have to get out of here.

Flames spreading into the hallway, blocking the exit.

Maybe if I run …

Choking smoke.

My arm is on fire!

She felt a nudge on her foot. "Dr. Taylor, are you asleep?"

Tori opened her eyes. *Where am I?*

She waited a moment as the fog cleared. She rubbed her left arm. She looked down to see a man with a familiar face. Tall. About thirty. Sandy blond hair. No white coat. *An administrator?*

"Dr. Taylor, are you okay?" His accent was British.

She rubbed her eyes. "Nightmare," she said. "I think it's all the medicines."

He nodded. He had the build of a runner. Lean. Hungry. "Is this a bad time?"

"A bad time for …?"

He reached out his hand. "I'm Phin MacGrath. I work on the transplant team with social services." She'd seen him a thousand times, but like so many others, she hadn't taken the time to learn who he was. He was outside her circle. The people she noticed were those in orbit around her.

"Okay." She took his hand. Callused, belying his hospital day job. She inspected his clothes. He looked like he had just stepped out of an Eddie Bauer catalog. Professional but contemporary. Casual but neat. "What's this about?"

"I visit all the transplant patients. We need to talk about your discharge." He sat in the chair next to her bed.

"Great."

"Are you single?"

"If that's a pickup line, it's a winner."

"It's a part of what I do," he said, smiling. "I need to know who will be with you after discharge. Dr. Parrish doesn't allow his patients to be alone for the first few weeks."

"Yes."

He looked confused.

"I'm single. I take care of myself. I'll be fine at home. I can live on the first level for a while. I don't think I want to take the stairs just yet."

"Hmm."

She didn't like his response. It was patronizing. "Look, Mr. MacGrath—"

"Call me Phin. Everyone around here does."

"Okay, Phin," she said, emphasizing his name. "I'll be fine." She reached for his hand, surprising herself, as she'd never been much for such physical gestures. *What is happening to me?*

His hands were strong and rough. She ran her finger across his callused palm, distracted from their conversation. "What do you do when you're away from here?"

"I swing a hammer for Habitat."

She let her hand rest in his for a moment and looked at his face. He had dark eyes set below a thick growth of brown hair gelled into submission. She offered a smile. "Just tell Dr. Parrish that I'll be fine. I'm not like his other patients. I'm a surgeon. I know what to look for."

He squeezed her hand and shook his head, then withdrew his hand to his lap. "You're used to getting what you want."

"I'm used to getting what I deserve. What I've earned."

"How about friends? Is there someone you can stay with? It would only need to be for a couple weeks."

Tori ran down a very short list. A fellow surgeon? No, her relationships were strictly professional. Jarrod? No, he'd moved on with a new girl. Besides, that didn't feel right. That left Charlotte. Charlotte would say yes, but Tori wasn't sure. The last time she'd lived with Charlotte was years ago, when Tori's life had been disrupted by her mother's death. She wasn't sure returning to that environment would be healthy. Too many memories. Too much of the baggage she had gladly set aside. Tori shook her head. "Not really anyone I'd like to live with."

"We can always go the nursing-facility route. I'll check for open beds," he said, standing.

"Wait! A *nursing home*?"

He smiled. "It's not just for old people."

"I know, but—"

"I understand. Just try to think of it as a place for people needing a little extra care."

She sighed. "I'll find someone."

"Think about your options. In the meantime, I'm going to contact a few of the local homes so I can reserve a spot for you." He placed his hand on the door to go.

Maybe a surgery resident will agree to live with me for a few weeks. Images of gorked-out, drooling old people in wheelchairs pushed ahead of Phin's good-bye.

She watched her door closing behind him. *I'm not going to a nursing home!*

5

A kiss.

Just a kiss.

In the end, that's all it took to nudge God from the top spot in Christian Mitchell's heart.

It's not like it came as a surprise. He'd thought about it, *dreamed* about it for weeks. One ride home from school had turned into two, then a lift back to school, and then a regular pattern. Who wanted to ride the bus when Emily Greene was offering curbside service in her convertible?

The progression just seemed so natural.

He went from hearing "Can you help me with this chemistry homework?" to "Stay for dinner" in a short week.

Laughter. Shared feelings. Walks along the Chesapeake Bay, during which the backs of their hands would just happen to brush.

His mother's questions were brushed aside.

"Is she a Christian?"

"Mom! They go to church. Her dad's an elder at First Baptist."

"Does she know about your love of Africa?"

"She loves Africa too. They sponsor a child from Kenya. She wants to visit him."

His mom would just turn away and stay quiet, continuing to wash the supper dishes.

It all unfolded in the strawberry patch. Carolyn Greene, Emily's mother, had invited Christian to pick a basket of strawberries to take home. It was Saturday, and the sun was straight overhead, baking the Eastern Shore. Emily and Christian picked and ate their way along, stooping over the low rows of strawberries until their baskets were brimming with ripe fruit.

Christian sat on the straw between rows and looked at Emily. Sticky with sweat and with her T-shirt clinging in all the right places, she did her best exaggerated pitch windup and fired a strawberry, catching him by surprise right on his forehead. Moist red strawberry flesh stuck to his left eyebrow.

Emily exploded in laughter and sat down on the straw beside him.

"Here," she said, still giggling. She wiped strawberry from his forehead with her index finger and quickly dropped her finger between her red lips and sucked the juice with a noisy smack. Then she moistened her finger with her tongue and wiped it across his face, cleaning his eyebrow of crimson juice. Leaning closer, she laid her finger against his lips. Without thinking, he closed his lips around it, tasting the strawberry on her skin.

She pulled her finger away but let it trail across his chin. He leaned forward. *Go ninety percent*, he reminded himself.

It was good advice. She went the extra ten.

Her lips were spongy, warm, and tasted of strawberry and sweat.

He knew only what he'd seen on TV since their furlough had started, but kissing Emily seemed easy.

And heavenly.

"I'm falling for you, Christian Mitchell," she whispered.

"And why would you do that?"

She giggled and shrugged. "What's that phrase you always use? I think it's a God thing."

Tori dreamed the smell of sweat and whiskey, the sound of a woman's cry and the *thump-thump-smack* of physical assault, and the sight of a bare bulb hanging at the end of a dim hallway.

He's in there.

Someday I'll make him pay.

A man with a bay-windowed belly yells in her face, spraying spittle from teeth rotting from meth.

She retreats. A stairway is on her right. *If I can just make it....*

A shove.

Falling.

Searing pain in my left ankle.

My foot isn't supposed to face that way.

Tori startled awake and wiggled her ankle. She sighed and struggled to sit up. *Just a dream.*

She pushed an IV pole toward the bathroom. Once there, she stared at her reflection in the mirror. Light-brown hair in need of shampoo curled in a tangle beside pale cheeks.

I'm a ghost. Maybe I can get Charlotte to bring my mascara.

She gently touched the pink scar that began at the lowest point of her neck and dived into the front of her hospital gown.

She toweled beads of sweat from her brow. *What's happening to me? How can a nightmare seem so real when I know it's just a dream?*

She pulled down the front of her gown. *Will I ever get to wear a low-cut top again?* She sighed. *Not without feeling self-conscious.*

"Knock, knock." It was Jarrod's baritone voice.

"In here." She washed her face and stepped back into her room. "Hey you." She smiled. "On rounds again?"

"Touché. No." He seemed to be staring at her scar.

She gathered her gown beneath her chin and sat in the recliner chair beside her bed.

"I'm on my own time." He hesitated.

She let the silence hang between them, not minding the quiet.

"I'll get right to it," he said, clearing his throat. "I know you need a place to live. I want you to come to my place. I have an in-law suite. It's all yours."

She studied him for a moment. He kept smoothing his white coat against his leg. "I don't think so, Jarrod. Things aren't like they used to be."

"But I want them to be. I screwed up, Tori. I should have been around. Let's start over."

She raised her eyebrows. "Start over by me moving in? That hardly seems appropriate. What about your new girlfriend?" She paused. "This hospital has ears, you know."

He looked down. "Didn't work. Way too emo for me." He sighed. "You know I don't do touchy-feely."

"I know. And I'm honored. I'm glad you want a new start. That feels good to me."

He appeared startled. "That feels good?"

"Sure."

"I'll prepare the room."

"I'm not moving in, Jarrod. *That* doesn't feel right. In fact, that makes me feel …" Her voice trailed off until she found the right word. When she said it, the surprise of it made her laugh. "Guilty."

"Wow," he said. "You?"

She looked into space, nodding. "Yep."

"What's happened to you?"

"I don't know. I just know that I'm not ready for such a leap." She reached for his hand. "You're a kind man," she said. "And I think it would be nice getting to know you better." She gave his hand a squeeze. "But let's not start by complicating the issue."

"I'm not exactly suggesting that we move in together. It was more of a spare-room offer."

"Right. I know how long that would last. One late night. The stress of work piles up. You need a break. I rub your back … well, you know the progression. And I'm not ready for that."

He stood up. "I don't get it. The old Dr. Taylor would have cut right through the feelings to see that this is an efficient, practical solution to your problem. You need a place. I have a spare room. I'm a doctor. I can look after you while you recover. It's perfect."

"Perfect, except it just doesn't feel right." She put her hand over her heart. "But the fact that you're concerned about me is touching."

A knock at the door interrupted them. It was a nurse from the cath lab, a cheery woman in green scrubs and a white coat. "I'm here to take you for your biopsy."

"Oh, joy," Tori moaned, looking over at a man she wanted to love. "Gotta run."

The nurse assisted her into a wheelchair. As Tori was about to be wheeled into the hall, she motioned for Jarrod. When he leaned down, she whispered a question. "Fresh start?"

He nodded. "Agreed."

In the angiography suite, Tori slid slowly onto the cold radiography table. She looked up into the face of her cardiologist, Dr. Eric Samuelson. "I don't want any sedation."

"I'll just slip you a little Versed. I want you to relax."

"No!" She held up her hand. "Really, I don't want to sleep."

Dr. Samuelson leaned forward and touched her hand, concern on his young face. "Tori, relax."

"It's just that being awake is better than sleep."

"Are you okay?"

She shook her head. "Nightmares. Every time I doze off." She hesitated, biting her lower lip to keep it from quivering. Her admission was tantamount to admitting weakness, something she'd never have done before her transplant. "Please."

A scrub nurse had set a sterile field up a few feet away. Now, as she pushed the table forward, she mumbled under her breath. "Not so mighty now, are we?"

The cardiologist cast a stern glance in her direction.

"It's all right," Tori said. "I see my reputation precedes me." She took a deep breath, trying to control emotions that threatened to take over. "Please just talk me through it."

Eric Samuelson nodded. "Sure."

She watched, alert.

"I'm going to touch your upper thigh. Cold. It's the prep solution." A minute later, Tori found herself beneath a tent of sterile paper sheets. "You'll feel a sting and burn in your groin. Numbing medicine," he said mechanically. "You may feel a little pressure here."

The angiogram to image her heart caused fire to spread inside her from her chest downward.

Fire. I remember a fire.

That's crazy. I've never been in a fire.

Or have I? I'm just remembering my dream.

"Your new heart looks great," he said. "We're going to do a biopsy. You shouldn't feel a thing."

Tori fought back tears, not from the good news, but because the nightmares that haunted her nights had just crept into daylight.

6

Dr. Parrish looked at Tori over half-glasses. "You'll have to keep your leg straight for the next few hours. We don't want to see any bleeding from your catheterization stick site."

Tori nodded.

Evidently, she wasn't very good at hiding her new anxiety. "What's wrong?" Dr. Parrish asked.

"Did Dr. Evans tell you he put me on administrative leave?"

"Yes."

"Listen, I know I've been hard on some of the nurses—"

He held his hand up. "You don't need to apologize to me. We need someone like you who will hold the staff's feet to the fire. I know you're a good surgeon." He paused. "I know who I'd see if I had cancer."

She took a deep breath. "Thanks," she whispered. "Listen, there's something else." She fought to find the right words. "Dr. Evans is requiring me to get a counselor to deal with anger issues." She held up her fingers and gestured quotation marks around "anger."

"I take it you're not crazy about the idea."

"That's an understatement."

He sighed. "I'll leave that to Dr. Evans. It won't affect my respect for you."

"The thing is, I'm here now. If I have to do this, I want to get started. Can you make a referral?"

"Why don't I have Phin MacGrath drop in?"

"The team social worker? I've met him."

He nodded. "He has a master's in counseling. He's familiar with the emotional issues that transplant patients deal with. I think he'd be perfect."

"Okay."

Dr. Parrish touched a stack of envelopes on Tori's bedside stand. "Wow, it looks like you get the prize for the most mail."

"Well-wishers," she said. "Seems at least my patients appreciate me. I'm averaging about twenty cards a day. Who'd-a-thunk-it?" She smiled. "I heard the nurses whispering about it. I don't think they can stand it."

He chuckled. "We should know something about your biopsy in a few days. For now, I'm keeping your antirejection regimen the same."

"I hope I can get off the steroids. I think I'm already looking fat."

"You? Not a chance." He stepped to the door. "Rest. You can't get up for two more hours. Take a nap."

She found herself wincing. What would once have been an afternoon luxury had become a minefield—one she wasn't sure she could cross without tripping a memory explosion.

Two hours later, Tori's discomfort had far more to do with the fact that her bladder was stressing and she still wasn't allowed up than from her postsurgery pain.

As a nurse finished taking vitals, Tori pleaded. "I need to get up to the bathroom."

The nurse looked at her watch. "Another fifteen minutes. Can I get you a bedpan?"

Tori sighed and shook her head. "I think I can wait."

But as soon as the nurse disappeared, Tori tenderly palpated the site of her recent femoral artery stick, the crease in front of her right hip. *No swelling. It should be safe.*

She gently rolled to the side and swung her feet over the bed to the floor. Slowly, she took a few steps toward the bathroom, padding on cat feet. Unfortunately, the movement intensified a need for speed. She realized quickly that her IV bag was still hanging on a pole by her bed. She groaned and turned to get her IV. *I need to hurry!*

In her haste, she knocked a plastic water pitcher to the floor. She grabbed the IV pole and slid it along with her, dragging a stripe of spilled water as a path to her goal where she eased herself down on the cold seat.

Made it. Sweet relief. And all without my nurse.

The trip back to her bed wasn't as stealthy. She slipped on the slick floor, sending a searing pain through her right groin. Tori tried to stop her slide to the floor by hanging onto the IV pole, but the pole was top-heavy and tipped. With a loud crash, the IV pole clattered to the floor, bouncing once on her side table and scattering her cards, a vase of flowers, and her phone. She ended up on her back, with a second ripping pain in her chest and the sensation of wetness on her leg. *Water?* She touched her thigh and examined her fingers. *Blood!*

Her door swung open, heralding the entrance of her nurse—a thirtysomething female with red hair—and an aide, an adolescent male with a face struggling with acne.

The nurse barked at the aide. "Throw me that towel!"

She threw Tori's gown back to expose her upper legs and pressed the towel down over a bleeding purple swelling.

"I told you not to get up!" Her teeth were bared, lips pulled back in a snarl.

Tori couldn't speak. The pain in her chest was nearly unbearable.

The nurse went on. "I should have known. You're above the orders. You know best, don't you, *Dr. Taylor?*"

Tori struggled for breath. "I … had … to … go," she whispered.

The nurse looked at the aide. "I want you to stat page the vascular surgery resident on call. If I can't get this bleeding stopped, she's going to need surgery."

The aide stepped toward the door.

"Bring me some sterile dressings!"

Tori felt warm fluid running down her leg. The nurse wasn't holding efficient direct pressure, and Tori was still losing blood. Tori placed her hand over the nurse's. "Here," she said. "The artery is more medial. Push here."

"Still need to be in charge, don't you?"

Tori's first impulse was to correct her, but as she began, she halted. "The femoral artery runs—" She took a deep breath and steadied her voice. "Could you cover me up?"

"You don't get it, do you? You could bleed out."

"I'm cold. Others can see me," she grunted. "The door is open."

The nurse didn't make a move to cover Tori. "It feels different being a patient, doesn't it?"

Tori reached out to touch the nurse's hand. She wanted to apologize. Instead, the nurse pulled away.

"Don't touch me! Your hand is bloody."

"I … I must have offended you."

"Oh, that's rich." The nurse appeared to be sweating. "What nurse haven't you offended, Dr. Taylor?"

"Thank you for taking care of me." Tori winced with pain. "I heard the nurses talking at the beginning of the shift. You must have gotten the short straw."

The nurse didn't respond. Evidently, she didn't expect Tori's honesty.

A minute later, a breathless vascular-surgery intern arrived. Dr. Ron Marsh had served on Tori's team the month she fell ill.

Tori struggled to cover her privates with her hand. "Hi, Ron," she said. "I slipped getting back to bed. I'm two hours postcardiac cath via a right femoral artery stick. I think I opened the artery again when I fell."

Ron quickly pulled on a pair of latex gloves and grabbed a sheet from the bed. He spread the sheet over Tori, leaving only her right groin uncovered. "Here," he said, nudging the nurse aside. "On three, take your hand away and let me put my fingers over her wound. I need to see." He paused. "One, two … three!"

The duo switched positions. "Hmm," he said.

"What do you see?"

"Most of the bleeding is under the skin. I think we can get this to stop without surgery, but you're going to have to live with a significant hematoma."

"I need heart biopsies each week for two more weeks," Tori said.

The intern frowned. "Then they'll probably have to use the other side or else use your arm."

"I'm worried about my sternal closure too," she said. "I may have ripped something."

"I can look if you want."

She nodded.

This time, the nurse cooperated and wrapped the sheet around to cover Tori's breasts while pulling up her gown to expose her sternal scar. Dr. Marsh leaned forward, still holding pressure over the hematoma. "It looks okay."

The intern looked at the nurse. "I'll need you to get some help to move her back to bed."

"Oh no, we're not moving her. It will increase her chances of bleeding." She shook her head. "Not on my shift. She stays on the floor."

"But it's wet and cold. Get that hard plastic transfer board and we'll log roll her onto it while I hold pressure."

"Not a good idea. I say hold pressure on the floor."

"But we need to do this for an hour."

"Not my problem." The nurse stood up and pushed past the young nurse's aide, who was wide-eyed and peering over Dr. Marsh's shoulder. "I've got charting to do." With that, she disappeared.

Dr. Marsh mumbled, calling her colorful names under his breath.

"Don't," Tori said. "I've not made many friends among the nursing staff. Now I'm paying for it."

"It's still not right." He flipped open his cell phone. "I'll call my team. We can get you back to bed without Nurse Coldhearted."

"Don't call her that. It's my fault." Tori couldn't help it. Tears began pouring down her cheeks.

"Dr. Taylor?" The intern's eyes were wide.

"Ever heard of the Golden Rule?"

"Sure," he said. "I went to Sunday school."

"Good," she said. "I didn't. So you should know better. This is what you get when you don't use it."

That evening, Phin MacGrath pushed open Tori's door.

She looked up. "You're keeping late hours."

He shrugged. "Gotta love the life of the single hospital social worker, eh?"

Her stomach tightened. Was Phin here for a counseling session?

Phin had changed from his hospital attire. He wore faded blue jeans and a print shirt opened to the third button. He read her anxious face. "Look, I stopped in late because I thought we'd be less likely to be interrupted. Dr. Parrish told me your dilemma. You're being forced into counseling." He chuckled. "My favorite situation."

"Seems the board has handed down an ultimatum. Get counseling or find a new job." She paused. "I'll be honest. I don't want to talk. I've never been much for bearing my feelings. I've handled my own problems all my life."

"Fair enough." He leaned back. "Let's not talk about feelings. Why don't you just tell me about what you want."

His approach disarmed her. His smile didn't hurt either. "Wh-what I want?"

"Sure. Tell me about your goals."

She shrugged. "That's easy. I want to get back to work, return to oncology surgery. I want to make a difference in the lives of my patients."

"But something has come up. There's an obstacle blocking your goal." He held up his hands. "This." He paused. "You need to work some things out before you can get back to the job you love."

She nodded, sighing.

"Do you want to talk about your anger?"

"I'm not angry."

"Look, I've been around here long enough to have heard the stories."

"The stories aren't necessarily true. I'm hard on the nurses. That part is true. But I don't discipline them in anger."

"You call them names."

"*Stupid* isn't a name. It's an adjective. And in most cases, an accurate one."

"So in your mind, anger is not an issue."

"Now we're communicating."

"Maybe we should talk about perfectionism, driven behaviors."

"Tell me something, Phin. If you were seeing a surgeon because you had cancer, wouldn't you want that surgeon to be perfect and to drive her team to be perfect?"

"I suppose."

"So I don't see a real problem."

He raised his eyebrows. "Really?"

She softened. "Okay, look, I'm pretty frustrated with myself right now."

He waited silently for her to continue.

"On the one hand, I know I haven't been sensitive to the nurses' feelings." She hesitated, searching his face for understanding. When he nodded, she continued. "This is new territory for me. While I know there have been times when the nurses should have been better, I know I've offended them when I come down on them." She touched her head. "I feel like I'm on a roller coaster. I still feel like things should be done according to the highest standard, but—" She stopped. "I think I've stepped on a whole lot of toes in the process." She sighed. "The nurses here don't even want to get me as an assignment. That tells me a lot."

"This sounds like progress."

She tried to smile. "Maybe."

"We work as a team here. So anything the team has discussed about you, I've been privy to."

She raised her eyebrows. "And just what does the team say?"

"Dr. Samuelson told me about your nightmares."

She stayed quiet.

"Can you talk about that?"

"Okay," she said, suddenly aware that her voice was tightening. She studied the social worker's handsome face. *I can do this.* "It's weird. I've never had such vivid dreams. I'm hesitant to even call them dreams. They seem so real. I wake up with the feeling that I've tapped an old memory."

"Something bad in your past."

"That's just it. Sure, I had some knocks growing up. My dad was killed in Iraq, and my mom died of breast cancer when I was a teen. But nothing ever like the stuff that haunts my nights."

"Tell me."

"Fire. Voices crying for help. A man's voice. A mean man."

"How do you know he's mean?"

She looked away. "I just know. It's like it happened to me." She took a deep breath. "He pushed me down the stairs."

"Wow." He sat quietly.

The silence between them was comfortable. She had to resist reaching out to brush his callused hands. "The last time I awoke from a nightmare, I had the distinct knowledge that someone wanted me dead." She studied his expression.

"What else?"

"A woman. Blonde. Green eyes. A tattoo of two hearts on her left shoulder. She gave me a number to remember." She reached for one of her cards on the side table. "Got a pen?" She wrote it in block letters, just like the number that had been handed to her in the dream. "It was like this. 3. 1. 6. Just like that. I don't write in block letters, but that's what the note looked like."

Phin ran his fingers through thick brown hair that was cut short over the ears.

"What? Why do you just sit there taking it all in? You think I'm crazy?"

He crossed his legs. A one-word answer. "No."

"What?" She leaned forward. "What aren't you telling me?"

He cleared his throat. "I've got an idea." Their eyes met. He seemed to be studying her.

She wouldn't look away. She waited for an answer.

"I think they *are* memories."

She coughed, something that hurt her chest. She reached up, tightening her fist over her gown. "I told you, nothing like that ever happened to me."

"Maybe not to you."

She shook her head.

He uncrossed his legs and leaned forward. "Ever heard of cellular memory?"

"No."

"It's talked about in transplant circles." He paused. "I think your memories may belong to your heart donor."

7

That summer, Christian Mitchell and Emily Greene were insepa-
rable. The closeness of their farms made it easy for them to spend
their evenings on the Greenes' expansive covered front porch.

"What do you do for all those hours?" his mom asked.

"We just chill, Mom. Talk." Chris shrugged.

And talk they did. About anything and everything. Everything
except the looming topic of their separation.

Christian knew it was coming, and it had become the unvented
lava beneath the surface in his family. He didn't want to return to
Africa. He loved Emily. He wanted to be with her. His father was
steadfast in his commitment. "If we don't return, the hospital will be
without a surgeon and will likely close its doors."

One day on Emily's front porch, he decided it was time to
face the future. It was dusk, and the summer air was heavy with
the buzzing sound of cicadas. Emily handed him a tall glass of
sweet iced tea, the sweat dripping from the cool surface. "My father
knows the hospital administrator over at Shore General. He's pretty
sure they've been looking for a surgeon. I think he can get your dad
a job."

Christian sighed. "Not going to happen. My father is set on returning to Africa. We've already got the tickets. We leave in six weeks."

"They can't just take you against your will."

"Sure they can. I'm their kid."

She sat on the porch swing beside him. "We're adults, basically. Let them go." She brushed his bangs back from his forehead with her hand. "Stay with me."

He looked back into her eyes and touched her cheek with his hand. "I believe in what my parents are doing. It's important stuff."

She pouted. "I'm important too." She brightened. "We could run away."

"We have no money."

"I know the combination to my father's safe."

"We can't start a life together like that."

"I want you to take me away."

"To Africa?"

"No, silly. America. But just away from here."

"You've got it made, Emily. Why would you want to leave this?"

"It may look great from the outside, but my father is too strict."

Christian squinted.

She straightened. "I have an idea." She set her tea on a small wicker table beside the swing. "If this works, your parents would never take you to Africa."

"What? There is nothing that would keep them from leaving." He sighed. "I hope you like letters."

"There is one thing," she said.

He shook his head. "It would take a miracle."

She shrugged. "Maybe." She leaned over and kissed his cheek and whispered in his ear. "Or you could just get me pregnant."

Tori looked down at the yellow legal pad in her lap. Phin had encouraged her to think about all the ways she sensed a difference about herself since her transplant, differences that couldn't be accounted for by medicine or surgery alone.

She'd written:

I can cry—can't remember the last time I cried before the surgery.

I've never been a "toucher" before, but now I want to hold hands with Jarrod.

She paused, not wanting to write down "and Phin" because she needed to show him her list. But the memory of his callused hand seemed dear to her. *Weird, because to want to do that seems so teenybopper to me.*

"What about different food, dress, or music preferences?" Phin had prompted.

She thought about her tastes. Nothing seemed to have changed there.

When she finished writing, she opened her laptop to do an Internet search on cellular memory. What she found was not only peculiar, it was downright creepy. A heart-transplant recipient who found a new love for classical music discovered his donor had been a classical violinist. Another had a new penchant for peppers and beer, *just like his donor*. Over and over again, there were anecdotal reports of changes in tastes, emotions, and even memories.

When Phin came by later that morning, she closed her laptop and folded the paper she'd been using. She wasn't quite ready to share this with him yet.

She smiled when their eyes met, and it struck her how easy it was for her to talk to him. She'd never really been able to open up and talk easily to anyone outside a very small circle. *Maybe another change?*

He held out his hand formally. She took it, letting her fingers trace the calluses on his palm. She took a deep breath and began, "If you are right about all this, I think I need to find out who my donor was."

"And why would you need to do that?"

Tori shrugged. "If I can find out about my donor, maybe I can understand these horrible memories. Maybe I can find peace again."

He scratched his head. She'd noticed that he did this when he didn't agree with her. "I don't know, Tori. If there was trouble in the life of your donor, how is it going to help you come to peace?"

"Because I'll have some truth to hang these memories on. As it is, I have only images, feelings of dread, and pain. What does it mean?"

"Maybe there are things you don't want to know. What if your donor wasn't a nice person? Would you really want to know?"

"What about the number? A woman made me promise to memorize it, saying she wanted to make—" Tori winced at needing to say the word—"that bastard pay."

"That's a problem," he said. "The records of donors are sealed from the recipients' knowledge unless the family wants recipient contact, and then only if the recipient agrees."

"Well, I'll agree. I need to talk to her family, to see if they can make some sense of these memories."

"I think it would be best if you could just accept that the troubling memories may not be your own and let that help you move on."

That idea didn't feel right to Tori. She'd never been much for intuition, but something inside told her she needed to push forward. "Look, Phin, I don't expect you to understand, but some woman died and gave me her heart. Don't I owe her anything? What if there is a police investigation into her death? Shouldn't I tell them what I know?"

"Oh, I'm sure that would go over big," he said. "I received a heart from Jane Doe and now I have her memories living in me." He shook his head. "I know I believe you, but I'm pretty sure that many others would laugh in your face."

Tori folded her arms across her chest. "Maybe I'm weird, but I can't walk away from this. I've got memories that I didn't choose. Maybe I'm *supposed* to do something about this." She laid her hand on top of Phin's, something she'd wanted to do since dropping his handshake. His hand was warm, and she enjoyed the fact that he turned his palm open to hers in response. "I need to talk to the transplant coordinator. I'll explain that I think someone may be in trouble."

He leaned forward. "This is new for you too, isn't it, the feeling that you are being led?"

She looked at the ceiling, thinking. "Yes. Yes, I think that's true. Another difference." She paused. "I'm going to have a talk with the transplant coordinator."

"Barb Stiles? She's pretty much a by-the-book gal."

"I need to talk to her."

Phin took his other hand and covered hers. Now he held her right hand with both of his. He didn't move to take them away when she spread open her fingers to receive his. "Let this go, Tori. Nothing good can come of it."

"I can't. My donor gave me life. I owe her this."

He shrugged. "Talk to Barb then. But when she turns you down, remember, I warned you."

"Okay."

"I hear you're being discharged tomorrow."

"Yep, my old friend Charlotte to the rescue."

He stood to go, pausing to put his card on her rolling table. "Call me. We still need to talk."

"You're going to hold me to this, aren't you?"

"If you want to go back to work," he said, smiling. "Look, it might be helpful not to let the dreams get to you. If you can accept that they may not be your memories at all, it may be less threatening to talk them through. Let's do that next time." He let the door swing shut and his chuckling faded with the closing of the door.

She watched him go, marveling at his intuition. *What was it he said? That I feel led?*

She shook her head and shivered. *Yes, that's exactly what I feel.*

The next afternoon, Tori sat on the back deck of Charlotte's old Richmond home. Her house was a place of solitude in the city, in an area known as the Fan because the streets extended west from downtown like spokes from a hub. She sat on a cushioned wicker chair surrounded by tall potted plants, looking out over a manicured garden of a back lawn, a place of greens, purples, reds, and orange bordered by a high redwood slat fence.

But Tori wasn't seeing the lawn, the flowers, or even the tall magnolia tree that scented the air around her. She'd been transported by a memory.

"If he comes, we'd better be ready to run." Fear flickered across green eyes. "Take this," she said, shoving the paper forward. "In case I don't make it."

Images blurred.

Smoke. Fire.

Screams.

Tori closed her fist and held it over her heart.

Just what does this mean? What have I been given beyond this organ of muscle?

"Tori? Are you okay?"

She looked up. The voice belonged to Charlotte.

"You're sweating. I'll set up a fan."

"No," Tori said. "I'm not hot." She looked at the pill-bottle collection on the glass-topped table in front of her. Cellcept, Prograf, Sandimmune, and Prednisone, all powerful drugs to keep her from rejecting the heart she'd received.

Charlotte sat in a second wicker chair and forced a smile, something that sprayed fine wrinkles from the corners of her eyes and creased the skin beneath her short white Afro. "What is it?"

"Not sure," Tori said, sighing. "Memories."

Charlotte leaned forward. "Something you need to talk about?"

Tori studied her old friend. *How to explain?* "This may sound weird, but I think I've gotten more than I wanted from my heart donor."

"More than you—"

"Transplanted memories," Tori interrupted.

Charlotte's expression revealed her confusion.

"It's been described in transplant literature. Some people believe it. Some don't. But there are unexplainable cases of new memories in transplant recipients." Tori paused, looking at her friend.

"And you think you have such memories?"

Tori nodded. "Some of the images are vague. I remember a fire. Screams."

Charlotte reached forward and touched a scar on Tori's arm. The skin graft.

Tori shook her head. "I know what you're thinking. It's not that." She shifted in her seat. "I burned my arm on a motorcycle muffler. I was very young. I don't even remember it."

Charlotte stayed quiet. After a minute, she spoke again. "You didn't receive a brain transplant, Tori."

She laughed. "But that doesn't seem to matter when it comes to memories. No one seems to really know how memories are stored. Is it physical? A molecule? A sequence of firing of nerve synapses?" Tori paused. "There is a complicated network of nerves that surround the heart. When a transplant is done, it all goes, heart, surrounding nerves, the whole network. Who's to say that the heart doesn't have its own memories?"

"You have other new memories?"

"Images mostly."

"Tell me."

"Some are detailed and sharp. A piece of paper with a number. 316. I was told to remember the number. It's a clue, something that will help convict a very bad man."

Charlotte's eyes went to the medicines.

"It's not those, either. Unless the medicines that keep me from rejecting my heart are keeping me from fighting off senseless hallucinations, too." She shrugged. "Maybe my defenses are down all around, even my mental ones."

"What does Dr. Parrish think?"

"I haven't told him."

"You need to do that. He may want to change your meds."

Tori didn't like the direction of their conversation. But she knew Charlotte's reaction of disbelief would be typical if Tori decided to share her feelings. "They seem so real."

"You've been under a lot of stress. Maybe you're mixing up some past trauma—"

"No!" Tori huffed. "I shouldn't have told you. You think I'm crazy."

"Tori, you almost died before your transplant. Your job is in jeopardy. You're on a boatload of powerful medicines. I'm the last one who would think you're crazy."

"But you think I'm cracking under the stress?"

Charlotte offered a meek smile. "Who wouldn't?"

"So why something so specific like the number?"

"I have no idea."

"That's why I need to figure this out. I left a message with Barb, the nurse who coordinates the transplant program. I need to find out who my donor was so I can make sense of these memories."

Charlotte looked out across her backyard as she spoke. "I brought lemonade. Dr. Parrish told me to be sure you were drinking plenty of fluids. He doesn't want you getting dehydrated."

Tori took the hint. Charlotte wasn't comfortable with Tori's theory.

Charlotte went back inside just as Tori's cell phone sounded.

"Hello?"

"Dr. Taylor, it's Barb, the transplant coordinator. I was told you called."

Tori took a deep breath and launched into the story of her new memories. After relating everything, she heard Barb's breath blow into the receiver.

"You know I can't tell you the identity of the donor."

"Look, Barb, I'm not sure I can get you to understand, but these feelings, these memories are very, very real to me. They frighten me." She sighed. "I need to make sense of this."

"You should talk to someone. A counselor. Finding out weird or dark things about your donor's life is not going to help. You need to trust me on this. There are things you may not want to know."

"Make an exception. I'm a surgeon. I know how these things work."

"Dr. Taylor, the system is set up this way for a reason. The donor family may not desire this kind of contact. News like you're suggesting may be very upsetting to the family."

"This is a special situation. There may be criminal and legal issues here."

Another sigh from Barb's end. "I'll ask a few questions. If the family wants to contact you, I'll let you know."

Tori looked up at the waxy leaves of the magnolia tree and felt her throat tighten with emotion. Fighting back tears, she coughed. "Okay. Let me know."

She set the phone on the table. *I can't expect anyone to understand. They don't feel what I'm feeling.*

She touched the front of her shirt, letting her hand settle over her new heart. *If our experiences define us, make us who we are, who does that make me?*

Am I the same person that I used to be?

8

Christian Mitchell looked up at the ceiling of his little bedroom, thinking about the question his father had posed at dinner that evening. *Who am I?*

His father had made the point that too often people pick the most obvious answer to that question. A person says "I'm a doctor" or "I'm a teacher" without thinking about the deeper spiritual issues. "God," his father said, "wants us to find our identity in him. Wrap yourself up in the idea that you are loved by God, created in his image, and made for the purpose of bringing him glory. Find your identity there."

Christian sighed. The truth was, he'd had a hard enough time trying to answer the question without getting spiritual. He thought about the typical ways he could define himself. *I have an American passport. But I don't feel American. I've spent most of my life living somewhere else.* When other kids talked about American TV shows, American football, or even the restaurants they enjoyed, Christian couldn't find a point of reference to understand. He didn't fit here, but when in Africa, thanks to his skin color and language, he didn't exactly fit there either. He was afloat between cultures without an anchor to fix his identity.

Emily was the first person to try to push past his awkwardness, the feelings of not fitting. She seemed to like the fact that he brought a unique perspective to problems. His answers weren't knee-jerk American. With Christian, it wasn't always about money or getting more stuff. He'd seen poverty. He'd never really had the "stuff" people seemed to spend all their energy wanting. For Christian, relationships took priority. For that, he could thank the influences of his African village and parents who were just crazy enough to think raising a family there might be a good thing.

Perhaps for that reason, his relationship with Emily was something he treasured. He suspected she'd have a hard time defining herself without all the stuff her parents had provided for her. He doubted that she could imagine life without the house, clothes, money, and car. But Christian looked past all of it to see the gem of who she was inside. And maybe her insane plan to begin their lives together wasn't so insane after all. They wouldn't be rich, but wasn't it all the material stuff in the world that caused most of the problems?

Christian looked at the illuminated dial on his Timex watch. 12:30 a.m. He peered through the kitchen window. All was quiet. Overhead, clouds obscured the moon. Inside, with his anxieties pushed aside, he attempted to focus on one thought. *I love her. Why shouldn't we begin our lives together now?*

He pulled the screen door, wincing at the squeak, an eerie report that seemed to echo even more loudly against the silence of the night. He waited until he'd crossed the backyard before clicking on the flashlight, pointing it ahead on the now well-worn path toward the Greene homestead.

He walked softly and wiped the sweat from his forehead as he anticipated the secret rendezvous. In the past week Emily had deftly countered his objections. *"We love each other, Chris. Why is that so wrong?"*

"We aren't married."

"Think about it. I'll bet some of those people you saw in Africa didn't have a piece of paper saying they were married, did they? Are you saying they aren't married? It's all just differences in culture."

"But—"

She silenced him with a kiss. "We can ask God to marry us." She pulled away. "You said you loved me."

In the end, he crossed a line that a mere month before he'd have sworn he'd never even approach. One by one his defenses fell like dominos, each one only enough to trip the next.

But what will my parents say?

His objections burned away in the fire of one thought that captivated his testosterone-driven frontal lobes: *Emily will let me touch her. See her. She wants it.*

After all, it is my life. I'm an adult. Why should I let others determine my destiny?

She'd whispered an invitation into the phone that afternoon. "I've been taking my temperature. I need to see you tonight."

His heart galloped at the memory. Hooves stamping against his chest.

At the fence bordering Emily's family farm, Christian flipped off the flashlight and hoisted himself chest first over the top board. As his right leg swung forward, he snagged his jeans, slowing his progress—not enough to stop him altogether, but just enough to send him sprawling onto the dirt. He uttered a rare curse and gripped his knee. His fingers explored the torn fabric and met moisture. *Dew?* He gasped. *Blood!*

He fumbled with the flashlight and peered through the cut edges of his favorite Levi's jeans. He frowned. The skin over his kneecap was folded back exposing a palate of red, yellow, and white. Christian moaned and pulled off his black T-shirt, one he'd selected to help him blend with the night. He pushed the shirt down over the wound as the pain proclaimed its presence, first with a whisper like a hint of smoke and then building until it seemed that his whole leg was on fire.

He contemplated his options. Dealing with the wound at home would certainly wake his mother. He looked toward the barn at the south edge of the Greene farm where Emily would be waiting in the loft.

He opted to continue. He limped onward, his mind temporarily diverted from an adolescent fantasy image of Emily leaning back on a blanket of hay. Naked. And asking for him.

Walking bent over, applying pressure to his knee with one hand, gave him an exaggerated limp. He paused and tied the shirt around his leg. Then, wiping the sweat from his forehead, he began again.

At the back door of the barn, he turned off the flashlight and slipped through the sliding doors, which were parted just enough. His knee brushed the door. "Ow!"

He knelt again, gripping his leg, his breath heavy.

A tiny voice came from the loft. "Chris?"

"I cut my leg on the fence."

"Come up."

"I'm bleeding."

He heard her sigh and the creak of the wooden ladder. A moment later, she knelt over him. She wore only a flannel shirt and a pair of very short shorts. "Let me see," she said, placing her hands on his.

He unwrapped the shirt and pointed the flashlight.

"Oooh. I think you need stitches."

"Emily, I can't. My parents—"

"You may need a tetanus shot."

"I'm up to date. Can you just get some bandages? I'll be okay."

"Come with me to the loft. We'll bandage it later."

He eyed the ladder. "I'm not even sure I can climb that with one leg. When I bend my knee, it starts bleeding."

"I'll bring down a blanket."

Christian sighed. His lustful anticipation had melted.

She started for the ladder.

"Emily, I'm not so sure." He gripped his knee. "I need to cover this."

"You can lie on your back. I'll do the work."

Christian watched her climb the ladder. His thoughts were the *Titanic*. Sinking fast. *How does she know so much?*

She came back a moment later with a blanket and a little candle in a simple black metal holder. "Turn that off," she whispered, lighting the candle and setting it on the floor.

Christian flipped off the flashlight.

"Come here," she coaxed. She spread out the blanket.

He took a deep breath. The smell of musty hay and diesel fuel provided the ambience. "Maybe we should wait."

"Lie down," she said softly. "You scared?"

"A little. This isn't how I imagined it."

"The time is right now." She pouted. "We've talked all about this. I thought we agreed."

"We did. It's just—"

She leaned forward, kissing him softly and interrupting his words. "I'll help you."

He surrendered to the pressure of her hand on the top of his shoulder and dropped down to the blanket. But something about her confidence made him hesitate. "You know what you're doing."

The candle cast large shadows against the tall ceiling of the barn. She only smiled and started to unbutton her shirt. "Here," she said, reaching for his hand, guiding him toward her skin.

He resisted. "I've got blood on my hands."

"We'll be sharing more than blood."

She added force. "Lie back. Relax."

He shook his head. "Emily, have you—I mean—before—"

"Shh." She put her finger on his lips and moved to straddle him.

He took her fingers in his hand and studied her face in the flickering light of the candle. "You've done this before."

She stayed quiet for a moment. "Christian, I love you."

He shook his head. "Get off me."

"Christian!"

"No." He stood up. "I need to go home."

That evening, Tori sat on the couch next to Jarrod Baker. He'd stopped by Charlotte's place bearing Chinese takeout, a flower arrangement, and a chick flick, *The Proposal*. She sniffed and wiped her eyes.

Jarrod looked over. "You okay?"

"Sure." She shrugged. "I don't know what's the matter with me. It's just that these two are just perfect for each other and neither one can see it."

"It's a comedy. You're not supposed to cry."

Tori ignored him and picked up another bite of General Tso's chicken.

Jarrod put his arm around Tori and stretched to look at Charlotte, who was banging around the kitchen. "Let's go back to my place."

Tori lay her head against his shoulder. "This is just fine."

He cleared his throat. "But there it could be just us and—"

Tori lifted her head. "Let's not go there."

"But you said you wanted a fresh start, right? I thought we could—"

"Listen," she said, pushing away and looking into Jarrod's eyes. "I just had major surgery. I'm not ready." She paused. "And even if I was strong enough, we're not at the same place anymore. I think we need to try friendship first."

"Friends with benefits."

"No. Friends. Period."

"But before—"

"This isn't before." She could sense his frustration. "Look, you can't just separate the physical from your heart. Sex comes with a lot of emotional content."

He frowned. "Emotional content?"

She nodded. "Commitment. Love."

Jarrod pressed the pause button on the remote. "What's with you? You cry at a stupid movie. And now you talk of love. We never cared about that before. In fact, we thought a relationship without complicated attachments was preferable." He pointed at her. "You said you didn't believe in love."

She sighed. "So maybe I've changed." She sat up straighter and watched Jarrod pace. "It just doesn't feel like it used to. I want you to care about getting to know me as a woman first." She hesitated. "What's my favorite color? What is my biggest fear?"

He held up his hands. "Blue."

She shook her head.

"I don't know. This isn't fair. I thought we could pick up where we left off."

She didn't respond.

Jarrod continued to pace for a minute, then quietly sat in a recliner opposite the couch. "Okay, I'll play. What's your biggest fear?"

She smiled. "You really want to know?"

He seemed annoyed. "I asked the question, didn't I?"

"This isn't a game," she said. "A woman wants to feel pursued. Worth your time."

He shifted in his seat. "Okay. I really want to know. What is the infamous Dr. Victoria Taylor afraid of?"

"A month ago, I was afraid of dying. But not anymore."

"And your favorite color?"

"I'm not finished with the first one."

He sighed.

"I'm afraid you're going to think I'm crazy. You won't believe me."

"I don't think you're crazy. You're one of the most grounded scientists I know." He leaned forward, squinting. "Just what am I not going to believe?"

She launched forward. "Ever since my heart transplant, I'm having vivid memories of terror."

"Memories?"

She nodded. "Fire. Screaming. Someone in trouble."

He tilted his head as if to ask for clarification.

"Look, Jarrod, I'm just telling you what I'm experiencing. But at the same time, I know nothing like that ever happened to me."

"Maybe it's your immunosuppressive drugs playing with your brain."

She shook her head. "I had the first nightmare just as I woke up in the ICU before starting the drugs."

"So what do you make of this, Doctor?"

"The memories are real. They're just not mine."

She could tell by the look on his face that he wasn't following.

"The memories are a part of the transplant. I've gotten my donor's memories."

"Okay, you're weirding me out. Where'd you get a crazy idea like that?"

She folded her arms across her chest. "This feels like a betrayal. I'm sharing my heart with you, not something I do lightly," she said, her eyes locked on his. "I'm trusting you here with something important to me, and you think I'm crazy."

"I didn't say that. I said you had a crazy idea. That's different."

"Doesn't feel different." She cleared her throat. "Phin MacGrath told me about the phenomenon. I did some research. I think he's right."

"The social worker? Not exactly a scientist, is he?"

"He's worked with a lot of heart-transplant patients. He's seen it before."

"Tori, think about how you sound. There's got to be another logical explanation."

"I've found a logical explanation. In fact, I think I may need to do something about this."

"*Do* something?"

"You can't understand."

"And maybe you shouldn't try either. Have you ever considered that there are some things about your donor's life that you might not want to know?" Jarrod stood again and resumed pacing, shaking his head. "Look, Tori, I think you've been under a lot of stress. Going out on a limb and talking about this publicly would not be good. What are people going to say?"

"I don't know—that I've helped solve a mystery perhaps?"

"More likely you'll lose your credibility. Your great reputation as a surgeon."

"This is important. I feel an obligation."

"Why?" He continued shaking his head. "Your donor is dead. Nothing changes that."

"You don't get it."

"I want to protect you."

"Someone gave up her life so I could live."

"Not on purpose."

"Doesn't matter. I need to know."

"Tell me why."

"I feel different. I'm changing. I need to know who I am."

"Come on, Tori. You know who you are. You just need to recover a little, get back to work, and life will resume for you just like it always has."

"It's not that easy. I can't explain it." She took a deep breath. "Not to you."

Jarrod continued pacing until he reached the front door. He rested his hand on the doorknob.

"So that's it, huh?" she said. "No payoff for the flowers so you're going to leave?"

"It's not like that," he said, looking at his watch. "I've got a big day tomorrow."

"I want to finish the movie."

"Fine. Maybe you could drop it in a Redbox."

She nodded. *Whatever.*

He paused at the door. "You've changed. I'm not sure I know you anymore."

She didn't know how to respond.

"Do yourself a favor, Tori. Don't pursue this craziness." With that, he opened the door and left.

Tori huffed, settled deeper into the couch, and grabbed the remote. A moment later, she couldn't hold back the tears.

Who am I?

9

Ten days later, Tori startled awake with a nightmare of falling.

Stark terror. A scream and then the sudden jerking of her limbs in anticipation of hitting the ground.

For the third morning in a row.

She sat up slowly, trying to sharpen the border between alertness and slumber. Bit by bit, the cobwebs in her mind broke away. Breathing fast, she steadied her runaway thoughts and wiped the sweat from her brow before standing. She gathered her robe around her and plodded to the kitchen, stirring about quietly so as not to wake Charlotte. She made coffee, dripping the first cup straight into a white mug.

She was recovering at a record pace. That was good and bad. Good because she wanted to get back to normal. Bad because she felt good enough to be active—and without a job, boredom was just around the corner. She felt that the sooner she could get back to normal, the sooner she'd have something else worth occupying her mind, hopefully something capable of forcing the night terrors back into hiding.

She needed a plan. Looking out the kitchen window on the early Richmond morning, she decided today was as good a day as any to venture out. She sipped coffee and thought about the transplant team.

Did the harvest team travel by air? If so, did they use the Learjet or the helicopter? If they had, there would be a record of the flight. When? Where? Knowing the location of her heart donor would be a logical first step in understanding her terror.

After coffee and a bagel, she dressed and took the Broad Street bus downtown, exiting near the main hospital. She walked slowly up the sidewalk, appreciating a newfound endurance. As long as she kept her pace down, she could walk without shortness of breath.

Once in the university hospital, she hoped to slip into the ER without much fanfare. The medevac flight-dispatch office was just inside the ER main entrance in a little cubicle run by a single person in radio contact with the helicopter crew and outside rescue units.

On that day, Tori smiled to see an empty chair. Rodney Smith was a constant charmer and was busy chatting it up with one of the new ER nursing recruits. His back was to Tori as she approached the door to the flight-dispatch cubicle. Slipping inside the office, she looked around for what she needed. Would the record be on a computer? Or did they have a physical logbook?

She opened and shut the top drawer below the desk. She eyed a filing cabinet, then spotted a logbook to the right of the radio. Opening the book, she paged back to a record on the night before her transplant. Running her finger down the page, she saw exactly what she wanted. "Organ harvest team, Baltimore City Hospital."

"Bingo," she whispered.

Hearing the door, she quickly closed the book and looked over to see Rodney.

"Dr. Taylor?"

"Hi, Rodney."

Rodney adjusted the bill on his Atlanta Braves baseball cap. "What are you doing here? You're about the last person I'd expect to see. How are you? You had a transplant, right?"

"Yes, yes. I'm fine. Bored, but fine. So bored in fact that I decided to look around the ER to see if anyone was stirring up trouble. When I saw flight dispatch, I thought I'd step in and see if you were flying anywhere memorable."

She watched his face. She was talking too much and didn't want to appear as nervous as she felt. She pointed to the logbook. "Looks like today has been quiet."

He chuckled. "The day is young."

"Yes, well," she said, edging past him to the door. "Great seeing you again. Take care."

She walked into the hallway and met two men, one she expected and one she didn't. The taller of the duo was Rick Harveson, an associate professor in Tori's department, surgical oncology. Rick was young but skilled and often sought Tori out for advice. The shorter man was Steve Brown.

"Steve?"

"Tori," the shorter man said, smiling.

Rick didn't smile. "I didn't expect to run into you."

Tori gave Steve the once-over. Steve had been a med-school classmate. He had aged. His hair, once black, was now silver. "Wow, how long has it been?"

"Too long."

"So what brings you to town?"

He looked at Rick and shrugged. "The surgical oncology chief. I'm interviewing for the job."

Tori tried to hide her surprise. *I wasn't told Dr. Fisher was retiring. That should be my job!* She cleared her throat. "I see."

"We should catch up sometime."

She couldn't think. She fought to focus. "Uh, sure."

Rick stepped between them. "I was just showing Steve around," he said, looking at his watch.

"Sure," Tori mumbled.

She steadied her weight against the wall as the men walked on through the swinging ER doors and the noise of trauma beyond. She took a deep breath.

A young orderly passed. "Ma'am, are you okay?"

Tori swallowed. "I'm fine."

She moved slowly down the corridor, aware that the breath that had seemed so easy outside on the sidewalk was now coming in labored gasps. She waited to enter a crowded elevator of shortcoats, the medical students on their third-year rotations. Fortunately, they hadn't rotated on surgery yet, so they didn't recognize her. She moved to the back of the elevator and listened to their banter.

"Jason spent the whole night in the ICU."

"He's kissing up."

"He got to do an arterial line."

"Wasn't Dr. Hinkle's lecture on physical exam hilarious?"

A student imitated the professor, holding up his finger. "The first rule of physical assessment is lights on, clothes off!"

Tori drifted as they droned on, complaining about their hours. *How did I not know that Dr. Fisher's spot was opening up?*

She exited on the floor of the surgery offices. Once on her hallway, she was greeted by her secretary, Valarie Herman. "Dr. Taylor? What are you doing here?"

She plodded forward, grunting through her teeth. "I'm here to see Dr. Evans."

Valarie trailed Tori like a toy poodle, barking warnings about the chairman's schedule, his clinic, and his other appointments.

Tori ignored her. "He'll see me."

She got to the receptionist's desk outside the chairman's office. The assistant, a woman of considerable stature, stood as a physical barrier between Tori and the chairman's door.

"I need to see Dr. Evans."

The secretary continued standing in the way and reached awkwardly for the phone. She pressed the intercom. "Dr. Taylor here to see you, sir."

She heard Samuel Evans grunt. "Send her in."

Tori offered a terse smile and moved toward the door. Once there, she took a deep breath and pushed her way inside.

She looked at the man behind the massive mahogany desk. He didn't raise his eyes from the stack of papers on his desk. Tori cleared her throat. "I want to interview for the division chief position." She sighed and wondered why the air seemed so *rare*.

He stayed quiet, sighing and rubbing his short crop of white hair. "Look, Tori, I was going to tell you."

"Well, it doesn't matter now. I know."

"Tori, you're on leave. You need to be concentrating on recovery. Counseling."

"Right now I'm concentrating on my career. You know everyone expects me to take Dr. Fisher's position. I've worked for this. I've earned it."

Dr. Evans looked up. "Tori, surgeons don't walk on water anymore. You can't just treat the staff like red meat and expect to get ahead."

She wanted to defend but held her tongue. "Agreed." She paused. "But I've changed, sir."

"Oh really? So why do I hear that you can't even obey a simple nurse's instruction to stay in bed after your catheterization?"

Tori was aghast. "That's crazy, sir. It has nothing to do with my ability to get along with the staff. I needed to use the restroom, so I got out of bed a little earlier than advised. End of story."

The chairman shook his head. "You're not making this easy on yourself." He tapped a designer ink pen against the desktop. "Why haven't you followed up with counseling?"

"I've talked to Phin MacGrath. I'm waiting for him to set up the next session."

The chairman sighed and pushed back from his desk.

"With all due respect, Dr. Evans, we have talked about this. I've served this department faithfully. No one has published more. No one carries my patient load."

"And no one has the file of complaints from staff that you do."

Her mouth was suddenly cotton-dry. She paused, trying to swallow the lump in her throat. "I don't deny that I've been hard on the staff. But I can learn better ways to deal with incompetence, sir."

Dr. Samuel Evans coughed and continued tapping his pen.

"You're supposed to make my life easy. Instead—" He halted with apparent concern.

She couldn't respond. Her face was on fire. She needed to find a Kleenex to wipe away the perspiration.

"Tori?"

She felt the room spinning and found it more difficult to get her breath.

"You're sweating."

She was aware of a feeling of tightness in her chest, a constricting pain in her throat. She reached for the corner of the desk to stop the spinning room.

She missed. And after that, everything went black.

10

Linda Mitchell stirred, nudged from sleep by the squeak of the back door. She'd gotten used to the sounds of the old house, the way the wind rattled the chains on the porch swing and the occasional creaking whisper of what her husband called "settling noise."

But this was different. The squeak followed by the rattle of the door had a human component. She poked her husband, who snored blissfully at her side. Her whisper was urgent. "Dan."

He moaned.

"Dan, I hear someone."

He sat up, rubbing his eyes.

The noise continued.

She followed her husband down the stairs. A light was on in the kitchen.

There, a shirtless Christian sat at the kitchen table. He leaned forward, his attention on his right leg where he had pulled his pants leg up to reveal a jagged gash.

Dan rushed to kneel in front of his son, who looked up with tears in his eyes.

"Chris, what happened?"

"Dad, I really screwed up."

When Tori opened her eyes, her chairman's face seemed to float above hers. She heard the voice of his secretary. "Should I call 911?"

Dr. Evans chuckled. "We're in the largest referral hospital in Virginia already. What do you think?"

"Oh," she said. "I could call a code."

"Don't do that either. She has a pulse." Tori felt his fingers on her neck. "Call the ER. Ask them to send up a nurse with a stretcher."

Tori tried to concentrate. *How did I end up on the floor?* She coughed.

"Oh my," the secretary said. "I think she's coming around."

"Tori?" Dr. Evans touched her forehead.

"What … what happened?"

"You fainted. I think you have a fever."

She struggled to sit.

"Stay down. I think your blood pressure is low. When's the last time you had fluids?"

"This morning. I had coffee."

Dr. Evans frowned. "Hmm. Coffee is a diuretic, probably not the best choice for a heart patient." He spoke as if she were an idiot child.

He stood and picked up his phone. "Operator? Page Dr. Parrish."

Thirty minutes later, Tori found herself the center of her transplant surgeon's attention. He held up his index finger. "Low-grade fever." He held up a second finger. "Fainting episode."

Tori raised her hand and inspected her IV line. "So what's the differential diagnosis?"

"Could be any number of things. The big two are acute transplant rejection and infection. Your immunosuppressive drug regimen puts you at risk for that."

This Tori knew. "My throat is dry."

"Sore?"

"A little."

He pulled a small flashlight from his pocket. "Say 'ah.'"

She obeyed.

"Wow. You've got a candida infection."

"And here I've never been across the northern border."

"Funny. If it's this bad in your throat, I'll bet you have it all the way down your esophagus. Very common in immunosuppressed patients."

"So give me some nystatin swish-and-swallow and send me home."

"Not a chance."

"But I didn't pack. I'll come right back if I have problems."

"Do you want me to spell it out? An acute rejection could mean sudden death. An infection while taking immunosuppressive drugs can be quickly fatal."

"I'm a doctor, okay? I get it. I'll be careful. Let me go."

"Not before we do a heart biopsy."

"But if we know the source of the fever—"

"You may still be in rejection. Too risky not to know. You're due for a biopsy in a few more days anyway."

Tori groaned. "This wasn't on my day planner."

Dr. Parrish folded his arms across his chest. "Is there anything you aren't telling me?"

"Am I that transparent?"

"I don't know. You just seem ... to be somewhere else." He paused. "How are the nightmares?"

"In a word? Vivid."

"I'm going to order a head CT."

"Looking for?"

"Central nervous system fungal balls."

"You won't find anything. The memories are real. They just aren't mine."

"If the CT is normal, I'm going to look into changing your drug regimen."

"It's not the drugs."

"How can you be so sure?"

"The nightmares preceded my first dose." She gathered the sheet under her chin. "And it just seems like something I know."

"Like it happened to you."

"Exactly."

He stood over her, his silence confirming her fears. He didn't believe her. And because she was also a scientist, she felt his disdain for her falling under the spell of such emotion.

She shook her head. "I can't imagine that you could understand."

"Look, I need you to be honest with me about these things. Just because I'm having a hard time with your theory doesn't mean I don't need to know about it. But I will look for another source for the problem."

She shrugged. "Sure."

He stepped to the doorway. "I'll be ordering your tests and some antifungal medication." He pulled open the doorway and then halted. "Say, I wouldn't mention these dreams to Dr. Evans. He certainly won't hear it from my lips."

Tori nodded. His unspoken message was clear. *The boss will think you're as crazy as I do.*

The next evening, Phin stopped by Tori's hospital room. They quickly covered her present situation: she'd undergone a cardiac cath and biopsy and the results were pending. In the meantime, she was being treated for an "opportunistic" infection, one that doesn't routinely cause problems in the healthy patient but, in a patient on immunosuppressive drugs, takes advantage of the lowered defenses to attack and cause illness. In her case, it was the common fungus known as candida, and it had attacked her mouth and esophagus with a vengeance.

After reviewing the present, Phin naturally steered the conversation to Tori's past. He seemed truly interested. He wanted to know everything about how she ended up in her chosen career of cancer surgery.

"I was a teenager when my mother developed breast cancer," she began.

Tori thought back over her mother's pitiful struggle and how a surgeon had made mistakes, reassuring her mother that she didn't need to worry about her mammogram findings.

She remembered the afternoon her mother came home from her first surgical consultation. "He said I'm okay. I don't need a biopsy after all."

Tori squeezed her mother tightly. "So all that worry was for nothing. Let's celebrate."

"How about Cold Mountain Creamery?"

The memory warmed her.

Three months later, Tori's mother started bleeding from her right nipple. She ignored it. "The doctor reassured me that it was okay, remember?"

By the time she presented back to her primary doctor, she had palpable lymph nodes under her arm and a chest X-ray showing lung metastasis.

Tori vowed she would become a surgeon and never make the same mistakes. She would dedicate her life to an aggressive surgical attack on cancer without regards to flim-flam emotions.

The memories tumbled down the mountain and picked up speed.

Chemo.

Surgery. The loss of a breast.

Her mother didn't feel sexy anymore.

And it mattered to Tori.

There were other losses.

Her mother's auburn hair.

A continuous dropping of weight. The fat fell from her hips. Yes, even from the butt she'd always complained was impossible to downsize, but in the end, she looked like a boy. Gangly. All knuckles and knobs. Bones sticking up under a thin tent of skin like moles poking up in a backyard.

More surgery. Cutting away a chest recurrence.

Dianne Taylor was sexless. No breast. No curves. No sexy auburn hair.

Tori cursed her mother's cancer every day.

And every other day: the God who allowed it to steal her away. In the end, when she found out that the surgeon had erred, warm fuzzy emotions became suspect to Tori because she feared another false hope. She grew into a skeptical, closed adult, suspect of any real hope, knowing the hammer of truth may lurk just around the bend.

By the time she finished telling her mother's story, Tori was glad she hadn't bothered with mascara. She blew her nose and looked up through watery eyes. "I'm a mess."

"Far from it," Phin said.

He stayed quiet throughout her story. Once, he reached his hand out and simply let it rest on hers for a moment.

She didn't mind the rough calluses.

"You still blame God?"

Tori stared off, above and beyond the social worker. "I don't think about it much anymore. But I never went to church after that either." She hesitated, then added, "I guess I'm mad because he didn't answer my prayers to take away the pain."

"God had an interesting answer to human suffering."

Tori didn't respond. When Phin stayed quiet, she shifted in her hospital bed. "Well, aren't you going to continue?"

"If you want," he said, with the corners of his mouth hinting at a smile. "God doesn't always deliver us from pain. God joined us in human suffering by coming as a man and experiencing pain and death for himself."

"You sound like Charlotte."

"She must be a good friend."

"She's gullible. Believes in fairy tales." Tori dabbed her eyes again. "I take a scientific approach. Pain is an important message, our body's way of telling us something is wrong. It's my job to figure out what is wrong and offer a solution." She smiled. "Fortunately, it's something I'm good at."

"Would you have become a surgeon if it wasn't for your mother's story?"

"Probably not. Until she got sick, I was planning on an Air Force career like my father. I wanted to be a helicopter pilot."

"Ever thought that God may have allowed some of this because he wanted you to do the good work that you do?"

"Okay, that's too Pollyanna for me. He could have just had me read an article in a magazine about cancer research or something. Why'd he have to take my mother away?"

"I doubt you'd have listened. As it was, he had your attention." He reached for her hand. "You'll probably never have an answer to the why questions until you get to heaven. For now, we have to comfort ourselves that while God doesn't always deliver us from pain, he joined us in it by taking on human flesh."

She let his words settle. Water filtering slowly into the sand of her mind. For some reason, she didn't fight. For the first time in a long time, she allowed herself to consider that Phin might be right. And if not right, at least his sincerity was touching.

After a minute, she turned her hand over in his so that they could rest palm to palm. "Can I change the subject?"

"Sure." He smiled. "I think we're making progress."

"Oh, great. Here it seemed like we were just two friends talking about life and I almost forgot that I'm in counseling."

"I didn't mean it like that. We can be friends."

She nodded. "Okay. I think I know where my heart came from."

11

Two days later, after Tori's discharge, Phin came to see her at Charlotte's place. On an old oak kitchen table, he spread out copies of the news clippings he'd photocopied and printed from online sources.

Charlotte looked on with a long nose over a mug of Earl Grey tea. "Are you sure you want to do this? They protect the identity of donors for a reason."

Tori leaned forward, looking at an article from the *Baltimore Sun*. "No, I'm not really sure." She picked up the article. "But I think I need to."

Phin shrugged. "We'll have to be careful. Donor families can be pretty funny about this stuff."

Tori looked up. "Funny?"

"We once had a white family upset that their daughter's heart was given to a black girl."

Charlotte set down her mug. Too hard. She huffed and picked up a paper towel to catch the spill. "Intolerance like that needs to be exposed."

"I'm just saying …," Phin said, his voice trailing off.

"What?"

"Let's say we start digging and actually find out who owned that heart of yours before you did. Aren't there some things you might not want to know?"

"That's a risk I'm willing to take to try to make some sense of all this."

"Maybe the memories just represent fears your donor had that weren't real. You know, like a fear of fire or falling and you just dream about it because you're afraid."

"So we just need to ask some questions," Tori said. "But I think the memories mean more than that. I can't get the number three one six out of my mind." She shook her head and stared at the ceiling. "I have the distinct memory of my donor telling me to remember it. I think it's the key to unlocking the mystery of her death."

Tori carefully wrote in block numbers: "316." She took the paper and stuck it to the refrigerator with a Papa John's Pizza magnet. "There. What it means, I don't know."

Phin scratched his head. "An address? A box number of some sort?"

Charlotte sat down. "What if your donor was a criminal? Is that something you really want to know?"

Tori nodded. "I'm alive because of her." She looked up and traded glances with her friends. "I'm not sure you can get this, but I feel I'm not really going to understand who I am until I know whose heart this was."

Phin shook his head. "You aren't defined by a muscle. Your identity is so much more. Think of the people you've helped. That's who you are."

"That's who I was. I feel different now."

Phin picked up an article to review. "You weren't responsible for what happened to your donor. You just happened to be the right tissue type."

"Look at this," Tori said, writing down a name from a clipping. "A twenty-year-old female by the name of Charlene McDonald was in an accident on the night before my transplant. She was taken to Baltimore City Hospital."

"The same hospital where the donor team flew to get your heart."

"One and the same," Tori said. "The article doesn't say if she lived or died." She read aloud from the article. "After a forty-minute extraction, McDonald was flown from the scene to Baltimore City Hospital with head and abdominal injuries." She paused, holding the clipping in her hand.

"There were four others." Phin pushed a second article forward. "A stabbing victim downtown. Taken to Johns Hopkins. Says she died shortly after arrival in their ER."

Tori studied the paper. "Doesn't mention transplant."

"Normally they wouldn't. Privacy is a priority."

"Exactly," Charlotte said. "These laws are in place to protect the families. They may not want to meet you."

"So maybe I won't contact the family. I could still go to the police and tell them what I know."

Charlotte sighed. "I bet that would go well. This whole thing is a stretch."

"So what am I supposed to do, just ignore the nightmares?" Tori pushed back from the table. "I think they mean something."

"Maybe they do mean something, child. What about your own past? Have you ever thought the dreams might be a distortion of something in your own childhood? Or maybe the fire is just a symbol."

"That's crazy. No one ever tried to hurt me."

"Here's one more," Phin said. "Two jumpers from the fifth floor of an old apartment building in northeast Baltimore. Apparently the couple jumped to escape a fire."

"Does it say they died?"

"Nope. Condition unknown. But the EMS took them to Baltimore City."

"Five stories. Not too many people survive that." Tori tapped her pen against the tabletop. "So that makes four possibilities. One car accident, one stabbing, and two jumpers." She scanned the article about the jumpers and studied the picture above the article. "Fire victim, Dakota Jones. The fact that they call her a victim sounds like she died." Tori touched the picture of Dakota Jones and thought about her nightmares of fire and falling. "Dakota, did you give me your heart?"

"There may be more," Phin added. "At least three outlying counties fly their trauma into Baltimore City and the shock trauma unit. They may not have made the papers."

"So how do we find out?"

"Do you know any of the docs at Baltimore City?"

Tori shook her head.

"What about other VCU docs? Someone is bound to know someone up there who can tell us something."

"Look, Phin, I'm not comfortable asking other VCU doctors to get involved. If it gets around that I'm snooping into this, it can't be good. I'm already against the ropes on my career. I can't risk another black mark."

"Okay, I'll enter their names and do some Internet searches, and I know an ex-cop who had a transplant who may be able to help us out."

"That's cool."

"Give me the names of the possible donors," he said, snatching a pen from his shirt pocket.

"Charlene McDonald was the accident victim." Tori lifted another article. "The stabbing victim was Nancy Chan." She slid the article toward Phin and lifted the third. "And the jumpers were Dakota Jones and …" Tori scanned the article. "Here it is. Christian Mitchell."

12

Emily stepped slowly toward her farmhouse beneath a condemning night sky. The planned rendezvous had been a disaster. What was supposed to be a night of exploration and ecstasy had turned bitter. A separation. Hurt feelings and disgust.

Her plan had failed. A rescue, once visible on the horizon, had vanished. She was stranded on the same island of tension.

She entered through the back door, wincing at the squeaking sound of the screen door. She froze, standing barefoot in the kitchen.

Above her, the floor creaked. She heard water running through the pipes. Her father must be in the bathroom. She tried to slow her breathing. It would not be pretty if he found her up.

She waited, listening to the night sounds. A toilet flushed. The groan of weight on hardwood floors and the muffled creaking of her parents' king-sized bed.

She waited another five minutes, a century in the darkness, before climbing the stairs. She only needed to get to the top and across the hall to her room.

At the top of the stairs, a lone figure stepped from the shadows. Her father, Billy Greene, stepped out of the darkness with a baseball bat.

Emily gasped. "Oh, Daddy, you scared me."

"Emily?" He lowered the bat but continued forward. "Where have you been?"

"I couldn't sleep. I was just getting a snack."

He shook his head and frowned. "Since when do you sleep like that?" He was inspecting her clothes. "You've been outside."

"I just wanted some air."

"You were meeting that boy, weren't you?" He grabbed her shoulder and pulled her forward, stretching open the neck of her flannel shirt. "What's this?" he said, reaching for her chest. "No bra!"

"Daddy, I don't sleep in—"

"Emily, tell me the truth!"

Emily pulled back, but her foot slipped onto the stairs. Her arms flailed in an attempt at balance, a fight that was hopeless against gravity. Her head struck the banister on the way down. *Was I pushed?*

Bumping and rolling, she bounced down the wooden steps. Pain assaulted her, stabbing her foot. She gripped her ankle.

"Billy?" It was her mother's voice.

Her father towered over her. "She snuck out to meet the neighbor boy." He snapped on the lights. "Look how she's dressed."

"Emily?" Her mother's voice was soothing. Quickly, she came to her side.

Emily stared at her right foot that pointed in an unnatural direction different from her knee.

"Your foot!"

Billy backed away. "She slipped. That's all there was to it."

Emily seethed. "I was getting away from *you*!"

"Oh, my baby," Carolyn Greene cried. "We need to get you to a hospital."

Thirty minutes later, Dr. Dan Mitchell watched every suture over the shoulder of the ER physician on duty as he carefully reapproximated the edges of the wound on Christian's right knee.

The doctor cleared his throat. "Why didn't you just stitch him up yourself?"

"I don't keep the instruments I need at home," he said. "The supplies I had on hand I've already packed and sent back to Africa."

The doctor nodded and used his forearm to blot the perspiration from his forehead without contaminating his sterile gloves.

"I hope I'm not making you nervous by watching."

Christian watched as the doctor rolled his eyes. "Of course not, sir."

The automatic doors to the entrance of Nassawadox General Hospital ER slid open. Christian looked up from his stretcher to see an orderly pushing Emily Greene in a wheelchair, flanked by her parents, Billy and Carolyn. He flailed to grab at the curtain beside him, desperately wanting to fling it closed.

The doctor cut the last suture. "Just what were you doing outside at this hour anyway?"

Christian ducked and propped a pillow in front of his face. "Long story," he grunted.

"Christian?" The voice was Emily's.

Busted.

Mr. Greene's face was the color of salmon. He pointed at Christian. "You?"

Christian felt a tightness in his chest. "Hello, Mr. Greene."

Mr. Greene took a step toward Christian's stretcher. Dan Mitchell stepped between the large man and his son. Mr. Greene looked at Dan. "Do you know what your boy was trying to do?" Mr. Greene's right eye was twitching. "You want to know what happens to a boy who violates my daughter?"

Christian held up his hands. "Nothing happened, sir. We just talked."

"That's not the story my daughter gives. She said she had to fight you off, and you cut your leg when she pushed you away."

"Emily!" Christian shouted, his eyes wide with shock.

Dan moved closer to his son. "He cut his leg jumping over a fence."

"Tell him, Emily," Christian pleaded.

"My daughter was assaulted by this young man. She hurt her ankle jumping from a hayloft, trying to get away from him."

Dan Mitchell stood his ground. "I'm going to ask you to leave us alone, Mr. Greene. We can sort this out later."

The doctor looked at the orderly. "Why don't you put this wheel-chair patient into the ortho room?"

"No!" Emily's voice was shrill. "I want to stay out here in the open."

Mr. Greene raised his voice. "Emily!"

She began to cry. "I made it all up, Daddy. He didn't assault me. Meeting in the barn was my idea."

Tori opened her eyes and fought for focus. More often than not since her transplant, she awoke with the premonition of fear. *Someone wants me dead.*

Pain in her ankle brought with it the memory of falling down stairs. She rubbed her eyes and sat up. In spite of the early hour—5:30—there was noise in the kitchen below. She worked the stiffness out of her ankle and mused that her nightmares were encroaching on her reality. *Must be the weather.*

She tested her feet on the floor, grabbed her robe, and walked to the kitchen. Charlotte was stirring a kettle of soup. The air was thick with the aroma of fried hamburger, onions, and green peppers.

Friday was chili day at the soup kitchen.

"Morning," Tori mumbled as she lifted the coffee pot.

"You're up early."

She didn't answer. Not that Charlotte had asked a question, but it had been inflected in her voice. Instead, Tori paused, touching the photocopies from the articles that Phin had brought over the evening before and still lay scattered on the kitchen table. She lifted the picture of Dakota Jones to her face. "I wonder if she has green eyes."

Charlotte opened the refrigerator and retrieved a block of cheddar cheese. "I've been thinking about your number here," she said. "What it means."

"A clue in a mystery, I think."

"Or maybe it's a message to you."

Tori sat at the table.

Charlotte busied herself grating the cheddar.

"Do I have to pry it out of you?"

"You'll think I'm preaching."

"It's never stopped you before."

"For God so loved the world," Charlotte began.

Something quickened within Tori. She picked up the refrain. "That he gave his only begotten Son."

They continued together in unison. "That whosoever believeth in him should not perish, but have everlasting life."

"John 3:16," Tori whispered.

"I wasn't sure you knew it."

She shrugged. "I seem to know it now." She hesitated. "By heart."

"You didn't memorize it. You left my home rebellious and stubborn, never once doing the memory verses I suggested. You just couldn't get past God allowing your mother to die."

Tori sipped her coffee. "Phin thinks God used my mother's death to get me to follow a path into medicine."

"What do you think?"

"I think you two are ganging up on me."

Charlotte laughed, her soprano heh-heh-heh staccato in the air like footsteps bounding down happy stairs.

"Can I serve soup today?"

"You gonna tell me what you think about my theory?"

"It's a nice verse, Charlotte."

"It's truth."

Tori sighed. "Can I serve soup?"

"Sure."

"How's Manny?"

"He hasn't been by in a few weeks. We can go by his place and take him some soup once the kitchen closes."

"I don't know."

"He's dying, Tori."

"Exactly why I don't want to see him."

"For a physician, you certainly seem to be spooked by death."

"Death is the enemy. I spend all of my time trying to keep my patients out of the grim reaper's bony fingers."

"Sometimes death doesn't have to be the enemy. Manny has been hurting. Death means the arms of Jesus and relief." She put her hands on her ample hips. "Have you ever been with a person at their moment of death?"

She cleared her throat. "No."

"Being a good surgeon isn't just a technical adventure, you know."

Tori waved her off. "Okay, I get it." She hesitated. "What would I do?"

"Just be there. Offer your presence."

Tori stayed quiet and sipped at the warm cup in her hands. When she spoke again, it was as if words were echoing across time from her childhood. Instinctively, they fell from her lips.

She began quietly, "For God so loved the world ..."

13

That afternoon, with the aroma of chili still clinging to her clothes, Tori reluctantly rode along with Charlotte to visit Manny Benson.

Tori had first known Manny as a patron of the soup kitchen. She was a teenager when she first started hanging out there, listening to his stories of survival. As a Vietnam vet, Manny never quite fit in after his return from the jungle. He couldn't seem to keep a job, fighting nightmares and posttraumatic stress. Then, in a blow that would have leveled most men, Manny suffered yet another devastating loss: his wife in an apartment fire. After that, he never seemed to find his footing. But that didn't stop a young Tori Taylor from admiring his grit. Eventually, after living on the street for the best part of a decade, he became a local celebrity of sorts when a *Richmond Times-Dispatch* reporter did a series on Manny's life, digging up several heroic reports where Manny had put himself in harm's way to save a fellow soldier. Here he was, recipient of a Purple Heart and surviving yet again in a jungle of sorts in downtown Richmond. He found part-time work as a maintenance man in a tobacco warehouse and found motivation to stick it out because they let him roll his own cigars. He had finally escaped the streets, but if truth be told, he always felt a little claustrophobic indoors and would favor a park bench to a couch if given the option.

Two years ago, Manny had turned pumpkin orange and started to itch. Charlotte corralled him into Tori's clinic where a CT scan told a predictable story: a mass in the head of the pancreas.

Tori operated, removing the cancer, carefully and meticulously dissecting the offending tissue from the vital vascular structures at the base of the liver. Now the enemy had resurfaced. This time, there was no cure. Like a bad neighbor, the cancer had set up residence in the liver. A tube inserted through his side diverted the flow of obstructed bile and relieved the itching, but survival now was a matter of time. Weeks, not months. "Don't buy green bananas," his doctor said.

As they entered his small apartment, Tori lifted her face toward an open window, a vain attempt to escape the smell of sweat, bile, and decay.

Manny was sitting in an old recliner with an Atlanta Braves fleece tucked under his chin. He brightened when he saw the two of them. He shook his head. "Leave the door unlocked around this place and you never know what kind of riffraff will find its way in."

Charlotte huffed. "Just you be glad God made riffraff like me." She set the Tupperware container on his kitchen table. "Got a pan? I want to heat this up."

"Chili day at the kitchen," he said, his voice threadbare.

Tori inched forward. "Hi, Manny."

"Look at you. You got a new heart."

She nodded.

"You don't have to stand by the door."

Tori edged closer and selected a kitchen chair. Somehow a wooden chair seemed a safer bet. Everything else was upholstered, and she could just imagine how the odor of death held the fabric with tiny bony hands. Worse, she found herself wondering if her immune system could handle the smorgasbord of bacteria in this place.

He held up his hand toward her. She approached, suddenly finding herself with the armor of a clinician. She wanted to check his drain, his incision, to ask about his bowel movements. Anything to put it back on a professional plane. Somewhere away from this place where friends needed a handshake or worse, to try to make sense of pain.

Charlotte clanked a pot onto the stove. *Why doesn't she come in here and rescue me?*

Manny took Tori's hand and didn't let go. "Here," he said, pointing to the ottoman where his feet lay. "You can sit."

She obeyed, sitting next to the sticks that used to be his legs.

"How are you?" he asked.

"I'm good."

"That's it? You just had a heart transplant."

She shrugged and concentrated on his hand, now held in both of hers. She felt each finger, cold skin stretched over bone, imagining that warm blood was reluctant to go all the way to the tips for fear of freezing. "It's been tough. I was back in the hospital once since my discharge. Seems my body wanted to reject such a nice gift." She hesitated, putting away all the clinical questions she would normally use to assess cancer. Instead, with her mind slate swept clean of data, she asked the first thing that came to her mind. "Are you afraid?"

His eyes moistened. "A little."

They sat quietly for a few minutes, and Tori just listened to the noise of Manny's breathing. He seemed to be grunting his way from breath to breath.

"Soup's on." Charlotte set a tray with a steaming bowl of chili on Manny's lap.

Manny took a few sips and set the tray on the coffee table. In leaning forward, his blanket pulled off to expose a bucket sitting beside his recliner.

Is that what I smell?

Manny belched, and then lifted the bucket to his chin. Leaning forward, he emptied his stomach.

It looked as if he'd gotten rid of a lot more than he'd taken in. Many more days like this and he'd be so dehydrated his kidneys would shut down.

Charlotte came running with a moistened washcloth. She patted Manny's forehead as he spit into his pail.

"Let me bring over some IV fluids," Tori said. "Some saline will make you feel better."

"For what?" Manny whispered. "So I can live a little longer like this?" He shook his head. "No thank you."

Tori brushed a tear from her cheek. She hated seeing him this way.

"That's the only saline I need," he said. "To see your tears means more to me than your doctoring." He reached for her again.

She thought once about the vomit he had wiped away from his lips with his hand. Her head told her to be careful.

Her heart told her something different.

They stayed two hours until a hospice nurse arrived. For most of that time, Tori just held his hand and listened to him breathe.

When they got outside, Charlotte pointed across the street to a park bench on the edge of a little playground. "Why don't you rest a few minutes? I need to pick up a few things at Checker's Grocery."

Tori sat but soon felt compelled to explore the playground. *Why do I remember this place?*

She listened to the children playing, their voices mingling with memories of a playground.

Just like this one.

She walked around an old set of swings and looked at three molded animals mounted on thick springs. A little girl with red hair bobbed back and forth on the back of a turtle, her voice rising and falling with the swaying beast.

At the edge of an enclosed twisty metal slide, Tori paused. She couldn't shake the feeling that she'd been there before. As an adult, she could look over the top of the slide. In her memory, the tunnel slide was much higher. She knelt in the sand at the exit of the slide and peered in.

Fire.

A bad man.

She gasped and pulled her head away.

A double tap on a car horn caught her attention. She looked up to see Charlotte wave through the open window of her VW Beetle.

She opened the door slowly, trying not to strain her chest.

"What's with you? Seeing old ghosts?"

Tori looked at her friend. *I'm that transparent?* "Just take me home. I need a bed." She lifted a small brown bag and inspected the contents. One bottle of Paul Newman's Caesar salad dressing. "You know you have a full bottle of this in your refrigerator?"

Charlotte didn't answer. She glanced in Tori's direction and turned her attention to the road.

This wasn't like Charlotte. Her kitchen was organized to the point of obsession. She knew what she had and what she needed, right down to every spice. Evidently, she felt Tori's eyes boring in on her, because when she spoke, she'd taken on a rare defensive tone. "You can never have too much Caesar dressing."

Tori stared through the window, letting the conversation drop. As they approached the end of the block, she turned to see the tubular slide one last time. A knot formed in the top of her stomach. *Why does that thing scare me so much?*

Social worker Stephanie Allen handed Emily a tissue. "You're safe. I need you to tell me exactly what happened."

Emily sniffed. "I need pain medicine."

"Why don't you just tell me what happened? Then I'll get the nurse."

Emily looked around the ER cubicle. The unit was quiet. Since Christian had left, only one other patient remained, a disheveled man sleeping off a drunk in the first stretcher. Across the nurse's station, she could see the closed door to the waiting room. The room where certainly her father would be pacing. "I snuck out to be with my boyfriend. My dad caught me sneaking back in. We had a fight at the top of the stairs. When I pulled away from him, I fell. That's all."

"Did your father hit you?"

She shook her head.

"Why did you lie to your father and tell him that your boyfriend assaulted you?"

"I was afraid my father would think it was my idea."

"What about the story about how you twisted your ankle?"

"I told you, I fell down the stairs. That's the truth. My dad told me to lie about it so that no one would think he pushed me."

"Why would they think that?"

"Because we were arguing when I fell."

"And now I'm supposed to believe you when you've just admitted making up two lies."

Emily nodded.

The social worker made a note and muttered something about being out at two in the morning to talk to a lying teen.

Emily looked up to see her father through a crack in the curtains. "My daddy wouldn't hurt me," she said. "Daddy loves me."

The social worker looked at her watch. She nodded. "Okay, I'll ask the nurse to get you some pain medication." She opened the curtain and nodded at Mr. Greene. "You may as well come in."

"Oh, Daddy, I'm so sorry. Don't take it out on Christian."

Mr. Greene eyed the social worker. "That's okay, baby, as long as you're going to be all right."

Stephanie stepped away from the cubicle just as Dr. Stanfield, the orthopedist on call, entered. After an introduction, he lifted an

X-ray toward a fluorescent light in the ceiling. As he leaned closer, Emily caught the scent of a heavy aftershave.

The surgeon pointed to the black-and-white image. "See how these bone fragments are separated here? A few screws should do the trick."

Emily hugged her chest and looked at her father.

The surgeon smiled. "Since your daughter is a minor, I'll need you to sign the consent, Mr. Greene."

Carolyn Greene entered and took her place at her daughter's side, between Emily and her husband.

Emily shook her head. "Mom, I'm afraid."

"Don't worry, baby. I'll be waiting for you after you wake up."

14

Tori knocked softly on the open door. Phin MacGrath looked up from behind his cluttered desk. "Hey, you're out on the town."

She smiled. "Can't stay away from this place, you know?" She looked at the stack of papers in front of him. "Got a minute?"

"Sure." He lifted his hand toward a chair across from his desk.

Tori sat. "I wanted to know if you've found out anything about our little investigation."

He leaned forward, squinting. "Are you in pain?"

"No."

"You were rubbing your chest."

"I'm trying not to scratch." She forced a chuckle. "My incision itches."

"My grandmother says that's a sign of healing."

"Smart woman." She purposefully took her hands away from her blouse and gripped the arms of the wooden chair. "So what do you know?"

"Not much. My buddy, the one that used to be a cop, remember? He talked to the police in Baltimore. The stab victim was basically dead when EMS picked her up, never even had surgery."

"Okay, so no time for a transplant. That leaves the car accident and the jumpers."

"No obituary for the car-accident victim. He found a phone number and confirmed that she lived."

"That means my heart came from Dakota Jones."

"Not necessarily. There could have been others that were flown in from somewhere other than the city who wouldn't be in the Baltimore paper."

Tori sighed. She studied the top of his desk. Her eyes paused on a small framed photograph. A slightly younger Phin and a smiling young woman bundled up in winter jackets and gripping a set of skis. She looked up to see Phin watching her. *Busted.* She cleared her throat. "She's pretty."

He didn't bite.

Tell me she's your sister.

"How's Dr. Baker?"

"Jarrod?" She made a dismissive wave. "I wouldn't know." She smiled. *If you aren't telling me about little miss snow skier, I'm not telling you about Jarrod.*

"We should set up another appointment to talk."

"Can't you just write the report? Say I'm okay?" She stared at him. "You know I'm okay, right?"

"That's cheating." He opened a file drawer in his desk. Moments later, he retrieved a folder.

"My file, huh?" Tori shifted in her chair. Somehow in her conversations with Phin, it hadn't felt like a professional counseling session. It felt more like talking with a truly concerned friend. This reminder caught her cold. *He talks to me because he has to.*

He opened the folder. "We're making progress." He appeared to be reading his report. "We still haven't gotten to the root of your anger."

"I thought I told you, I'm not angry. I'm just demanding."

He smiled. "Not very tolerant of imperfection."

"Not in myself or others."

"Fair enough. But when that driven behavior affects the way you interact with others, it becomes an issue. If we understand what has caused it, then we can help you control it."

Tori sighed. "Look, I watched my mother's cancer being mismanaged. I think that would be enough to understand my resolve not to err."

He just looked at her with that same annoying smile.

"What? You think there's more?"

He shrugged. "Maybe." He closed the folder. "You haven't shared with me about your childhood before your mother became ill."

"Not much to know," she said, shrugging. "Typical childhood." She stood. "Well, I'll let you get back to work. I just really wanted to see if you'd found out anything else."

His voice stopped her at the door. "About that appointment?"

She didn't want to look at him. Why it even bothered her that he seemed to want to keep this professional was so not her. "When are you free?"

"I could come by Charlotte's place tomorrow evening."

She shook her head. "You're confusing me."

He stood. "What?"

Clueless male. "I don't know. It's stupid."

"Help me out here."

"I've liked talking to you." She looked at the floor. "But it didn't seem like a counseling session. It seemed like I was talking to a friend. Then you started helping me with a search for my donor and I just thought—" She stopped talking and looked at his expression.

"I shouldn't have come by the house, is that it?" he said. "It wasn't professional."

"No, I liked it, but—"

"We could meet here."

"Maybe I should just find another counselor."

"Don't do that." He cleared his throat.

"So all of our time together, it was just counseling? What about looking into finding my donor?"

"I thought your memories could be important to explore. Looking into it might be helpful."

She felt a lump growing in her throat. *Of course, he's just being a nice guy. He knows my ice-princess reputation around this place. I'm stupid to think he thought of me as something other than a patient.* She didn't want to cry. This was crazy, way out of bounds for her. She didn't let down. Dr. Taylor didn't cry. "I'll give you a call."

"Sure. We'll set something up."

Her composure was back. "Fine."

She walked away, juggling her hurt. *What did I expect?*

Tori's next stop was in the surgical department on the hallway that contained the offices of the cardiothoracic surgeons, a place the residents just called the mauve hallway because of the hideous color of the carpet. At the end of the hall, the wing widened into an open area in front of the chairman's corner office. Here, office cubicles divided the space. Casually, she sauntered past the CT secretaries and paused at the cubicle of the transplant coordinator, Barb Stiles.

She cleared her throat. Barb looked up from her desk. Tori scanned the cubicle. "Hi."

"Dr. Taylor. Good to see you're up and about."

Tori smiled, seeing what she wanted pinned to the far wall. The master schedule for the transplant residents. *Who was on call the night before my transplant?* Trying not to stare, she nodded. "Were you able to contact my donor family about my request?"

She nodded. "About that," she began. "The family has not yet decided to allow any contact."

Tori took a small step toward the calendar. "Did you tell them about the memories?"

"Of course not!" Barb shook her head. "I'm not about to tell them something unsubstantiated that might upset them. Donating organs is an intensely personal decision." She pushed back from her desk. "You'll just have to wait on this. If they want any contact with you, I'll let you know." Barb looked down at the paperwork on her desk, but not before Tori detected a subtle shaking of her head and a little grunt.

"You don't believe me."

"It doesn't matter." She sighed. "My only concern is this program and the protection of the rights of the donor family."

"What if I agree not to contact the family? I could just talk to the police. It was the jumper, wasn't it, Dakota Jones?"

Tori watched for a reaction.

Barb's right eye twitched. "Look, I don't know how you're getting your information, but I've got to caution you to stop." She raised a finger in the air. "If it gets out that this department is leaking confidential information about donors, we could lose our accreditation."

"But—"

"Stop!" Barb's eyes locked on Tori's.

"Is that a threat?"

"Look, the chairman is a friend of mine. We all know you're under evaluation here. Don't do something stupid to jeopardize your future."

Tori offered a plastic smile. "Wouldn't think of it." She began a turn, but her small black handbag slipped from her shoulder to the floor. "Clumsy me," she said as she leaned forward slowly to gather it up again. As she did, she steadied herself against the desktop in front of the calendar. Hesitating, she slowed her breathing.

"Are you okay?"

"Getting stronger every day." Her eyes fell on the name of the resident on call the night before her transplant. *Bingo.*

Tori turned to leave. "I'm just not quite as fast as I used to be."

She smiled to herself as she went back down the mauve hallway. *But I'm fast enough for you.*

Phin MacGrath pushed the stack of papers to the side when his cell phone vibrated. The phone's screen revealed the source of the call: "Randy."

He smiled. Randy was the pastor at Hope Community Chapel. He and Phin had been casual friends until two years ago when Randy assisted Phin through a personal tragedy. Since then, the two had been like brothers. They held each other's feet to the fire. This was an expected call, an accountability check-in.

Phin picked up the phone. "Hey, bro. What's up? You all ready for Sunday?"

"Getting there. I still have some work to do." A moment of silence followed. "Listen, I know August 10 is coming up. You okay?"

Phin touched the corner of the small picture frame and cleared his throat and paused before answering. He knew better than to try and bluff a "fine" in response to Randy's question. "Home has been tough. Memories everywhere, you know? I've been working a lot."

"Sally said she'd seen you at the cemetery."

He felt his throat thicken. "Yeah."

He let the silence hang between them for a few moments. Randy was like that. Skilled as a listener, he didn't feel the need to fill every silent moment with advice.

Randy spoke next. "You want to run the list?"

"Sure," he responded, glad to think of anything else.

"You keeping up with daily quiet times?"

"Yep."

"How's the thought life? Temptations? Any problems with porn? Internet? Movies?"

The questions were a routine part of their interaction, touching on the main areas where Christian men struggle. "No, I'm good. You?"

"I'm okay as well. Remember, Phin, temptation often hits when we're wallowing in sorrow. It's almost like we feel we deserve to indulge ourselves in some secret delight because we've seen hard times."

"I've been there. I'll stay aware."

"I know you will. And I'll be praying for your heart. We all loved Missy. She was a very special woman."

Phin stayed quiet. *Understatement of the year.*

"You finding any chances to date? What about that lady you mentioned? You know, the surgeon."

Phin sighed. "I've been tempted for sure, but there are land mines with that one. Turns out that Dr. Parrish gave me an assignment to do some counseling with her to help her work through some personal issues."

"Oh wow, so now you can't cross the line because she's your patient."

"Right. I can't exactly ask her out. Taboo, you know?" Phin looked away from the photograph on his desk. "Besides, she's pretty much off-limits anyway."

"Come on, a surgeon isn't out of your league."

"It's not the job, Randy. After I talked to her more, I realized she's not a believer."

"Oh."

"So I really can't go down that road."

"Something will come up. God's got a plan."

Phin nodded as if Randy could see. He held back a verbal response. *But God sure does take his time, doesn't he?*

That evening Tori took the number 7 bus downtown to Legend Brewing Company, a local Richmond microbrewery, home to an award-winning brown ale. There, she met two thirsty chief residents, Paul Griffin and Daniel Freeman, the two surgery residents who had participated in her operation. Paul had gone out with the harvest team and operated on her donor. Dan had stayed and operated with Dr. Parrish on the transplant.

The atmosphere was perfect. A little noisy. Casual. Friends enjoying a variety of local brews and comfort food.

Tori hoisted a frosty mug of Belgian White and tapped the mugs of the two residents. "Here's to you, boys. Thanks for your great work."

"To your speedy recovery," Paul said. He had the hungry look of a runner. He had his eye on a career in academic surgery and had the drive to succeed. His shirt was wrinkled. He probably hadn't slept the night before.

Dan, on the other hand, was an obsessive neatnik. He was still in a white shirt and tie although he'd left the hospital two hours before. He looked well rested and sported a red goatee over a generous chin. He never missed a meal, a feat worthy of praise at a busy university hospital. Many times Tori had seen him gather his interns in the cafeteria to make "card rounds," so named because the interns kept data cards for each patient. Dan's card rounds were legendary, and he grilled the students and interns while each patient was discussed over a load of carbs.

She caught the eye of their waitress. "Could you bring us another order of these wings? And how about a plate of those loaded fries?" She looked at the duo at her wooden table. "You boys good with that?"

There were smiles all around.

The waitress nodded. "I'll get that order right in. Could I bring you another round?"

"I'm still nursing this," Tori said.

Dan looked up. "Absolutely. Could you bring me a pale ale this time?"

"Porter for me," Paul said.

The waitress disappeared.

Dan chuckled. "I've been at VCU Med Center seven years and never once has a patient said thank you in such a nice way."

Tori smiled and sipped slowly. She didn't even bring up the subject of her transplant until the boys were on their third round of brews and a platter of bratwurst, warm pretzels, and mustard sat on the table in front of them.

"Have you guys ever heard of cellular memory?"

Blank stares.

Dan belched quietly into his hand. Paul yawned.

"We don't really understand all the intricacies of stored memory," she began. "But it's much more complicated than we previously thought. There is a complex neural network surrounding the heart, and there are some interesting reports in the literature about heart recipients receiving transplanted memories from their donors."

Dan conquered the last of a bratwurst. "Hmm."

"In some cases, it's merely a transplanted like or dislike—a new taste for a certain food, for instance. In other cases, it's much crazier, a transplantation of a complete or partial memory from the donor."

Paul looked sleepy. He drained his beer. "That is freaky."

Dan shrugged. "Do you believe it?"

She leaned forward. "It's happening to me." She watched as the boys exchanged glances.

"What do you remember?" Paul asked.

"A fire. Falling." She didn't elaborate.

Dan straightened his tie. "When did you first notice this?"

"As I was waking from my operation. I thought it was a nightmare at first, but it wasn't like a normal dream. The images persisted beyond the night."

"Wow."

She sipped her beer and slid the mug across the table. "Maybe I'm just going crazy, huh, boys? The big surgeon has finally lost it."

"No way," Dan said. "We wouldn't think that."

"I don't know. I'm having a hard time with it. It's really making it difficult to sleep." She watched for a reaction.

Well lubricated by this time, the boys seemed reluctant to offend the one picking up their bar tab. "No, no," Paul said. "You're not crazy." He pushed back from their table. "Heck, you're practically a hero among the residents."

"I don't know," she said, sighing. "Maybe I should just hang it up. I can't be trying to conquer cancer if I'm troubled with these images of fire."

Dan seemed to be studying the golden ale in his mug. "Don't say that."

"You know, you guys could help convince me I'm not crazy."

Dan finished his beer.

"Want another?"

"Not me."

Paul shrugged. "What can we do, Dr. Taylor?"

Tori forced herself to breathe. This was it, the whole point of this little thank-you celebration. She was all in, no turning back. She reached into her purse and pulled out a copy of the *Baltimore Sun* story of the jumpers. She laid it on the table in front of the boys. "Look, I know you can't tell me the name of my donor, so I'll make this easy for you. I know the helicopter took the harvest team to Baltimore." She pushed the paper closer to Paul, the resident who had been on the harvest team. She tapped the paper. "Just tell me if I'm wrong. This is where my heart came from, isn't it?"

She watched as Paul looked at Dan. Finally he looked back and shrugged. "You didn't hear it from us."

"You didn't tell me a name," she said. "Just tell me if I'm wrong. Am I crazy here?"

Paul shook his head. "No, Dr. Taylor, you're not crazy. And you're not wrong."

15

Tori sat in her favorite chair stroking the front of her shirt with her finger, nervously tracing her sternal scar. Her eyes were wide open, her gaze jumping from object to object as if searching for a lost item. But she did not seek car keys, a wallet, a comb, or any material object so easily lost. She sought the unseen, the meaning of her current life's craziness, the inevitable but illusive deduction she loathed to consider. A minute later, she was on her feet, restless, and unable to curl her fingers around a conclusion she'd been avoiding since her horrible nightmares began. She paced the floor, facing for the first time the sure knowledge of her heart donor's identity: *Dakota Jones.*

Memories carried her back to a moment just before her transplant, the few seconds of her life chiseled into the stone of her mind when she saw the donor heart as they carried it into the operating room for her transplant. She relived the moment and her vision of two intersecting lifelines, colliding in the controlled violence of surgery. The sounds of conversations on fast-forward accompanied the lines as they raced toward the inevitable union. One line was Tori's; the other belonged to her donor, an unfortunate soul kind enough to sign the back of her driver's license to indicate her willingness to give life to a stranger. But now, for the first time, the other line had an identity, and the whispers of pain, fire, and threat screamed to reveal the experience of Dakota Jones.

Tori looked down at her chest where her hand still rested over her heart. She whispered into the stillness of the room. "Dakota, what have you given me? What happened to you?"

She thought of the mysterious number, the feeling of threat and dread, of fire and pain.

And at that moment, she just knew. The floating dread, the nightmares and images of fire and pain settled into place, each puzzle piece now locking with the other, each providing a letter that spelled out one conclusion: MURDER.

The thought crept upon her, settling over her soul with a sense of finality. *Yes*, she thought. *Dakota Jones was murdered.*

The conclusion locked into place. Tori shook her head. *Am I crazy?*

But her own feelings told her she was finally embracing the truth.

In the next moment, in the dim light of the den, she accepted a new responsibility. In her mind, she spoke to her heart. *Dakota, I owe you my life.*

I will find the person responsible for your death.

Christian didn't want to say good-bye. He didn't really want to have to explain his feelings. The truth was, he was conflicted, and he didn't want the adorable and beautiful Emily Greene talking him into another crazy adventure.

The evening was heavy with moisture. The cicadas started their symphony as Mr. Greene's BMW disappeared down the long lane.

Christian glanced over at Emily as she sat on the porch swing with her cast propped on a frilly pillow set up on the wicker coffee table. She looked at him. "So this is how it ends, huh? I thought you didn't want to return to Africa."

He shifted in his chair. "I wasn't sure for a while. You gonna be okay?"

"I guess."

He nodded. "I'm sorry."

"For what?"

"I should've been a better, you know, leader."

"I'm a big girl, Chris."

He looked down the lane toward the setting sun. "Sure."

"What happened to all the talk about us? You said you wanted to be with me."

"Yeah, well, I thought you were a, you know—"

"Say the word, Christian. The word is virgin."

"I can say it."

Emily adjusted the pillow under her foot. "I was fourteen, all right? The guy was a senior, a real jerk. He used me."

"I don't need to hear this."

"I felt so contaminated. Down on myself. I didn't feel worthy of saving myself anymore. I started giving it away 'cause I wanted someone to love me."

Christian dropped his head between his hands. He didn't want to know.

"Christian, that was before you, don't you get it? You showed me real love."

"Yeah, well, maybe I don't know anymore."

"Come on, I remember how you talked. How you wanted our relationship to be a picture of something bigger, of Christ's love for the church."

Christian shook his head. "Sounds pretty silly now. You used to tease me, saying it was cute, all my God talk."

"But I listened, didn't I? You didn't think I got it, but I did."

"You just wanted me to help you get away from your dad."

"Okay, that was a stupid idea. But that doesn't change the way I feel about you."

Christian looked up. He felt his heart softening. *God, she's so beautiful.*

He didn't know what to say. He just listened to the sounds of dusk and breathed in the smell of honeysuckle.

"Say something."

He felt his throat tighten. What was it about this girl? "I'm leaving tomorrow." He shrugged. "Everything is packed. Dulles. London. Nairobi."

She pressed her fist to her upper lip. "If I could change my past, I would."

"It is what it is."

"What about forgiveness?"

"I'm not Jesus. Ask him."

"I have. A thousand times." She crossed her arms.

"You need me to say it?" He shook his head. "I can say it, but it won't be enough. It doesn't change things."

"Say it."

"Come on, Emily. You don't need my forgiveness."

She started to cry. "I want you to love me."

Christian felt the ice around his heart begin to melt, beads of sweat on a surface of rock. He closed his fist, trying to find the resolve he'd mustered to walk away. He shook his head and stood. If he kissed her, he'd stay for an hour. Kisses would linger as he tasted her tears. He'd lose himself in her emerald eyes. He'd say things he'd regret. Sweet things that would make little sense in the light of morning.

He looked at her only for a moment and spoke as he started down the porch steps. "I'll never forget you, Emily Greene."

Tori awoke at four a.m. *What's that noise?*

For a moment, she was the surgeon on call and the phone nudged her from sleep. She sat up and rubbed her eyes. The fog began to clear, but the sound of the phone continued. She began plodding toward the kitchen. *Can't Charlotte hear the phone? And who is calling at this hour?*

She lifted the phone from its base. "Hello."

"Hello, this is Mary Fiorino. I'm the hospice nurse. Is this Dr. Taylor? I think we met the other day at Manny's place."

"Yes, this is Tori. Let me get Charlotte for you."

"Actually, I'm calling for you."

"Me?"

"Look, Manny doesn't have long. He's asking for you."

Tori sighed. "Okay." She looked through the window above the kitchen sink, seeing only her reflection. "Give me a few minutes. I'll call a cab."

"You'd better hurry."

The line went dead. Evidently, Nurse Fiorino was all business at this time of the morning.

Tori prepared the drip coffeemaker and trudged back to her bedroom to change. She found jeans and a colorful top that she could button up above her sternal scar. She washed her face, called a cab, poured coffee, and waited.

Let me be in time.

Tori straightened. The words that had just formed in her mind had been more than a thought—they had been a prayer. And the impulse to mentally express that prayer had felt very natural, even though it was far from her normal routine.

Maybe it just comes with facing the death of a patient ... something I always avoided before.

A yellow cab pulled up on the street in front. She scribbled a note to Charlotte and entered the darkness of the Richmond morning.

She gave the address to the cabbie, who turned and shook his head. "Not the safest part of town for a young lady at night."

She hesitated. *I should have brought my mace.* She cleared her throat. "I have to go."

The cabbie appeared to be Middle Eastern, possibly Arabic, possibly Somali. She wasn't sure. She didn't take him for the type to turn down a fare, even into a war zone. He shrugged and hit the meter. "Have it your way."

"Where are you from? You don't have an accent."

"Ethiopia," he said. "But I've lived here since I was five."

She settled into the backseat and stared out at the vacant streets. The statues on tree-lined Monument Avenue kept a silent vigil. Robert E. Lee sat proudly on his horse. Motionless. Offering neither comfort nor warning. Jefferson Davis, however, looked eerie, his hand extended into the air palm up in a gesture that seemed to suggest surrender. Or a plea for help. Tori doubted the artist responsible had anticipated how creepy Davis would look standing alone in the darkness.

Soon, they turned away from the trees, skirting Virginia Commonwealth University and up Broad Street. A man in a worn jacket leaned against a building. A woman with too much lipstick and a short skirt bent forward to talk to the driver of a luxury car. It was the nightlife that Tori rarely thought about. Seeing it now brought an ache to her soul. *The poor. The homeless. Sex for hire.* The woman looked up and her eyes followed the cab as they passed. In spite of an application of rouge and eye shadow, her cheeks were pale, eyes hollow. "I'm lost."

The message startled her. She looked at the cabbie to see his reaction, but if he'd heard her cry, he didn't react. "Did you hear that woman?"

She watched as the cabbie glanced in the rearview mirror. "Didn't hear nothing. The windows are up." He squinted. "Was she talking to us?"

"To me—" Tori halted, realizing that perhaps it had only been in her mind. *Okay, so now I'm officially hearing voices.*

They passed an adult theater. A liquor store still open in spite of the hour. A man was exiting with his prize in a brown bag, promising a momentary reprieve from a hard life. He smiled at the cab as they crept past, his snaggletoothed dentition framed by unshaven cheeks. His soul whispered to her. *I'm lost.*

Tori closed a fist over her heart. *We're all lost, aren't we?*

She found herself on the verge of tears.

This is crazy. I've lived around this stuff all my life.

But she'd insulated herself, building up a fortress of armor, warding off *feeling*.

She opened her purse and felt for her stethoscope. Why had she brought it? Certainly a doctor should have a stethoscope at the bedside of the dying. In the darkness of the cab, she clutched the plastic tubing as if to hold onto the science she relied on to explain everything. Science framed her world, offering an explanation for human suffering. Pain was only a neurologic message, right? A transmission of information about pathology that needed to be changed. Medicine and surgery offered a cure.

But Manny is dying.

In spite of my surgery.

What's on the other side?

Is there an other side?

The cabbie drove up a long hill away from the VCU hospital complex and into a neighborhood of government project housing where Manny lived. He pulled up to a curb opposite the small playground, the one with the swaying turtle and the scary tubular slide. The cabbie turned around. "Twenty," he said.

"But the meter says twelve fifty."

"It's a risky neighborhood. Some cabbies won't come here at all. I risked my life and my cab." He stared at her, unblinking, with a yarn hat pulled down over his ears and repeated his demand. "Twenty."

Tori looked through the window toward Manny's apartment building. It was a little scary out there. She tossed a twenty over the seat. "Thanks."

She passed a sleeping drunk outside the elevator on Manny's floor. An exposed fluorescent tube buzzed and blinked, measuring her progress in jerky images. Her mind floated as if caught in déjà vu. She hurried to escape the feeling that she'd been there before, not just a few days ago, but years ago.

She paused and steadied herself against the wall. *Dakota, were you here?*

Mary opened the door after a soft knock. After letting Tori in, Mary excused herself. "I've been here most of the night." She pointed at the morphine. "Use this if he gets agitated. He's been a little delirious." She shook her head. "Keeps talking about a fire."

Tori only mumbled an echo of Mary's words. "A fire."

Manny had been set up on his old brown upholstered couch. The room smelled of bile and urine. Tori imagined he hadn't the strength to get to the bathroom, but took it as a positive that his kidneys must still be functioning. He was propped up on three pillows, covered with a quilt in spite of the warm temperature.

"Manny," she said, sliding a kitchen chair to the edge of the couch. "I'm here."

He squinted in her direction.

She took his hand. "Are you in pain?"

He didn't reply. His respirations were shallow.

She looked in his eyes. His constricted pupils were rimmed in muddy brown irises that floated in a sea of yellow. She counted his respirations. Six in a minute.

The hospice nurse had been generous with the narcotics, and Manny was barely breathing as a result.

"At least you're comfortable," she whispered.

She watched him, paced, made coffee, and watched the sun rise over downtown Richmond.

After an hour, he stirred, and Tori returned to his side.

"Nadine," he said, reaching for her. His eyes were unfocused, looking through her to a memory.

Your wife's name. What to do? She toyed with correcting him, then just took his hand and replied softly, "Rest, Manny."

"The smoke was too thick." His breathing quickened. "Too hot."

She lifted the quilt from beneath his chin. His forehead was slick with sweat. She inspected his biliary drain. The bag was milky and yellow-brown. *Infection has set in.*

"You've got a fever." She put her fingers on his radial pulse. It was a few moments before she convinced herself that she could feel the thready runaway rhythm tapping against her finger.

"I tried ... to ... save you." His words erupted in a broken staccato.

"Shh, Manny, don't try to talk."

"We're together again."

Charlotte had told Tori about Manny's wife, a strong woman who'd tried to help him after Vietnam but had failed to escape an apartment fire.

He began to shake, the rigors of fever. The doctor in her wanted to keep him cool, but she knew it was only a matter of time, so she let him have the quilt again. "Here," she said, tucking it up under his chin.

After a few minutes, he relaxed again, and his eyes rolled upward until only yellow slits of sclera remained. He appeared horror-film spooky that way. She imagined the yellow color erupting into lasers.

Girl, you are losing it. She stood and walked to the window. She looked down at the small playground. Even from her vantage point high on the fifth floor, the image held a strange anxiety for her. *What is it about that playground?*

Manny grunted, and she returned to her vigil beside the couch. She took his hand again. This time, he squeezed back. Hard. His grip was crazy strong. Startling, not like that of a dying man.

He pulled her hand to his chest and looked in her eyes. With the light of the morning falling on his yellow eyes, the effect was chilling. Even before he spoke, Tori's heart was in her throat. "God knows what you did," he said.

Tori pulled away. "What?"

He didn't repeat it. *Was he speaking to his dead wife? Or to me? What did I do?* "What, Manny? What do you mean?"

His eyes were sad. "I forgive you."

She didn't understand. "Forgive me? For what?"

But Manny didn't answer. Instead, his countenance brightened. He sat up, the first time he'd shown any strength. Reaching toward the light streaming in the window, he grinned. "Oh, Jesus!"

With that, his face relaxed. Then his shoulders. And he sank back onto the couch. She watched his chest. It didn't rise again.

Tori gasped. "Manny, no! Tell me what you meant!"

Silence. Manny was gone.

And for the very first time, Dr. Tori Taylor, one of Virginia's premier cancer surgeons, had been there at the moment death snatched life from one of her patients.

But what had just happened?

How could science explain his hallucination of Jesus?

She took a deep breath, not even trying to hold back the tears. She touched his chest. "What did you mean?"

She looked toward the window and let the sun bathe her face. Instead of comfort, she felt the sting of guilt. *God?*

What did I do?

16

Tori spent the next two hours interacting with the hospice home-health staff and a local funeral home that came and picked up Manny's body. By the time Charlotte appeared to give Tori a lift back to her place, Tori was exhausted.

"I knew this was coming," Charlotte said. "It's a relief, really."

Tori stayed quiet.

Charlotte seemed to be studying her. "Did he talk?"

Tori shrugged. "He was pretty much out of it. Didn't make much sense."

Charlotte nodded. "Well, cliché as it sounds, Manny's one that I know is in a better place. His faith really carried him through."

Tori sighed, unable to get the image of Manny's sunlit face out of her mind. For a moment, she was convinced he'd seen beyond the veil. She walked slowly behind Charlotte to the elevator. "What do you think happens? After we die?"

"Child, you know what I think."

Tori held up her hands. "The good guys go to heaven. The bad …"

"If that's what you think, I know you haven't been listening to me."

"But that's it, isn't it? God sends you to heaven or hell, right? That's what you believe."

"Well, yes, I believe in a heaven and a hell, but heaven isn't a place for the good guys, Tori."

"But you always—"

Charlotte held up her hands. "Heaven is for the bad guys, Tori. For those of us who realize we're bad and in desperate need of some help. No one can be good enough to earn heaven."

"Manny was a good guy."

"True. He was honest. A good friend. But that alone didn't make him fit for heaven. His relationship with Christ did."

"That's where I stumble," Tori admitted. "Why does it always come down to Jesus?"

The elevator doors opened and the duo stepped in. Charlotte punched the *G* button. "What do you mean?"

"Christians shouldn't claim to be the only way. What about the Buddhists, Jews, and Muslims? They deserve a chance." Tori looked over at Charlotte. "Christians are intolerant."

"Hey, Christians didn't make up the claim that Jesus was the only way. He said that himself. 'I am the way, the truth, and the life. No man comes to the Father but by me.'"

"Doesn't seem fair."

"Why are you suddenly on the attack? You're feeling guilty."

"Oh, just because I attack your faith, you think I'm feeling guilty? You're not supposed to judge, remember? I seem to recall you teaching that to me."

"*Are* you feeling guilty?"

Tori looked away. *Yes. But I'm not sure why.*

What did I do? What did Manny mean?

"Watching someone die makes you think, huh? I mean, life and death, eternity, what's it all about?"

"Whatever," Tori mumbled.

They stepped off the elevator. They walked down the hall and out into the sunshine. The day was clear. Outside, children played, a squirrel ran up an oak tree, and a maintenance man was mowing grass, smiling as he saw the two women. Death may have stolen Manny away, but outside, life marched forward, going on as if nothing had happened. Tori wanted to scream. *It's so unfair. The good die too young.*

Once they were in Charlotte's car, Tori changed the subject. "I'm going to Baltimore. I want to talk to the police about my donor."

"Your donor?"

"It was the fire victim, Dakota Jones. The consensus is that she died trying to escape the fire. But I believe someone wanted her dead. It wasn't an accident."

Tori listened as Charlotte sighed. Charlotte turned on her blinker and pulled into the traffic flow. "Can I be completely honest with you?"

Tori shifted in her seat, pushing the shoulder harness up and away from the scar over her sternum. "Could I stop you?"

"Probably not."

"Well?"

"I think this is a diversion, Tori. You've got enough trouble in your life right now, what with dealing with recovery from surgery, these issues surrounding your job, and sorting out your anger. Why can't you just leave this obsession with your donor alone?" She paused. "You need to focus on your own life."

Tori stared through the window. "That's what I'm doing." She shook her head. "I'm not sure I can expect you to understand. For the first time in my life I feel like I'm doing something for someone other than myself. Dakota Jones gave her life. I owe her."

"No, you don't. She died in an accident. She didn't willingly give up her heart so you could live. She signed a donor card, that's all."

"I don't expect you to get this."

"Think of her parents. Do you think they want to know that you think their daughter may have been murdered?"

"Do you want her murderer to go unpunished?"

Another sigh. "Of course not."

"I didn't ask for this, okay? But there are memories that keep bubbling up, stuff that scares me, Charlotte." Tori touched her friend's arm. "Don't you get this? If I can find out what happened to Dakota, maybe I can put this torture to rest."

Charlotte didn't respond. At least not verbally. Instead, she flipped on the radio, a station that played her favorite gospel music.

Outside, Tori examined the population of Richmond's downtown. Scores of unsmiling workers clipped along with phones welded to their ears. A hot-dog vendor argued with a customer over change. Tori lowered her window to listen.

A middle-aged woman directed a dozen preschoolers down the sidewalk toward a McDonald's. A white woman wearing gray sweatpants stepped away from an approaching businessman. She looked at Tori to reveal a face caked with too much makeup. Her eyes danced with fear. "My husband beats me," she said.

Tori touched Charlotte's arm. "Stop the car."

"What for?"

"Don't you want to help her?"

"What are you talking about?"

"Didn't you hear her? The woman in the gray sweats. Surely you heard her."

"Nope."

"She talked to me. She said, 'My husband beats me.'"

The woman walked on down the block. Traffic was slow. The woman paused at the front of a building and glanced back at Tori one more time before entering. The sign on the door said "Arms of Love."

Charlotte turned down the radio. "Why would she speak to a stranger? Abused women don't just tell random people their problems."

Tori rubbed her eyes. "I know what I heard."

"Arms of Love. It's a women's shelter. Maybe you just had a stroke of intuition."

Tori took a deep breath. "The way she stepped away from that man, makeup that could cover a black eye, the fear in her expression … all of it spoke to me."

"Has this happened before?"

She nodded. *This morning. I felt the lost.*

"Tori, that's a gift."

"No. I'm falling apart. I've got nightmares. Now people talk to me without words."

"You've been up since four. Have you eaten?"

"No."

"Your meds?"

"I left them at your place."

"Okay, kid, let's get you home, get your meds, feed you, and let you nap."

Tori nodded again. *Maybe that's it. I just need food and a nap.*

But somehow she knew things had changed. Life was different somehow. Effervescent trouble bubbled from the surface of her life like the sparkling gas escaping from soda on a summer day.

She brushed a tear from the corner of her eye. This trouble was far, far deeper than anything that could be cured with a sandwich and a nap.

For most teenagers, Saturday morning meant a chance to sleep in, but for Christian Mitchell, Saturdays meant a chance to go on hospital rounds with his father. They'd fallen into a comfortable routine, including a stop in a little hospital cafeteria where Christian ate *mandazis*, the almost-doughnut-sweet fried Kenyan bread washed down with chai, sugary tea steeped in half milk and half water.

After that, he would follow his father, Dan Mitchell, as he saw patients on the men's and women's wards. Often, a Kenyan intern and a medical student or two accompanied them. Today, the team was Dr. Mitchell, Christian, an intern named John O'mollo, and a medical student, Charity N'ganga.

John greeted them warmly. "We have a patient in ICU."

Dr. Mitchell nodded. "We'll start there."

As they walked up the long hallway, John explained. "This is our lymphoma patient."

"Mr. Wanjiku?"

"Yes. He began struggling to breathe. He has cough and fever. I thought he might have had a pulmonary embolus."

Christian's father paused. "It would be a relief, really. I don't want him to suffer." He looked at his intern. "He shouldn't be intubated. We can't use up a ventilator on him."

Christian met his father's gaze. "Why?"

"He has AIDS, son. And an advanced cancer that has spread throughout his abdomen and, I suspect, to his brain. There is no cure for him."

Christian followed the team into the small high-dependency unit. In the third of six beds, Jeremy Wanjiku was clearly struggling to breathe.

Dr. Mitchell used his stethoscope, placing it on the patient's chest, front and back, on both sides. "Diffuse rales. He sounds wet to me." He then uncovered the patient's lower legs. "Equally swollen, but not tender, so I don't think he has a venous clot. He probably hasn't had an embolus." He added quietly, "If he has, it would be a mercy."

A nurse, a female whose name tag identified her as Purity, approached the team.

"Let's try Lasix," Dr. Mitchell instructed. "Use morphine generously to keep him comfortable." The team stepped away as the intern wrote the orders. When they were out of earshot of the patient, Dr. Mitchell spoke to the nurse. "No ventilator for him. He doesn't have long."

She nodded.

Outside the door to the ICU, Christian paused. "I think I'll stay back with Mr. Wanjiku. He doesn't have any family here."

His father shrugged.

Christian pushed back through the door and looked at Mr. Wanjiku. *He seems so lost.* He felt an urgency. *I want to give him one final chance to know the Savior.*

Christian made his way to the bedside where the nurse injected the man's IV with a syringe full of clear fluid.

"Lasix," the nurse said. "It will help him get rid of extra fluid. Maybe he will breathe easier."

Mr. Wanjiku's eyes widened. Muscles in his neck flared as he braced his arms against the mattress, struggling for air.

"Does he understand English?"

Purity shook her head. "Kiswahili and Kikuyu."

Christian sighed. "Will you talk to him with me then?"

Purity moved closer.

How to start?

"Mr. Wanjiku, I am Christian Mitchell. My father is your surgeon."

Christian waited as Purity interpreted.

"It doesn't look like you will survive very long." He paused. "Do you know what will happen after you die?"

The patient seemed annoyed. Or perhaps it was only because all of his effort was in grabbing for his next breath and he couldn't be bothered.

Christian continued, pausing to let the interpreter follow each phrase. "You are going to face God's judgment for all of your earthly activities, good and bad. You will be sent to heaven if you put your faith in Christ and the cross." Christian struggled, wondering if the patient could understand such terms. "No one gets to heaven by being good on their own. It is only because Jesus paid for our bad deeds by dying on a cross."

Mr. Wanjiku looked at Christian and grunted out a few phrases in Kikuyu.

Christian looked at Purity. "What is he saying?"

Purity reached up and silenced an alarm with the push of a button on the cardiac monitor. The patient's heart rate raced along at 155 beats per minute.

Sweat drops beaded the patient's forehead. The air around him was thick with the smell of his breath. It was an odor Christian hadn't yet learned. An odor of death. Decay, sour and bittersweet, mixing in with the antiseptic odors of the cleaning solutions used for disinfection.

"What does he say?"

Purity stared at Mr. Wanjiku. "He says he's made choices. He's made his decision long ago."

"So he's already a Christian?"

Purity shook her head and looked back at Christian. "No. He does not believe."

Christian took the man's hand. "It is not too late. Even a criminal who died on a cross next to Jesus turned to God in his final moments and was admitted to heaven."

The nurse translated.

Mr. Wanjiku pulled his hand away.

Purity touched Christian's arm. "He doesn't want to believe."

Christian shook his head. "He will burn in hell."

The patient grunted out a few more phrases.

Purity looked down. "He wants you to leave."

The heart-rate alarm sounded again, a high-pitched note keeping time with the patient's racing heart. Christian watched the monitor and slowly backed away. Regular narrow blips, sharp and jagged, were replaced more and more often with widened ones. First one, then in twos and threes.

Christian sat in a chair behind a counter in the center of the unit. He felt useless. He'd failed.

Purity came to his side and placed her hand on his shoulder. He looked in her face, a nice face the color of coffee with milk. Her complexion was smooth and her teeth even and white. Her lips were full, the kind that in Hollywood, women pay to emulate. "Perhaps the Lasix will work."

But the monitor didn't lie. Blip, blip, blip, each one running toward an inevitable free fall from the precipice between life and death.

Christian stayed an hour.

To pray.

But heaven was closed.

He watched the patient, the monitor above the patient's head like a gravestone proclaiming his final moments. A second alarm sounded, this one a register of a critically low oxygen in the blood.

Mr. Wanjiku's right hand lifted to his chest. His mouth twisted in a snarl of fear. With eyes wide, he collapsed against the sheets that were stained with an outline of his sweat. His chest rose and fell in diminishing heights. Two minutes later, an eerie cry parted his lips one last time.

Christian imagined the patient leaning over hungry flames of eternal separation from God.

The rhythmic dancing line of Mr. Wanjiku's heart ceased, ironed flat by the invisible hand of death.

Purity turned off the monitor and looked back at Christian. *"Asante."*

Thank you.

He rose and walked from the unit. He needed escape. Into the African morning with sun on his face and the dust of a rocky path beneath his feet, Christian stumbled forward beneath a silent sky.

17

Just after sunrise on Saturday morning, Tori sat on a bench waiting for the city bus, the first leg of a day trip to Baltimore to find out more about Dakota Jones.

As she sat, she replayed her argument with Charlotte from the night before.

"Don't do this, Tori."

"I didn't imagine you'd understand."

"Her family could be hurt."

"They deserve to know the truth."

"You've had a heart transplant. You're on multiple drugs. These things affect the mind. Your nightmares could mean anything."

"Then investigating this won't hurt anyone, will it?"

"You're going to get hurt." Charlotte put her hands on her hips. *"Or you're going to hurt yourself."* She walked toward Tori and placed her hand on her shoulder. *"What about finding out about your own childhood? You've seen some tough times. Maybe—"*

"I never had these nightmares before! You knew my mother."

"Tell me about kindergarten."

Tori scoffed. *"What does that have to do with this?"*

Charlotte held up her hands. "I'm just asking."

"This isn't about my past. It's about a debt I owe to a woman who gave me her heart."

"I wish you'd slow down. You're not ready for this."

"I'm a big girl."

A big girl. Tori sighed at the memory. Sitting on the bench, she felt anything but.

She tried to think about kindergarten, but it was a big, empty black box. Why on earth did Charlotte want to know that, anyway?

She let the number 21 bus pass. She needed 19 to take her to a downtown bus terminal. In truth, she hated to take a bus, but she'd been warned not to drive for another week, and she feared that if there was any problem and her surgeon got wind that she wasn't cooperating, it could only come back to sting her. All she needed was Dr. Parrish telling the chairman that Tori couldn't be trusted to follow instructions.

A few minutes later a gray Honda Accord approached and slowed with the passenger window rolled down. "Hey, stranger, where are you headed?"

She looked up to see Phin MacGrath, smiling and motioning her to get in.

A bus was approaching behind him. "My bus is here."

"Come on, get in. I'll take you."

She looked once at his smile, glanced back at the approaching bus, and yielded, opening the passenger door.

Inside, there were two cups of Starbucks coffee in a cupholder between the bucket seats. "Phin, what are you doing?"

"I hope I'm taking you to Baltimore."

She thought back to their last encounter. Phin had been Mr. Professional—distant and direct. "I'm taking the bus, Phin. You don't need to do this."

"I know. I want to."

"Let me guess. Charlotte?"

"She asked me to help out."

"She refused to take me herself. She wants nothing to do with my search. She thinks I'm stirring up trouble, concentrating on distractions when I should be trying to recover."

"She loves you. She didn't want you to go alone."

"She wants to keep tabs on me."

"We should all have friends like Charlotte."

"But you're my counselor. This doesn't seem much like something a counselor would do."

He nodded. "Agreed."

"That's it? You agree?"

"So maybe I'm crossing a professional line." He shrugged. "You want to report me?"

She smiled. "Maybe."

He handed her one of the cups. "I'm willing to risk it. If it gets too crazy, I'll just refer you to someone else for counseling."

"Or you could stop crossing the line."

He glanced at her. His face said he'd rather make the referral.

He sipped his own coffee as they sat at a traffic stop. When the light turned green, he put it back in the holder. "So, Sherlock, what's your game plan? Why are you suddenly so sure you know your donor's identity?"

"I got the information from the resident on the transplant team." She positioned her cup just below her nose so she could savor the rising smell of the coffee. "A little beer and a few carbohydrates did the trick."

"I'm still part of the transplant team, remember. Maybe I don't really want to know." He hesitated, and she could tell he was irritated. "This was a violation of patient confidence. You know that."

"I also know that if an attending surgeon asks a resident a question, there is too much pressure to stay in the attending's good graces not to answer."

"You took advantage of your position as an attending."

She shrugged. "Perhaps."

"I hope not. You shouldn't have told me."

"Hey, you're a part of this now. If I go down, I'm taking you with me."

He chuckled. "Well, if it's just the same to you, we have to be very careful not to let the donor's family, or anyone else for that matter, think that the transplant team is giving out confidential information. That could spell huge trouble for us. The program could get suspended."

Tori tapped her thigh with her fingers and thought about Phin's statement.

She stared out at the passing traffic, trying not to look at the faces. *Wow. If that happened, I won't just be on temporary leave, will I?*

They drove on in silence for a few minutes before Tori spoke again. "If I'd known you were going to rescue me, I wouldn't have needed to leave so early."

"So we'll take our time." He glanced in her direction. "You could fill the time by telling me about your family."

She shrugged. "Is this a question from a friend or part of our counseling?"

"I want to know for me." He hesitated. "But it's both, I guess."

"I've told you about my family."

"You told me about your mother. How about your dad?"

Tori felt her gut tighten. "I don't remember that much. He died when I was twelve."

"Certainly you have memories."

"He was fun. He took me to the movies. But he was deployed a lot." She sighed. "I remember thinking I should cry when he died, but I didn't."

"Your father died and you didn't cry?"

She continued staring through the window. "I guess I wanted to be strong for my mother."

"When was the last time you cried?"

"I cry all the time now." She hesitated before adding, "Since my transplant."

"How about before?"

"I didn't cry." She looked back at Phin. "You think that's weird?"

He seemed to be choosing his words carefully. He looked as if he was rolling something around in his mouth, perhaps trying it out for taste before responding. "Unusual. Not exactly weird."

"I used it to my advantage. While others are getting bogged down in their emotions, I've been able to move forward. As a cancer surgeon, it was a plus. I didn't let all that baggage interfere with the decisions I needed to make to cure cancer."

"Hmm."

She didn't like the way he responded. It sounded judgmental. "What do you mean, 'Hmm'?" She imitated him.

"You've been closed down."

"Maybe losing your parents can do that." She sipped her coffee. "Don't make a big deal of it."

"But you were closed before that."

"Okay, Mr. Counselor, what do you make of that?"

"Not sure," he said. "But I'd say it's a protective response, usually a defensive mechanism to prevent hurt, caused by exposure to some sort of bad experience. Something traumatic."

"Well, that's where you're wrong. I had a happy childhood, parents who loved me."

"Your dad was deployed a lot. Maybe you closed down to prevent yourself from missing him. Maybe you'd been worried so long that he would die that when he did, you were already proficient at protecting your heart."

"I think you're reaching. I think I was just made tough."

Phin tapped his fingers on the steering wheel. "And I think twelve-year-old girls aren't supposed to be that tough. Did you have lots of disappointments?"

"Disappointments?"

"You know—your father was away in Iraq, missed your birthday, that kind of thing."

"I don't remember. He was gone a lot, so he probably missed my birthday, but my mother always had a gift that was from him and told me he was such a hero. I think I understood."

"Did you cry when your mother died?"

"I told you I didn't cry. Not till I got this new heart."

"What do you make of that?"

She sighed. "Only that I got a lot more than I imagined when I got this heart." She let her hand rest on his as it gripped the gearshift. "I think Dakota Jones was a crier." She squeezed his hand. "And a toucher. That wasn't me before, but now it just seems … natural."

"Seriously. Don't you think there could be another explanation for all this?" He picked up his hand and gestured in the air. "You're in a serious brush with death. It could make you think seriously about what's really important, help you get in touch with your emotions."

"Good try. But you seem to remember, we're on this trip because this same heart not only made me a bit more emo, I've been the recipient of some pretty scary memories."

He tapped the steering wheel. "Right." He glanced at Tori. "So it was the jumper after all."

"I'm not sure she jumped. I remember falling. I remember fire."

"Hmm."

"I wish you'd stop doing that. It sounds judgmental."

He put his fist to his lips and chuckled. "I almost did it again."

She smiled. "Okay, this should go both ways. I want to know something about you."

"Fair enough."

"You get to know all about my life. I want to know about yours. What about Phin MacGrath? Happy life?"

"I'm an only child. My mother is a hairdresser, the stereotypical small-town stylist who knows everyone's business. My father is a civil engineer. He works with a construction firm designing concrete walls."

She decided to give him his own medicine. "Hmm," she said, trying her best imitation.

She watched as the corner of his mouth turned up before he turned sober again a few moments later. A reflection of pain flashed behind his dark eyes. "I married my college sweetheart. She was killed by a drunk driver three years ago next Sunday."

"Oh, Phin, I'm so sorry." *The ski picture on your desk.*

He stared straight ahead and stayed quiet. Eventually, he coughed and spoke again. "That's pretty much the high and low points."

Tori didn't know what to say. In spite of her occupation, she'd always found herself uncomfortable when dealing with her patients' emotional pain. In fact, she'd always avoided it, said it was something she left for the hand-holding nursing staff.

But just then, as she found no words adequate to comfort him, she naturally let her hand rest on his again. Skin on skin, a practical encouragement without words.

And for Tori, it just felt like the right thing to do.

That afternoon, Tori and Phin walked into the Baltimore Central District Police Station. A female uniformed officer looked up from behind a counter. "Can I help you with something?"

Tori cleared her throat. "I need to talk to someone about a crime."

"What sort of crime?"

"Murder."

The officer, no older than thirty, stood.

Phin put his hand on her arm. "Maybe you should explain."

"There was a fire in this district a few weeks back. Two people were reported to jump from the fifth floor to escape being burned."

The officer nodded. "I remember that. A break in some old wiring or something caused it."

"I don't think it happened like that. I think someone started the fire in order to kill one or both of the jumpers. The woman may have been pushed."

"And you know this how?"

Tori hesitated. "I remember it like I was there."

The officer squinted.

"Could I just talk to the on-scene officer who responded to the fire?"

"Why don't you just try explaining to me what you're talking about?"

Tori took a deep breath. As much as she didn't want to, she knew she'd have to convince this officer in order to get further. "Look, this may sound weird, but the woman who jumped—well, she was a heart donor. And I'm the one who received her heart." Tori smiled meekly. "And along with her heart, I have received some memories. These memories tell me that my donor was in trouble and was likely murdered."

The officer sighed.

Tori could see she didn't believe. Or understand.

"So you don't really have evidence of foul play?"

"Other than my memories, no."

"Look, our homicide division is really busy. Why don't I take your name—"

"Can I just talk to the officer who was on scene?" Tori retrieved a copy of the news article from her purse and traced her finger down the print. "Officer Bundrick."

"Officer Bundrick is on patrol." The officer turned away for a moment and snapped open the drawer of a tall filing cabinet. Tori watched her as she slowly walked her fingers across the top of several files before depositing a paper into one of them. Even if the police-woman didn't roll her eyes, Tori felt her negative attitude. The officer glanced over her shoulder. "If you insist on staying, have a seat. I'll have dispatch see if Officer Bundrick is available."

Tori sat next to Phin in a row of wooden chairs. "She thinks I'm crazy."

Phin shrugged. "We knew this was going to be a hard sell."

"She made me feel stupid."

"You've got to admit, when you try to explain it, it sounds pretty crazy."

Tori couldn't keep the sarcasm from her voice. "Thanks."

She settled into her chair and looked around the crowded wait-ing area. Two officers wrestled an angry drunk in handcuffs. "I know my rightsss," he slurred.

A tattooed man sat on the floor, slumped against the wall. A woman with too much mascara tugged on the edges of a short leather skirt. A young couple stared straight ahead, their shoulders slumped in despair. A teen with hair spraying out from a knitted cap closed his eyes and bobbed his head, a response to whatever was booming through the cord leading from the pocket of his jeans to his ears.

Tori shook her head. A message seemed to rise from the people around her. *I'm lost.* And it was a message she didn't want to hear.

Phin seemed to be studying her face. "What's wrong?"

She shook her head. "Let's get out of here."

"We can't leave now. We came all this way."

"They think I'm crazy." She waved her hands toward all the people. "And all of this."

"What?" He leaned toward her. "You feeling claustrophobic?"

"No." She searched his face. "Don't you feel it? All these people," she said slowly. "It's like I feel their despair." She shook her head. "I don't like it. I want to leave."

"Ma'am?"

Tori looked up to see the policewoman standing behind the counter. "Officer Bundrick should be here in a few minutes."

"See," Phin said. "You can't leave now."

Tori took a deep breath. "Maybe if I get some water," she said. "I think I saw a fountain down the hall."

With that, she walked slowly away, trying to build a defense against the clamor of human noise.

Phin walked behind her. When she reached the fountain, she turned. "Don't you feel this?"

"What?"

"Hopelessness. It's overwhelming."

He looked back at the people in the lobby. "You're depressed."

"I'm not depressed. It's like I feel—" She hesitated. "Like I feel their pain."

Phin's expression reflected his confusion and concern.

"Come on. Let's step outside for a minute. I need some air."

They walked into the Baltimore sunshine. Phin smiled. "We should go down to Inner Harbor. We can relax, get some seafood."

"Don't."

"What?" he said. "I like seafood."

"You're trying to distract me. You think I'm crazy too."

"It's not like that, Tori." He huffed and looked up the street, busy with traffic. "I'm just being a friend."

"Oh, so maybe we should just forget about this mess and go grab a hot dog and a beer, take in an Orioles game. Forget about the pain."

"Lighten up, Tori. We're here. We're dealing with your old memories, okay? I didn't come all this way because I think you're crazy. I'm with you in this." He shrugged. "But everyone deserves a little fun."

She sighed. "I know," she said, shaking her head and squinting up at the sunshine. "That cop just made me feel silly. I shouldn't take it out on you."

A few minutes later, a police officer paused at the front steps to straighten the front of his uniform. Tori read his ID pin. "Bundrick." She tapped Phin's shoulder. "That's our guy. Let's go."

Tori followed him in. "Officer Bundrick."

He turned. He was only five foot seven, Tori's height, but muscular, like a man who spent too many hours in the gym. His chest was broad, his neck thick, almost making his head look a size too small. His hair, what she could see of it, was clipped short, only an inch of it visible below his cap.

She held out her hand. "I'm Dr. Tori Taylor," she began, hoping that her title would help build a little weight to her story. "I believe you're here to see me."

"Doctor?" He paused, and his eyes quickly moved from her head to the floor, taking in everything along the way. "You're the woman reporting memory of a murder?" His voice was too high. She found herself expecting it to crack like an adolescent's in puberty.

This is better, she thought. His voice wasn't as intimidating as his muscled physique.

He took her hand, and she nodded. "I'm an oncology surgeon at the Virginia Commonwealth University Medical Center."

He raised his eyebrows and glanced at Phin. "You're Mr. Taylor?"

Phin smiled. "Just a friend."

The officer nodded. "Follow me."

He led the way past the throngs of waiting people, down a hallway decorated with pictures of uniformed men, something akin to an officer-of-the-month display. He opened the door to a small room with a mirrored glass wall, a small table, and three chairs. It was straight out of a movie set, a 1980s interrogation room. Tori walked in and wondered when he was going to switch on the bright lights. *"Tell me where you were at eight o'clock on the night of June 14th!"*

"Officer Detweiler tells me you have some information about a possible crime." He held up his hand toward two seats on one side of the empty table.

Tori sat opposite Officer Bundrick. "Let me begin by telling you about cellular memory. It is a recognized and respected theory about how memory transfer takes place after heart transplantation." Tori really didn't know that the theory was respected, but she didn't want to be turned away again.

The officer leaned back in his chair. This didn't seem to interest him.

Tori explained the theory, then leaned forward. "I received a heart from Dakota Jones, the woman who was reported to have jumped from an apartment in this district to escape a fire."

"And you believe that to be false?"

"My memory tells me differently."

The officer shifted in his seat and cleared his throat. He pulled a small notebook from his shirt pocket. "Just what does your memory say?"

"I remember the fire. I remember being afraid. Dakota felt threatened."

"By whom?"

"I'm not sure. Someone she wanted to expose. There was a number. Three one six. I think it's a clue to uncovering what really happened."

The officer wrote the number down and grunted. "Uh-huh." He looked up, unable to hide his skepticism. "And you know this how?"

"I remember her voice. She said, 'Memorize this. It's the proof. I want to make that bastard pay.'"

"Three one six."

She nodded. "I think it's a PO box or something."

"This is all you have?"

Tori squirmed. "Did she have green eyes?"

The officer seemed to brighten. "Yes."

"I knew it. That proves the memory is accurate."

He raised his eyebrows in question. "Proves it, huh?"

"How about a tattoo? Did she have a tattoo, a little one with two hearts?"

"I have no idea."

"I can tell you she did. I remember."

"And you think all of this points to a crime?"

"Someone wanted Dakota Jones dead." She leaned forward. "Why else would I feel such fear?"

"Maybe because she forced herself to jump to escape being burned alive?"

Tori thought about that for a moment. "That doesn't feel right. She definitely felt threatened by a man."

"Who?"

"Don't know."

The officer shook his head then rose from his chair. "I'll look into it. Can I have a number in case I need to contact you?"

Tori handed him a business card as she stood to keep his line of sight.

"Fine," he said. He scrutinized the card then placed it in his little notebook and folded it closed.

"I'm a surgical oncologist," she explained. "A doctor who operates to treat cancer."

This seemed to impress the high-pitched talker. His gaze traveled over her again, floor to face, face to chest, where his eyes stopped to rest. The thought that she was both beautiful and a surgeon seemed hard for him to digest. He brightened and pulled up his sleeve. "Hey, doc, would you look at this mole?"

She stepped forward, but he laughed and rolled down his sleeve again. "I was just yankin' your chain."

They stood together without talking as the officer chuckled over his own joke.

"So that's it?"

"I said I'll look into it. That's all I can do." He paused. "Why is this so important?"

When she hesitated, he continued. "Let me play devil's advocate. This girl, Dakota Jones, was a nobody, a drug addict most likely, and no family has come around showing any concern. Why should I spend my time on her?"

"She wasn't a nobody to me." She paused. "And I doubt she was a serious drug addict or she couldn't have been a heart donor."

He turned and opened the door. Apparently the conversation was over.

"A woman died to give me life. A woman that I think was killed. I think I owe her a chance at justice."

"Thanks for coming in."

"How can I contact you? I want to know what you find out."

He handed her a card. "Now, if you'll excuse me."

Tori and Phin stood motionless. "That's it? We're done?"

"If that's all you know, we're done." He smiled and reached out his hand.

Tori shook it, but something in his demeanor spoke to her, something layers beneath the tough-guy surface. It was something that chilled her.

Behind his plastic smile. *I'm afraid.*

18

On Saturday morning, Christian sat at the breakfast table staring into his cereal bowl.

His father set his coffee mug on the counter and picked up his stethoscope. "Coming?"

Christian shook his head. "Not today."

"I could use your help. Keep the kids on peds occupied with a magic trick while I talk to their parents."

"I need to work on a paper for English."

His dad knew better. He sat opposite his son. "You know it's not up to us who lives and who dies."

Christian looked away. "I know."

"And people can accept or reject our message."

"Sure."

His father sighed. "Why are you torturing yourself? If a man dies without Christ, it's not like it's all on your shoulders. You were obedient. You gave him his chance."

"I know that!" Christian stood and walked to the sink, dropping his bowl with a clatter against the other breakfast dishes.

"So what is it?"

"Voices."

His father raised his eyebrows in question. "Voices?"

Christian nodded. "It's crazy." He stared out the window beyond a loquat tree toward the dusty path leading to the hospital.

"Help me understand."

"It's like I hear their souls calling to me. Not an actual voice, but it's like I just know their feelings."

"The patients?"

"I feel their loss, their sorrow, their lack of hope."

"It's a hospital, Christian. Everyone feels that."

"Not like I do. It scares me. It's overwhelming."

Dan Mitchell walked up behind his son, laying his hand on his shoulder. "Maybe it's a gift, son."

"A gift? Well, maybe I don't want it. I didn't ask for it."

"Compassion is something I need more of."

"You can have it. Remember last week? I left after five minutes on the peds ward."

"I remember. You didn't feel well."

Christian stepped away from his father's touch. "I wasn't sick, Dad. I just didn't want to cry in front of everyone."

"Maybe it's just the stress of the move. You had to leave your friends. Emily—"

"This has nothing to do with her."

"Sometimes when I'm tearful about one thing, and I hold that thing dear to my heart, it seems like just about anything can bring on the tears at a moment's notice."

"That's not it." He shook his head. "I do miss Emily. But I'm not spending every night crying in my beer."

His father chuckled. "You'd better not be drinking beer."

"It's only an expression."

Dan moved his hand up and down as if weighing his stethoscope, his eyes intent on Christian's face. "So I'm on my own today, huh?"

He nodded. "Most people don't think about hell."

His father gave a quick shake of his head. "Where'd that come from?"

Christian shrugged. "A lot of people die around here."

"It's a hospital, Chris. We don't win every time."

"It's not a game you win or lose. Die and you face eternal judgment, right? That's what you taught me."

"True."

"I can't stand the thought of people on fire."

His father took a step toward the front door. "Maybe it's a reality that Christians need to think about more often." He paused. "But don't let it paralyze you. Let it motivate you to love people."

Christian pinched the bridge of his nose, trying to block out an image of fire. *Voices calling for mercy.*

"Harness it, son." His father left, and Christian watched him disappear up the path.

He sat back down at the kitchen table, covered his ears, and started to cry.

Tori and Phin stood on a downtown Baltimore sidewalk. Phin looked toward a stretch of yellow crime-scene tape. "You can't just go in there."

"That tape isn't intimidating me." Tori looked past a series of sawhorses and yellow tape around the perimeter of an apartment building. "The doorway isn't exactly barred."

Phin MacGrath squinted down the street. Opposite them, an Asian couple entered a small grocery store. On the next block, a half dozen teens played basketball on an asphalt court behind a chain-link fence. An elderly man with a gray beard and a heavy winter coat wheeled a shopping cart beneath the summer sun.

"Worried about them?" Tori shook her head. "They couldn't care less what we do."

Phin followed as Tori walked down an alley between two apartment buildings. A stray dog ran ahead of them and disappeared behind the building. Halfway down the alley, a boy leaned against a green city dumpster.

Tori paused a few feet from the boy. There was something strangely familiar about him. He was black, with skin the color of mahogany. His hair was a short Afro, and his T-shirt and jeans couldn't disguise his stick-like build.

The boy looked up. "Don't tell me," he said. "You're lawyers. You want to know about the jumpers."

Tori and Phin exchanged a look. "No," she answered. "We're not lawyers." She folded her hands in front of her. "You know about the jumpers?"

"You're lawyers."

"Why would you say that?"

"Because after the first few days, the only people to come around here are wanting to sue the landlord."

Tori knelt in front of the boy, who appeared to be about ten years old. "I'm a doctor. Did you know the—" She hesitated. "The people who jumped?"

"You mean Dakota. I know her. She's my mom's friend."

Tori reached out her hand. "I'm Tori Taylor."

He shook her hand. "I'm Mike."

He pointed to a broken window high up on the side of the apartment bordering the alley. "That's where she jumped."

Tori followed his gaze, then examined the alley below the window. The concrete was stained to be sure. Whether it was old blood, dirt, or something else, she wasn't sure she wanted to know.

"The man landed there," he said, pointing. "Dakota hit the top of the dumpster."

She looked up at the building and back to Phin. "I want to go up there."

"The elevator don't work 'cause the electricity's off. But you can still go up the stairs."

"You've been in there?"

He nodded. "My mom won't let me go again."

"How do I get in?"

"That door leads to the stairs."

She looked at Phin. "You in?"

He shrugged. "This is a bad idea. You can't climb five flights of steps." He shook his head. "Besides, it may not be safe."

"It's dark, but nothing is burned except on the fifth floor." The boy rubbed his right leg. "You friends of Dakota's?"

Tori smiled. "Not exactly." She hesitated. "But I'm interested in finding out about her."

"Did you know that doctor?" The boy stood and scuffed his foot against the alley. "The man that was with her."

Tori shook her head.

"He was a good doctor, but I think he was in trouble. I heard them arguing."

"Really? When was this?"

"A day before the accident." He squinted at them. "You sure you're not lawyers?"

"No."

"Police?"

"Of course not. Why?"

"My mama doesn't want me talkin' to police."

"Mike, how old are you?"

"Thirteen."

Evidently, Tori's expression revealed her doubt.

"Okay, I'm twelve." He put his hands on his hips. "But I'm small for my age."

"The man that jumped was named Christian Mitchell. Did you know him, too?"

"I met him at the clinic. Dakota took me to see him."

"You said he was in trouble. Do you think he wanted to hurt Dakota?"

"I don't know. She sounded mad at him. I saw them in the grocery store across the street."

"What did she say?"

"She was crying, telling him to leave her alone, that he had her confused with someone else."

"Dakota took you to a clinic?"

"On Sixth Street. That's where she met Dr. Mitchell."

Tori looked back up at the windows.

"I think he was dealing some drugs."

"What makes you say that?"

"'Cause I heard Dakota and my mom talking about the clinic helping some addicts get drugs."

"Mike, do you think your mother would talk to me?"

"She might. She sleeps a lot during the day."

"Where do you live?"

He pointed to the next building across the alley. "We live there, just across the alley from Dakota's place. My mom used to talk to her through the window."

Tori pulled out a notepad and a pen. "Can you write down your mother's name and number?"

Mike wrote the number and his mother's name: Kesha.

She looked up at the windows again. "If I wanted to get to Dakota's apartment, how would I get there?"

"Go up the stairs. On the fifth floor go straight down the hall. Second door on the right."

The boy limped toward the yellow-taped door. "This is the way. Mama would be mad if I showed you."

Phin tried the door. "Shouldn't this be boarded up?"

"It was, but some dudes broke the door so they could sleep in there."

Phin peered into the darkness. "I've got a flashlight in my car."

"I'll wait," Tori said.

While she waited, she studied her new young friend. What was it about him that seemed so familiar? Tori pushed back a feeling that was becoming all too familiar: déjà vu.

"Can I ask you a question about Dakota?"

The kid shrugged.

"Do you know if she had a tattoo?"

"Everyone around here has tattoos."

"How about Dakota's? What was it?"

He wrinkled his nose. "Two little hearts." He pointed to his back, over the right shoulder. "There."

Tori knew it. She'd seen it. She *remembered* it.

Two minutes later, Tori followed Phin into the darkened stairwell. "You set the pace," he said.

She did. Slowly, step by step, waiting for her new heart to get the message to speed up and deliver more oxygen. This was something she needed to get used to. It seemed to take more time for her heart to respond when she exerted herself.

Their progress was methodical. Six steps, rest, another six, rest again. Midway up, Tori noticed a definite aching pain in her left ankle. She paused, rotating the joint and pushing back images of falling from a similar set of stairs. After another five minutes, they arrived on the fifth floor. The smell of burned wood seemed to permeate everything.

Tori stepped into the hallway, shining the light a few feet in front of her. The wall on the right of the hallway was essentially gone. Ahead, she could see light from windows facing the alley. Somewhere in the distance, she heard her name.

"Dr. Taylor! Dr. Taylor!"

It sounded like the boy. She walked toward the sound, eventually discovering that it came from an open window across from the room where she now stood. Mike was waving his arms.

"Run, Dr. Taylor!"

She heard footsteps behind her. She turned to see a uniformed officer.

"Are you Dr. Tori Taylor?"

She nodded, startled.

The officer shook his head. "You shouldn't be here." He spoke into his radio. "It's her. It's Taylor." He looked back at the duo standing in the room. "Ma'am, you're under arrest."

19

Standing outside a Baltimore high-rise apartment, with the Miranda warning statement still fresh in her mind, Tori vented her frustration at her arresting officer. "I don't understand. How did you know I would be in there? Why were you looking for me?"

The officer was pleasant, a twentysomething patrolman, fit, with a perfect uniform. "Dispatch warned me to look for you, to bring you in. That's all I know."

He opened the backseat to the police car.

"Why just me? Why not him?" She asked, tilting her head toward Phin.

Phin's mouth fell open.

"Whose idea was it to enter a condemned building?"

Tori put her hands on her hips. "Mine."

"Exactly." He shrugged. "I have my orders. They were to arrest you and bring you back to the station for questioning."

"No one knew I would be here."

The officer adjusted his hat. The name clipped to the front pocket of his uniform said "Robins." "Evidently someone thought you would. Otherwise, I wouldn't have been alerted."

She looked at Phin. "Do something."

He held up his hands. "There's nothing to do. Go with him. I'll follow in my car."

She sat in the backseat.

"Put your seatbelt on."

She looked at the young officer in his rearview mirror through the Plexiglas that separated them. *Make me.* She grumbled and complied.

"What were you doing in there?"

"Whatever happened to 'whatever you say can be used against you in a court of law'?"

"It applies. I just thought you might like to tell me the story."

"I wanted to see, that's all."

"You could get hurt. The building is condemned for a reason. What did you want to see?"

"I wanted to remember."

"You lived there?"

"Not exactly." She shifted in her seat, noting that there didn't seem to be any way to get out of the backseat. The door didn't have a handle. "What happens now?"

"You'll be allowed to give a statement if you wish."

"Do I need an attorney?"

"I can't imagine why you'd want one. This is a simple thing. You were trespassing."

"So why make a deal of it?"

"Someone at the district office wants to talk to you. That's all I know."

As they drove, Tori's mind spun ahead, thinking of the consequences if anyone back at VCU learned of her activities. *This is crazy. A disaster.*

A few minutes later, Officer Robins led her into the station she'd left earlier that day. Some of the same faces still populated the waiting area. As she walked, she avoided looking at their eyes. She didn't want to think about their plight. She didn't want to feel their pain.

She was fingerprinted and photographed, then placed in another nondescript room with a table and two chairs. There she waited, patiently at first. But after what seemed like an hour, she started pacing the little room, back and forth, until finally, another officer entered. This one had more stripes on his uniform. Gray salted his short hair. "I'm Captain Ellis," he said. "You must be Dr. Taylor."

She nodded. "Look, all I did was trespass." She held up her hands toward her surroundings. "I'm being treated like a criminal."

"Oh, don't worry about all this." He paused and sat, gesturing toward the opposite chair.

"Don't worry? I've never been arrested before." She sat.

"Dr. Taylor, I'm sure my department can move beyond that. We can overlook a simple trespass as long as you are willing to cooperate with us."

She leaned forward, resting her hands on the table. "I don't understand."

He rotated a silver pen through his fingers, rolling it around first one and then the other, cartwheeling the pen forward and backward over his knuckles. "I had an interesting conversation with Officer Bundrick this morning," he began. "Your information may be useful to us."

Tori nodded. "I'm glad someone thinks so."

"Mr. Bundrick tells me you think Dakota Jones was murdered."

"The short answer is yes."

"Why don't you give me the long answer?"

Tori explained how she'd received Dakota Jones's heart, gave a brief report on cellular-memory transplant, and the new nightmares and memories she'd had since her surgery.

The captain felt the surface of his flattop gray hair. Evidently satisfied with its smoothness, he smiled. "What do you make of the numbers?"

"I'm not sure. I just think it's a clue somehow to unlocking information that Dakota had. I think she knew of something bad going down and she was silenced because of it."

"And you know this because—"

"Because I *feel* it."

Captain Ellis tapped the silver pen against the table. "How committed to finding the truth are you?"

She paused, searching the captain's face. "I feel like I owe Dakota this."

"Fair enough. Would you be willing to talk to a psychiatrist? I have a consultant who may be able to help bring to light any information you have."

"Repressed memories."

He nodded. "Are you okay with that?" He slid his chair away from the table. "Because if you just want to forget the whole thing, I can have the deputies give you a court date to discuss your trespassing before a judge."

"And if I talk to this psychiatrist?"

"I'll tell my staff to ignore the trespass."

"You're threatening me?"

"Let's say I am more inclined to show favor toward those who are helping us. Call it a plea bargain."

"And you want this information for what reason?"

"Look at this from my viewpoint. Wouldn't you want to know if someone was murdered? It wouldn't look good if we just ignored that, would it?"

"Why didn't you look into it before now?"

"We weren't aware that there was anything to investigate. Officer Bundrick was first on the scene and didn't find anything suspicious."

Tori sighed. "I can talk to your psychiatrist." She shook her head. "Anything to stop these nightmares."

The captain nodded and smiled. "That a girl."

She glanced at him quickly before looking away. The whole thing felt a little … well, *greasy* was the only word she could find. "I'd like some information as well," she said.

He shrugged. "Like what?"

"Who was Dakota Jones?"

"Who was she?" He stared above Tori's head and seemed to be seeing something in his mind. "A drifter. A druggie. Single. No family." He looked back at Tori. "Probably not what you wanted to know about your transplant, huh?"

"I was one of the lucky ones. Some people don't get a match from anyone."

"I wouldn't want a woman's heart," he said. "No disrespect to you, of course."

She ignored his comment. "What do you know about Christian Mitchell? I talked to a boy who knew Dakota Jones down at the apartment this afternoon. He said he heard Dakota arguing with this guy. Maybe he's the one who wanted her dead."

"He was a doctor, some sort of resident physician at Johns Hopkins. I can look into it, but at first glance, he seems pretty clean."

"Just check him out."

"Very well," he said. "You're free to go. Just stay away from that apartment building. You'll be hearing from Dr. Mary Jaworski. She's the psychiatrist I mentioned."

"So I can leave? Just like that? What about the arrest?"

"What arrest?" he said.

She walked out, shaking her head in disbelief.

Behind her, she could hear the captain laughing, first almost under his breath, and then rising to a crescendo.

She saw Phin in the waiting room. "Let's get out of here."

"What gives?"

She didn't explain until they were in the car. "I don't get it," she added. "When I talked to Officer Bundrick, he barely acted interested. Now, I get brought in under the pretense that I was being arrested only to talk to this captain who tells me my arrest will be forgotten as long as I talk to a psychiatrist."

Phin pulled into traffic.

"It was like the whole thing was orchestrated to scare me."

"Why do you say that?"

"For one thing, why didn't they arrest you? We were both trespassing."

"It does seem strange." Phin patted her hand. "Why don't you relax? I'm sure they will check into things now that you've started the ball rolling." He let his hand rest on hers and gave her another gentle squeeze. "And maybe an interview with this psychiatrist will help you sort out your memories. It could help you know the truth."

She turned her hand over and explored his, palm to palm, tracing her fingers against his.

She closed her eyes, content to let her hand lie in his. "I hope so," she whispered. "I can't take much more of this."

A minute later, as Phin was changing lanes to get on the interstate, Tori looked at her watch. "Let's go back to the apartment," she said. "I want to talk to Kesha."

She listened to Phin sigh, so she gave his hand a friendly squeeze. "Come on. For me?"

He glanced at her. "You're used to getting your own way, aren't you?"

She shrugged and offered a little giggle. "Only child. I didn't have to share."

They made a U-turn at the next intersection. In five minutes, they were back at the condemned apartment. She scanned the street and a dozen occupants. Across from the apartment high-rises, she saw the boy leaning against a storefront. "There's Mike."

They parked, and Tori made her way across the street, pausing to let a city bus pass.

Mike looked up. He didn't smile. "So they let you out of jail?"

"I didn't go to jail, Mike."

"A brother would have gone to jail."

She didn't want to go there. "I want to visit your mother."

He tilted his head. "She's up." He paused. "Fifth floor. 502."

He didn't seem to want to talk. She shrugged and looked at Phin. "Let's go."

Across the street, they took the elevator to the fifth floor. 502 was the first door on the left.

She knocked. She could hear loud rap music coming from inside.

No response.

She pounded harder.

After a minute, a young woman opened the door against a restraining chain lock. She wore short shorts and a T-shirt that ended above her navel. Without makeup, even with her caramel complexion, she looked washed out. She pressed her face to the opening. "What you want?"

"Kesha?"

"Who's askin'?"

"I'm Tori Taylor. I'd like to ask you a few questions about Dakota Jones." She nudged Phin forward so Kesha could see him through the opening. "This is a friend of mine, Phin MacGrath."

"You police?"

"No. A friend." Tori wasn't sure how to answer, and she didn't want to explain it while standing in the dim hallway. She hesitated. "Can we come in for a moment?"

"Dakota's not around."

"I know. Your son told me that Dakota was your friend and that she may have told you about some suspicions she had about the man she was with when she—"

"I know what happened. You sure you're not police?"

Tori held up her hands. "I'm sure."

The woman closed the door and reopened it without the chain latch. "You can sit there."

The room was furnished with an old green couch. The TV was on. Several glamour magazines were on the floor by the couch. The room smelled of body odor, fried food, and something else. Maybe garlic.

"Why you want to know about Dakota? She in some trouble?"

Tori exchanged glances with Phin. Tori squinted. "You do know what happened."

"I know about the fire." Kesha frowned. "That was horrible. They should have fire escapes on all the windows." She pressed a button on the TV remote to mute the sound. "How she doin'?"

"Kesha," Tori began. "Dakota didn't make it."

Her hand flew to her mouth. "No!" She shook her head. "Did you tell my baby?"

"No." Tori reached for her hand. "I thought you knew."

"I just knew she'd been taken away. They don't tell us nothing 'round this place."

"Look, I'm trying to figure out exactly what happened. I think someone may have started that fire in order to try to hurt Dakota. I think someone wanted her dead." Tori paused, not really wanting to explain her reasons.

But Kesha probed. "Why would you think that?"

Tori took a deep breath. "Kesha, Dakota was a heart donor. When she died, they took her heart and gave it to me." She hesitated, searching Kesha's face. So far, she seemed to be tracking. "But when I woke up after my surgery, I had new memories, memories that I believe came from Dakota."

"That's wild."

Tori nodded. "Exactly. Your son mentioned the man that was with Dakota, a doctor, I believe."

Kesha nodded.

"Do you think that this man would have had reasons to want Dakota dead?"

She shook her head. "No. He was a doctor, a good man, I think. He saw my son down at the clinic."

"Your son doesn't think he was such a good man. He said he saw Dakota arguing with him."

"I don't know nothin' 'bout that."

"Mike said that Dakota told you something about people getting illegal drugs from the clinic."

Kesha wiped at her eyes. "I can't believe this. She cared about my son."

Tori placed her hand over her own heart. "Did she tell you anything?"

"Dakota had a drug problem. She was interested in how people were getting OxyContin on the street. She mentioned that she thought the clinic might be involved somehow."

"And what about this doctor, Christian Mitchell? Was he involved?"

"He worked at the clinic. That's all I know." She stood and walked over to the window, staring out at the apartment building across the alley. "That was Dakota's apartment." She turned back to face Tori. "Why would that doctor jump if he was trying to hurt Dakota?"

"I don't know. I'm just trying to figure out what happened, that's all."

"I don't think I can help you." Kesha looked down. "Dakota wasn't a bad girl. She helped my son, took him to the doctor."

"Is your son okay?"

"He got something in his leg."

Tori nodded. She remembered the boy's limp.

"Don't tell him that Dakota is dead. I want to tell him myself."

Tori and Phin stood. "Of course." They stepped to the door. "If you can think of anyone that might have wanted to hurt Dakota, could you call me?" Tori handed her a card.

"You a doctor?"

Tori nodded.

"Maybe you can help my son."

Your son has cancer. Tori shook her head to dispel the thought. *Where did that come from?* "What's wrong with him?"

"They're not sure. It might be cancer."

It was several weeks before Christian went back to the hospital to round with his father, and several months before he learned how to deal more effectively with his "gift."

He called it that because that's what his mother had dubbed it. "Call it what you want," she said. "But your ability to see below the surface and feel people's real needs is special. It's God-given."

At first, Christian was skeptical, but more and more, as he tested it, he was dead-on with his accuracy. In one situation after another, he applied his discernment. With one person, he'd sense loneliness. With another, a broken heart. With another, an unforgiving nature. Gently he probed his friends in conversations that plunged beneath a surface of calm into the cold water of their pain. Their reactions were similar. *How did you know? I've never told anyone.*

At school, it became obvious that an interaction with Christian Mitchell would be more than a flippant banter about sports or the weather. Classmates sought him out for advice.

At the hospital, his father respected Christian's impressions. If Christian sensed that a patient needed extra attention, he was free to stay behind during rounds and pray.

Over time, he learned not to bear the burden himself. His mother taught him the necessity of unloading his concerns on God, taking him back to one of her favorite verses in the Bible, *Casting all your care upon him for he cares for you.*

His joy returned.

In April, he received his acceptance letter to the University of Virginia, where he planned to study biology as a premedical student.

Throughout high school, after Emily Greene, Christian didn't date. Mostly, he found the girls in his class to be consumed with the daily drama of who liked whom, clothing, and sports, while he wanted to understand the whispers of the Holy Spirit and the Bible.

On spring nights he liked to lie out on the rugby field and look at the dusting of the Milky Way. *Show me your ways.*

And sometimes he wondered if Emily gazed at the same stars, thought the same thoughts, or dreamed the same dreams.

He remembered her kisses.

Those he would never forget.

20

As they neared Richmond, Tori pointed at an exit sign. "Get off here."

Phin flipped on his turn signal. "What's up?"

"I'm going home."

"But Dr. Parrish—"

"Phin, I'm tired of imposing on Charlotte. I've recovered enough to be on my own again."

Phin looked over. She met his gaze. He held up his right hand in surrender. "Whatever."

"She doesn't believe me."

"Charlotte's known you for a long time. Don't let this become a rift."

"That's all the more reason to move back home. I need my own space to work this out."

"You know I'm a part of the transplant team. It puts me in a funny place knowing that you're not complying with doctor's orders. Dr. Parrish wanted you to have help until—"

"He isn't God. He doesn't know what's best." She paused, study-ing his face. "Look, Phin, I appreciate all you're doing. Especially taking me all the way to Baltimore. You've been a friend. So if knowing what I'm doing is going to be a problem, I just won't tell you. As far as you know, you just dropped me at my house to pick up a few things and I took the bus back to Charlotte's."

"Except I know that that isn't true."

"I need things to normalize. I need to be in my own place again."

"Is this a control issue?"

"No." Tori huffed. "Charlotte's been great. But we don't see eye to eye on everything. I need my own space."

They drove in silence for a minute. "Here," Tori said. "Turn right. I live in Windham Estates." She sighed. "What's happening to me, Phin?"

"You thinking about Mike?"

"Him and everything else. Sometimes I don't even recognize myself. I'm so different since my transplant."

"People can change, Tori, even without transplant surgery."

She looked out the window and didn't reply.

"So what's changed? You seem more in touch with feelings. More intuitive."

"I cry. I never used to cry."

"That's a good thing. But all of these changes could just be a result of you coming face-to-face with death. You were this close," he said, lifting his hand and holding his thumb and index finger out, barely separated.

She waited until he pulled into her driveway. "You've spent enough time with me to know. Can you write a report and tell my chairman that I'm okay? Tell him that after a few more weeks, I'll be good to go."

"Maybe you should stay off until the nightmares are controlled."

"Phin, I *need* to work."

"That sounds like the old Tori." He touched her arm. "Driven."

"Hey, I'm going to see that Baltimore psychiatrist, okay?"

"I'll write my report. I'll say you're good to go. But they still have you on administrative leave. I doubt they'll let you back before that expires."

She let her hand rest on his. "Thanks."

"So that's it. Our counseling sessions have finished. I'm no longer your counselor."

They looked at each other for a moment. Phin cleared his throat.

Tori broke the silence. "Thanks for the ride." She reached for the door handle. "I guess your duties have been fulfilled, huh? No more Tori Taylor."

"It's not like that. I had hoped that I could keep seeing you, but not in the same way."

"The same way?"

"Not professionally. You see, there's something I've been thinking about for a long time, but something I couldn't consider if we were in a professional relationship."

She raised her eyebrows and turned back toward him. "And just what, Phin MacGrath, have you been thinking about?"

He reached for her cheek, touching her tenderly with his palm. She pressed in toward his hand. His voice was quiet. "I've been wondering what your lips would feel like." His thumb passed across her mouth. She pushed her lips against his finger.

"There is a better way to experience this," she said, her eyes locked on his.

He leaned forward slowly, teasing her with a closeness that was beyond physical. Soon, she felt the warmth of his breath. She would not pull away. She exhaled into his mouth, blowing across his lips. His nose grazed hers. Finally, their lips met and she sucked his lower lip between hers.

When they separated, she could not keep the new Tori beneath the surface. She sniffed and let the tears flow.

He kissed her cheeks.

She saw the moisture of her tears on his lips. Her throat tightened. She found her voice in a husky whisper. "I'd better go."

Tori entered her house, locked the door behind her, and placed her purse on the island in the kitchen. She'd not been home other than to gather her clothes since the week before her operation, the week her heart began to fail.

That day marked a step toward a normality she desperately wanted. She walked from room to room turning on lights, turning down the thermostat, and closing the drapes. A light coating of dust had settled over the bookshelves. She grabbed a dusting rag from underneath her sink and ran it across the surfaces.

She paused at a picture of her father in uniform. The one next to it was one of her favorites. Tori after a junior high play, sandwiched between her parents. Another showing Tori, the valedictorian, at her high school graduation with Charlotte. She noticed the arrangement of the pictures. *Before.* On the left of the bookshelf divide. *After.* On the right.

Charlotte's words came back to her. *Tell me about kindergarten.*

Tori paused to think. Nothing. A big blank. *My teacher was Mrs. Rohrer, wasn't she?* She nodded an affirmative answer to her own question.

Why can't I remember the details?

She moped back into the kitchen. The refrigerator contained ketchup, mustard, a bottle of habanero hot sauce, a half-empty jar of mayonnaise, and a few eggs. She sighed. *I need to go shopping.*

The challenge of resuming normal life meant driving.

She plodded to her Mazda 3 parked in the garage. She sat in the driver's seat. *I can do this.* She inhaled the car scent. It had been her first purchase after landing her attending job at VCU. She loved her little car. It boasted a 2.5 liter engine, heated leather seats, and a Bose stereo system that could blast away any nagging doubts about upcoming cases as she cruised to the hospital.

Ten minutes later, she pushed a cart up and down the aisles of her local Food Lion, making selections. *It was all supposed to be so routine,* she thought. *So why does something as mundane as grocery shopping feel so special?*

She told herself that it was crazy, that experiencing commonplace activities should fall into the category of the humdrum, but she couldn't push aside the feeling of excitement she had from being back in a routine. She picked up a box of cereal and studied the nutritional-contents label. *Is it my new relationship with Phin?*

Is it the fact that I haven't been able to do this for weeks?

Or is it deeper? Her hand traveled to her blouse and rested over her sternal scar. *Is an appreciation for the ordinary another change?*

As she shopped, she thought about Phin, what he would choose, what he might like. She smiled. Six months ago, she might have felt a date with a social worker to be a mismatch, a step down on the social ladder.

A young mother with an infant in a car seat on her grocery cart approached from the end of the aisle. Tori looked twice. The woman seemed to be radiating … peace. Tori looked again and discreetly watched as she worked her way down the column of cereals. After she passed, Tori turned around and followed her, listening as she hummed an old and vaguely familiar tune. Although she didn't know the words, Tori felt certain it was something she'd heard Charlotte sing, probably one of those Christian hymns.

Perhaps her intuition was only the recognition of a familiar and comforting tune. How else could she have any idea what a stranger felt?

She lingered in the store, comparing, shopping, watching customers, and filling her cart. When she finally slotted herself in a checkout lane, a man in front of her turned and smiled, exposing a too-generous offering of teeth and gums. His only purchase was a case of Keystone beer. "You must be fixin' to entertain," he said, looking at her purchases.

She looked at her cart. Somehow she'd selected black smoked salmon, Brie cheese, Tuscan wheat crackers, capers, imported Dijon mustard, chopped walnuts, caraway seeds, and a ten-year-old bottle of Pinot Noir. She offered a weak smile and picked up the caraway. "Never know when a recipe might call for this." She set down the seeds and let her hand graze over a bottle of imported olive oil. She felt like a poser. *I've never even tried caraway seeds before.*

Shopping before her surgery had always been quick in, select premade frozen dinners, quick out, and avoid eye contact because she didn't like running into the families of all the cancer patients she'd treated. Her choices had always been straight Americana. If it was microwavable, she'd probably tried it. She glanced self-consciously at her cart. *When did I ever start liking capers?*

Outside, the sun was setting on the Richmond skyline. Back in her Mazda, she adjusted the radio. The classic-rock station didn't seem quite right anymore. She pressed the scan button until something Mozart-like filled the air. She nodded. That just felt right.

She drove home the long way, enjoying moving the manual transmission through its five gears. The dreary had been gilded, blessing replaced the tedious, and surprise seemed to lurk just inside the dull and ordinary. Was this the result of just one kiss?

Or was it something more?

Again, she touched her chest.

Will I ever be the same?

Her next thought surprised her and came out in the closest thing to a prayer that she'd uttered in a long time. It was her first conscious positive response to the change.

"God, I hope not."

21

Stacy Williams lifted another forkful of flaky flounder to her lips. "Oh my," she groaned. "I'll follow you anywhere."

Wes Harris clapped Christian on his back. "Oh, you'll never compete with Chris's ideal woman." He closed his fist over his heart and pined, "Oh, Emily."

"Shut up," Christian responded. "I should have never told you that story."

Wes smiled. "It's good you did. We were all starting to think you're gay."

Christian ignored him.

"Seriously," Stacy said, lifting another bite to her mouth. "What's the secret? This is amazing."

"I picked out the fish this afternoon at the Inner Harbor market. Use rye flour, just a light coating before you fry it. Most people use too much and it blackens and makes a mess when you fry it."

"What's this topping?"

"Just lemon and a touch of dill."

She poked at a small green ball. "And this?"

"They're called capers."

"It's magical." Stacy lifted her wine glass. "I do have someone I'd like you to meet."

Christian groaned. "Not again."

"She loves fancy foods."

Wes mumbled under his breath. "'Loves food.' Code word for fat."

"She's not fat. She's very sweet. But you have to promise not to overanalyze her in the first five minutes."

"I don't do that."

"Oh, yes you do. Every time I introduce you to another girl, it's like you read their innermost thoughts after one conversation." She laughed. "With Claire, I think you had her figured out before she opened her mouth."

"Anyone could have done that. I knew she was a skeptic, a vegan liberal, just by the way she dressed. One look as she stepped out of her hybrid, and I knew she wouldn't like me."

Stacy frowned. "Come on, say you'll give me another chance. My friend would love your stories of Africa. Say you'll meet her."

Christian groaned. "Maybe after I get done with this ICU rotation. You guys are lucky I make time to cook at all."

She mumbled, "Medical students."

Wes nodded. "It's all about the priorities. Books, carbohydrates, and sex."

Christian sipped his Pinot Noir. "Maybe for you."

Stacy clinked her glass against his. "Two out of three ain't bad."

On the way home, Phin's thoughts ping-ponged between opposite poles.

What was I thinking?

Oh God, she's beautiful.

But so off-limits. She's not a believer.

Her kiss. Phin put his hand to his face and tugged on his lower lip, thinking of how Tori had done the same.

She's successful. Smart. Pretty.

Pretty scary to the nurses.

Scary how quickly she could wrap up my soul.

After a few minutes, he slowed as he passed a familiar place, a place where he had poured out what seemed to be a lifetime's worth of tears.

Guilt hit him full in the face.

He walked through the rows of headstones, memorials to the beloved dead. His feet took him straight to her. Fourteen rows in, second one on the right.

He glanced at an awning in the distance, a family gathering beneath the approaching night. He smelled the flowers placed at nearby sites. How long had it been since he had left flowers in her memory?

He looked down at his wife's gravesite.

I've met someone—

His cell phone rang.

He looked at the readout. Pastor Randy. Great timing.

"Hello."

"Hey, Phin. I saw your car. I figured you were heading to the cemetery. You okay?"

Phin sighed. "Yeah."

Randy let the silence hang. Unwelcome, prodding silence.

"I kissed her."

"Uh-huh. The surgeon?"

"That's the one."

"Is this a confession?"

"Maybe. She's a great girl."

"So you're sharing a blessing?"

"Yes. Both." Another sigh. "I don't know."

"You telling Missy about her?"

"Startin'."

"You need to talk?" Phin listened to Randy tapping his finger against the phone.

"I know I have to watch my step." He paused. "But she has so much going for her."

"What about the doctor-client relationship thing?"

"We're done with that."

"Just in time, huh?"

"I've got it under control."

"Really?"

Phin was irritated. Randy had a knack for going right for the sore spot.

"A threefold cord, bro," Randy said.

"I know, I know." Phin sighed again. He knew what Randy referred to. It was a verse in Ecclesiastes commonly used to describe the strength of a marriage that was made up of man, wife, and God. At best, a life with Tori would be a twofold cord.

"Okay, Phin, I'll be praying."

Phin nodded. Randy would be praying for him. Unlike many Christians, Randy didn't promise to pray with no intention of following through.

"Thanks, bro."

He closed the phone, not wanting to face the truth Randy had pointed out. More than anything, he wanted to share a deeper relationship with Tori.

But eventually, he knew that her absence of faith would create a chasm between them.

I've got to tell her good-bye.

Tori moved from room to room on cat feet. For some reason, the noise, even of her shoes against the hardwood, seemed to echo against the stillness and set her soul on edge. Her day had been crazy. Her meetings with Mike and his mother, Kesha. Her encounter with the police. Kissing Phin. Moving back home. All of it filled her with emotion, a guaranteed moat that would keep sleep away at least for the next few hours. She opened a bottle of wine and decided that a late supper didn't sound so bad.

She prepared a spinach salad, topping it with microwaved bacon, blue cheese crumbles, and a hard-boiled egg. She sipped her wine and sautéed the salmon, pouring a little of the Pinot Noir into the pan along with butter and a clove of garlic. Steam rose to greet her.

Satisfied, she covered the pan with a glass lid.

Somewhere, her cell phone sounded.

Who would call at this hour? Her heart responded with hope. *Phin?*

She followed the sound to the bedroom where her phone lay on the dresser. As she entered, the call ended. She looked at the readout. One missed call. Number restricted.

She carried it with her to the kitchen.

She needed to eat. She felt the wine hitting her without a food buffer. Her forehead felt fuzzy, her lips thick. She kissed her fingers to feel her lips tingle.

In a few minutes, as she was sitting before a plate of fish and salad, her phone sounded again.

She flipped open the phone. "Hello."

She didn't recognize the voice. A man. "I think it's time for you to stop," he said.

"Who is this? Stop what?" She looked quickly at her windows. No one could be watching. The drapes were drawn.

"Just stop," he said. "You know what, Dr. Taylor. Or should I call you Dakota?" He laughed with a booming voice. "Stop before you get hurt."

The call ended abruptly.

She felt a chill. She slid away her plate.

Had she ever heard that voice before?

She still held a wine glass in her hand. The surface of the liquid quivered. She set the glass on the table and clutched her trembling hand. She slid from her barstool, noticing a sharp pain in her ankle when her foot reached the floor. She pushed aside the feeling of pain.

Who was that?

And what do I need to stop?

Who knows about Dakota?

She lifted her phone again, dialing a number by memory.

"Hello." His voice was thick from sleep.

"Phin, it's me. I'm scared."

"What's wrong?"

"Really scared."

He sighed.

"Can you come over?"

Twenty minutes later, Tori opened the door. Phin was dressed in blue jeans and a T-shirt with a Nike logo. He carried a small gym bag.

Good, she thought. *Ready for an overnight.*

He sat opposite the couch in a recliner. "Tell me what this is about."

"It was a phone call on my cell. A man warning me to stop. I asked what he was talking about, and he said I knew. Then he called me Dakota and told me to stop before I got hurt."

Phin rubbed the back of his neck. "Wow."

"Someone doesn't want me looking into Dakota's death."

"But he didn't say that."

"What else could it mean?"

Phin shrugged. "I guess you're right." He tapped his knee. "Who knows about your donor?"

"It has to be a short list." She held up a finger. "The transplant team. Charlotte. The Baltimore police. Kesha."

"Let's assume for a moment that your theory is correct, that someone wanted to harm Dakota Jones. If that's true, whoever tried to hurt her would naturally be the one who wouldn't want someone discovering the truth."

"Makes sense."

"You should talk to the police in Baltimore. It might convince them that this is legit."

"What if he calls again?"

"Try to talk to him. Find out as much as you can." Phin yawned. It was past midnight.

"Can you stay?"

He nodded.

"Come next to me," she said, patting the couch cushion.

Phin sat next to her. She rested her head against his chest.

That lasted all of thirty seconds before Tori lifted her face to his. She kissed him, and she felt him respond in kind. His kisses became searching, warm. After a moment, he tried to untangle his hand from her hair. "Tori, we can't—I can't—"

She searched his face. She knew he wanted her. His kisses said as much. *So why the ambivalence, cowboy?*

"It's late," he said.

She nodded and stood, trying to hide her hurt. "I'll get you a blanket. You can stay on the couch."

22

When Tori rose the next morning, she heard Phin stirring in the kitchen. He was already dressed for work and the coffee was brewed. She trudged past him straight for the pot.

"Wow. You make coffee," she mumbled. "You can stay."

The morning after. Only without the before.

After nothing, Tori thought.

Phin cleared his throat and rinsed out the cereal dish he had used. "Good morning." He seemed uncomfortable. He didn't meet her gaze. "I take it your caller let you sleep."

She nodded. "All night."

"I, uh, I need to get going." He picked up his gym bag.

She walked to his side. She hadn't bothered to change out of her PJs. She kept her old robe pulled tight up around her neck. She could imagine how unflattering it looked, but she didn't care. That too was new. Before, she would have at least spent time with eyeliner, lipstick, and a chic outfit before walking in front of someone she cared about. But with Phin, there were no pretentious airs. "Thanks for staying over. I was a little freaked out."

She kissed his cheek.

Their eyes quickly met, and then he looked away again.

It wasn't the promising good-bye she wanted.

Phin seemed out of his element, on a wire, afraid of falling. He cleared his throat again.

"Go," she said. "I'll be okay."

He nodded and let himself out.

She watched through the front window. Her across-the-street neighbor, Evelyn Barkley, was at her paper box, her eyes following Phin to his car.

Tori sighed. *Let 'em talk.*

She clutched her coffee mug up under her chin. *Okay, I'm back home. I'm recovering. I've got a new chance at life.*

She looked around, unable to fight the sadness that came from not needing to go anywhere. No job demanding her presence. No patient waiting for her skills. No medical students to lecture or rounds to make. She felt … adrift.

Now what?

She picked up the blanket that Phin had folded and left on the couch. Beneath it, a small leather book had slipped between the armrest and the cushion.

Phin's Bible. He must have been reading it this morning. The cover was worn, the edges of the pages dog-eared and dull.

She held it in her hand, weighing it. Thinking.

She sat, intrigued. *Why would a smart guy like Phin need a crutch?*

She opened the cover, feeling a bit like she was peering into someone's private life, but wanting to continue just the same. She paged through, letting the book fall to the natural creases, the places

Phin had turned to over and over again. Her eyes fell on the verses highlighted in yellow.

"Trust in the Lord with all your heart, and do not lean on your own understanding."

Why would I trust God if he took my mom and dad from me?

She flipped a few sections to the next natural opening.

"And we know that for those who love God all things work together for good...."

She lifted her gaze to the photographs of her parents. *No. How can my mother's death work for good?*

She thought about Phin, how he had lost his wife, yet in his suffering he seemed to be moving in the opposite direction from Tori. She had become angry and blamed God; Phin had nestled in closer, clinging to the words he'd highlighted.

What was it that Phin had said?

"God doesn't always deliver us from pain. God joined us in human suffering by coming as a man and experiencing pain and death for himself."

Why can't I feel the same way about God that Phin does?

Tori took inventory, something that seemed to come more naturally now too. She did feel something. Not belief. More of a desire to believe.

That was new. Before her surgery, she prided herself in her objective, scientific approach. She excused the belief she saw in others as an evolutionary biologist would: beliefs were simply chemical reactions that in some way conferred a survival advantage to the carriers. It didn't necessarily mean that the belief was true, only that the belief made it more likely that the person would survive, and therefore the tendency toward that belief would be passed to the next generation.

But if it's true that a belief does not have to be true in order to provide a survival advantage, my belief in evolutionary biology must not necessarily be true either. I have to apply the scalpel equally ... both to a theory about other people's beliefs and my own.

God, I wish I could believe in you. She looked from the book in her hand to the ceiling. *I want to know the truth.*

Her cell phone sounded. She rose and found it on the island in the kitchen. "Hello."

"Tori Taylor? My name is Dr. Mary Jaworski. Captain Ellis asked me to call. It seems he has put a rather high priority on getting some information from you."

"You work as a consultant on police matters?"

"Yes. I also have a small university practice at Johns Hopkins. The captain tells me you're a physician."

"Yes. I work as a surgical oncologist at the VCU Medical Center." She didn't feel like telling the psychiatrist about her official leave status.

"Ohhh. So I'm going to have to work around your schedule."

Tori stayed quiet. *Okay, I'll let you assume that.*

"Listen, I'm not sure why the captain wants this done so quickly, but I guess he's a little concerned that a crime doesn't go unrecognized. He told me a little background."

Again, Tori just listened, not sure exactly how to launch in or whether it was appropriate to start the discussion over the phone.

Fortunately, the psychiatrist was chatty and filled the silence. "I understand you've had a heart transplant. Of course I've heard about cellular-memory transplantation, but I've never actually interviewed someone who is experiencing it."

Great, so now I'm a fascinating case.

"Listen," Dr. Jaworski continued, "I need to be in Richmond later this week to visit some family. Can I stop in to see you on Thursday?"

"Thursday is fine." *Every day is fine. I'm unemployed.*

"Would it be okay to conduct the interview in your home? I find that a familiar setting is conducive to these sorts of interviews."

"These sorts of interviews?"

"Induction of trance states."

"You mean hypnosis."

"Yes." She laughed. It sounded like something nervous and forced, not a joyous giggle. "But I avoid that term. It's so misunderstood."

"Are you calling me from a cell phone?"

"Yes."

"Fine," Tori said. "I'll text you my address. How about two in the afternoon?"

Tori listened to flipping pages. "Okay, two is fine. Oh, this is just fascinating! I look forward to talking to you."

"See you Thursday." Tori closed her phone. The psychiatrist seemed a bit too enthusiastic. "Fascinating," Tori muttered.

I hope she's as interested in finding the truth as she is in exploring an interesting medical phenomenon. I'll probably end up as the subject in a journal article.

She walked around the house sipping the coffee Phin had made, feeling a bit uneasy, wishing she had an agenda.

Now that she was sufficiently recovered and felt good enough to work, she missed it with an ache the size of Texas. Surgery was her life, her identity. It had given her purpose, but more than that, surgery had been her platform, an excuse to allow others to orbit around *her*.

But now, she wasn't the center of anyone's orbit.

And she wanted to be.

She waited until noon to call Phin, hoping to catch him on a lunch break.

He picked up after two rings. "Hello."

"Hey. It's me."

He didn't respond right away. "Oh, hey."

Not so enthusiastic. Tori frowned and clutched at the edge of her shirt at the collar. "I found your Bible. It was on the couch."

"Oh, sorry about that. Can I stop by after work to pick it up?"

"Sure. Why don't I fix dinner? I owe you for helping me out."

"You don't have to—"

"I know, silly. I want to."

"Uh, okay, sure." He cleared his throat. "I finished my report about your counseling. I've sent it to your chairman."

"Thanks." She paused, then added, "I think."

"No, it's all good."

"Are you sure you're not biased?"

He chuckled, but it didn't sound natural. "Biased? Me?"

She didn't know how to respond.

Phin added, "I wouldn't ask him about it until at least the end of the week. I recommended they let you start whenever Dr. Parrish releases you."

"Good. Maybe he'll let me start soon. I could go stir-crazy around here. I—"

"Tori, there's something you ought to know."

His voice was somber. She felt a shortening in her breath as if someone tightened a lasso over her chest. "What is it?"

"I heard Steve Brown was offered the surgical oncology chair."

She huffed. "That was my job! I've been standing in line for that job for six years." She paced around the island. "Evans didn't even interview me for the job after I asked for an interview."

"You fainted in his office."

"Yeah, well, that should have impressed him."

Phin sighed into the phone. "Listen, I just don't want you to get hurt. Evans doesn't really need you back right now."

"So what? You think I should give up?"

"I didn't say that."

Tori paused after taking another lap around the island. "You didn't give me an answer. About dinner."

"Wow, Tori, you don't need to—"

"Phin, what's going on? I thought something good was happening between us. Then last night, you acted like I had something contagious."

"Something good is happening. It's just …" His voice trailed off.

"I'll tell you what. I'll make it easier on you. I'm making dinner. You're welcome. Or not. Six-thirty."

She snapped her phone closed with more force than she'd intended.

She felt the tears beginning to well up. This was so unfair! Her life seemed to pack trouble on trouble like a snowball rolling downhill. First her health, then her job, then the mystery and terror of new memories, and now the news that she wasn't even needed back at the hospital.

She wandered into the foyer where she stared into a full-length mirror. She loved that mirror. She'd found it at an antique shop, so the glass had minor irregularities, but nothing that distorted the image. She'd painted the bulky frame a rich gold-leaf satin. In her old life, she stopped for a final inspection before leaving the house each morning at six.

She'd hoped that Phin would help her make sense of all her misery, or at least slow the rolling snowball. At first, she'd thought he might be bringing a little healing to her heart. Instead, she felt like he'd just given the snowball a shove. *Attaboy, Phin, just pack on more snow.*

She frowned at her reflection. No makeup. She lifted her hair and let it fall again. Flat.

No wonder Phin put on the brakes last night.

She thought about dinner. *Candlelight?*

No, that would be too much.

She unbuttoned the upper buttons on her pajama top. Her sternal scar was far from mature, slightly raised and pink, like a kindergarten child had smashed a worm of Silly Putty to accentuate her cleavage. *Oh, that's sexy. No wonder my social worker didn't want to steal second base.*

She gathered her robe up under her chin and tried to remember if she had anything remotely sexy that wasn't cut so low it would reveal her scar.

She pouched her lips toward the mirror, remembering how Phin had kissed her in the car.

You acted like you wanted me.

Until last night.

She sighed. *I'm calling my hairdresser. If he runs from me tonight, it won't be because I scared him away with my appearance.*

23

Christian Mitchell, MD, placed a cool washcloth on the forehead of his bald little chemotherapy patient, Brian Phillips, and resumed his vigil holding the boy's hand. On the nightstand were Brian's favorite things, including a baseball signed by Baltimore Oriole great Cal Ripkin Jr.

"Baltimore plays Atlanta tonight," Christian said. "We should be able to pick up the game on MASN."

Brian nodded but didn't speak or open his eyes.

Christian looked up as his resident walked in. Toby Henson, a West Point grad who was letting the government pick up the tab for his education in exchange for future service, shook his head and said, "There you are. The phlebotomist can't get blood on the Yarborough kid. I need you to do a femoral stick."

"Okay."

Henson stared at him. "Now?"

Christian squeezed the hand of his little patient. "I'll be back after a while and check on you again."

"Don't leave," he whispered.

"Sorry, sport. I'll be back soon."

In the hallway, Henson turned and pointed at Christian's chest. "I can't have you sitting here all day holding hands with the patients while there's work to be done."

"I finished all my admissions. Dr. Smith knew where I was."

He leaned forward. "And what is it with you? Your eyes are wet." He shook his head. "You can't expect to be able to help these kids if you get so attached."

"Brian was having a bad day, that's all. His mother had to leave for a few hours, and I had—"

"Get a spine, Mitchell. If you really want to help kids with cancer, you can't be crying over each one."

"Empathy can be helpful. When the patients know I care, they respect my recommendations."

"Yeah, well, if you let your emotions get involved, you'll never be able to be objective. And that's your job," he said, pointing again at Christian's chest. "You let these kids get under your skin and you'll never sleep at night. Bad things happen, Mitchell. Kids with cancer die every day."

"And maybe they should die with someone holding their hand."

"Let a nurse do that. You've got to make the hard decisions to use chemotherapy to give them a chance."

"But I—"

"No arguments from you. Now get to the ICU and draw that blood. And don't cry about causing your patient a little pain." Henson sighed. "What is it with you? First I find you praying for a patient; now I find you holding hands and getting tearful. If you want to pass this internship, you'd better start acting like a real doctor."

Chris nodded and held his tongue.

I am.

That afternoon, Tori carefully prepared Caribbean chicken with pear and cranberry chutney, using a rub of allspice, fennel, and cloves. At six, she'd just begun to fry chicken breasts in fresh ginger and chopped onion when the doorbell rang.

She checked her appearance in the foyer mirror and smiled. She'd found the perfect little black dress, one that covered her sternal scar and contained a side slit just high enough to keep things interesting. She wore a single pearl necklace, positioned so that the pearl fell right at her suprasternal notch. Not extravagant. Just right in a classy sort of way.

She took a deep breath and opened the front door.

Charlotte stood between two suitcases, obviously surprised at Tori's appearance. "Well, well, aren't we fancy?"

Tori stepped forward. "I wasn't expecting you."

"Obviously." She held up her hands. "I brought your stuff." She lifted the bags and entered. "Something smells wonderful."

"I'm planning a little dinner."

Charlotte raised her eyebrows. "Jarrod coming over?"

Tori shook her head. "No." She wasn't sure she wanted to share the news with Charlotte until she knew there was news to share. Tori needed to figure things out a bit first.

Charlotte barged her way forward, following her nose to the kitchen. "Wow. What smells so good?"

Tori shrugged and turned the burner down to low. "Caribbean chicken. I got the recipe online."

"Since when do you cook?"

She wrinkled her nose. "Since now."

"You could have told me you were moving out."

"I didn't think you'd approve."

"I don't." Charlotte looked around. "But obviously you're doing okay." Charlotte dabbed the end of her index finger into a small bowl of chutney and returned it to her mouth. "Mmm. Maybe I was cramping your style."

"It's not that. I just needed for things to get more normal."

"This is normal?"

"Not exactly. But here I'm in control." She put her hands on her hips. "Regaining control is an important part of recovery." She lifted the lid off the frying chicken. "I really need to pay attention to this."

Charlotte waved her hand in the air. "I'll get out of your hair, then. Do I need to camp down the street to find out who's coming to dinner?"

"Phin."

"Your counselor?"

"It's not what you think. He's a friend."

Charlotte stomped toward the front door. "I'm your friend and you don't dress that way for me."

"I'll tell you about it later."

"Be careful, Tori. You're going through a stressful time. Don't—"

Tori held up her hand. "I'm a big girl," she said, shooing Charlotte toward the door. "I need to work."

She watched Charlotte crossing the lawn and Phin arriving at the same time. Charlotte gave an exaggerated wave with an even more exaggerated grin. Tori stayed at the front door and opened it a moment later.

Phin stood there like a model out of an L.L.Bean catalog. He held a bottle of wine. "Wow," he said, looking at Tori.

Good start. She smiled and took the bottle. "Come in."

"I hope that's okay. I wasn't sure what you were fixing."

"It will be perfect."

He followed her to the kitchen.

She watched as he inspected the table.

"Tori, you didn't need to do all of this. Really, I just needed to pick up my Bible."

"Oh, and for that you bring me a bottle of wine?"

"You mentioned dinner. I just thought ..."

She turned the chicken and looked back at him. "I'm glad you decided to come. I thought you would."

He shifted his weight back and forth. "Look, I guess we should talk about this—"

She stepped toward him and placed her index finger against his lips. "Not now. Let's have dinner first. Then talk." She pointed toward a drawer in the island. "I have a corkscrew around here somewhere. Why don't you open the wine?"

Phin worked on the bottle. Tori walked into the other room and came back holding his Bible.

"Can I ask you a few things?" she said.

"Sure."

She opened the worn Bible. She smiled slyly. "I liked seeing the things you underlined."

"Those are meant for me."

"I know." She paused, hoping he was okay with it. "That's why I liked seeing them." She pointed to a verse he'd underlined. "This bit about not leaning on your own understanding—does that mean Christians just blindly trust and put their brains in neutral?"

"No. I've chosen to believe the claims of Christ because I've examined the proof and I think they're true. But I haven't abandoned my mind." He hesitated. "I underlined that after my wife died. Her death wasn't something I could understand. Why would God allow my wife to be taken from me?" He took the book from her hand. "So I just had to hold onto the things I believed, like 'God loves me.' I just had to believe he knew best."

Tori turned around. "I want to know more about the proof," she said. "But right now, I think this chicken is ready. Let's eat."

During dinner, they talked about their trip to Baltimore and Tori's upcoming interview with the psychiatrist. They talked about hobbies, Phin's work with Habitat for Humanity, and Phin's church. They talked about everything … except their relationship. That's the way Tori had planned it. She didn't want Phin to feel anything but at ease.

After eating, they retired with their wine glasses to a couch in the den. Tori didn't wait for Phin to speak. She took their glasses and set them on a coffee table. Then, she positioned herself so that she faced him on the couch. She stroked his cheek with her hand and leaned forward until her lips touched his.

She felt her breathing quicken. The kiss was heaven, tenderness wrapped in softness, wrapped in longing. But soon Phin put his hands on her shoulders and gently held her away.

"What's wrong?"

"I ... I," he said, twisting away. "It's just that I can't."

"But we're just beginning to click. You understand me. I thought we were ready to take—"

"It's not right. I can't do this." He disentangled himself from her arms and stood. "I'm sorry. I don't want to lead you on."

"Phin, talk to me. You don't like me in that way?"

"No. Yes, I mean, no, it's not that." He shook his head. "Missy." *Your wife.* "She's gone, Phin."

He stuttered. "I should go."

"No, we should talk," she said. "What did I do? Did I move too fast? We can go at your pace." She touched his hand. "Tell me about Missy."

"I ... I—" He shook his head.

"Have I misread you? Have I completely lost my ability to read men?"

"It's not you."

He walked toward the door. When he reached the front foyer, he turned. "Dinner was great. Thanks."

She couldn't quite believe he was leaving just like that. For a moment, she watched. Stunned. But then, just as he closed the door, she called his name. "Phin."

He paused.

"Take this," she said, reaching into the kitchen. "Your Bible. I wouldn't want to give you an excuse to come back."

She dropped the book into his hands, slammed the door after him, and began to cry.

24

Thursday morning, psychiatrist Mary Jaworski sat on the leather couch in Tori's den and smiled. "I don't want you to feel anxious about this."

Tori studied the petite woman in front of her. Her long, straight hair was streaked with gray. Not highlighted, streaked. Mary didn't seem the type to care. She wore a denim wraparound skirt, a plaid blouse, and one of those yellow "Live Strong" wristbands that indicated she'd donated money for a cancer cure. Her eyelashes and complexion weren't completely inadequate, but Mary hadn't used an ounce of effort to augment her natural strengths. Her build was slight and the knuckles on her hand seemed too prominent. On top of everything else, her smile revealed a set of clear braces, the kind that are supposed to be invisible but capture your attention and make you look even closer to see what's wrong.

"I'd like to start with some general questions. Later, if we conclude that it will help, I'll do the trance induction. I'll need to videotape it all, just in case the captain needs it for evidence."

"Will I remember what I reveal under hypnosis?"

Dr. Jaworski pushed her shoulder-length hair behind her ears. "You may not. If there are important discoveries, you and I can watch the video at a later time when we can process it together.

"I'd like to talk about your background. Childhood, education, that sort of thing."

Tori reclined in her favorite leather chair with her feet on the matching ottoman. "Is that really necessary? What I really want to know is the meaning of the transplanted terrors."

"I need to know about your own past, so that I can distinguish between the two. If you've got memories from two different lives, I need to know yours first." She paused and smoothed the denim skirt over her legs. "I've done some reading about transplanted cellular memories. This is really a fascinating area. If what you tell me can be documented, I'd say we have a reportable case."

"Wonderful." Tori let the words drip with sarcasm.

When the psychiatrist looked hurt, Tori explained, "I couldn't care less about whether medical science benefits from this. I just want to assist in bringing justice if someone was really trying to hurt Dakota Jones."

"Okay," Dr. Jaworski said, "let's begin." She opened a laptop and poised her fingers over the keyboard. "Tell me about your earliest memory."

Pastor Randy Slaytor folded his hands in his lap and looked at Phin. "It doesn't sound like you're being fair. You're leading her on by your actions."

"That's just it—I don't *want* to lead her on. In fact, it doesn't feel that way. When we kissed, it was something that I really wanted to do. It's just …"

Randy hesitated and finally finished the sentence for him. "You just don't think it's right."

"She's a great lady, don't get me wrong. But we don't share the same faith. She's a scientist. She believes in what she can see and feel."

Randy leaned back. "And did you tell her that the faith issue is what's holding you back?"

"No." Phin shook his head. "I didn't want to see her exploring faith out of a motivation to get on my good side."

"So you really think you have that much influence?"

"I think it's pretty clear that she liked me. But now I'm not so sure."

"She sounds hurt."

Phin nodded. "My fault, bro."

"I think you know where I stand on this. I'm concerned about whether you're being fair to Tori."

"I know." Phin paced around Randy's small office. "I should never have let things go so far."

"You need to give her space."

"Oh, believe me, that's no problem. I'm not sure she'd want to see me at all anymore."

Randy sighed. "Maybe that's best."

Phin stared out the window across the empty parking lot. "I think it is. But it doesn't really *feel* best."

Kesha watched Mike limp over and plop onto the couch. "Are you hurtin', baby?"

"A little."

"We need to take you back to the clinic."

"But my doctor's dead."

"There are other doctors, silly."

"Can you call that lady doctor, the one that was looking at Dakota's place?"

"She works in Richmond, Mike. That's a long ways."

"But she told you she'd see me, right?"

"She said 'if' I could get you to Richmond, she'd make sure you were taken care of."

"We can take a bus. Willie did it."

"Willie has money."

"You have money. I've seen the jar under your bed."

"You need to stay out of my things."

"Call the lady doctor. I don't want to go back to the clinic. They just want to give me drugs."

"The drugs helped, didn't they?"

"The pain, maybe, but the lump is still there."

Kesha opened her purse on the kitchen table and began to search. A moment later, she lifted a small card. "Here it is," she said, reading the card. "Victoria Taylor, MD, FACS, Department of Surgical Oncology. I wonder what all those initials mean."

"That's her degrees or something."

Kesha nodded. How did her son get to be so smart? "Go bring me that jar," she said. "I'll see if we have enough for bus fare."

Her earliest memory?

It was to be *the* trip of her young life. A trip to Walt Disney World. Breakfast with Mickey Mouse. The Magic Kingdom.

But somewhere in the throngs of people, six-year-old Tori Taylor stood in line with her mother so she could ride on the spinning teacups. Again. Tori looked at the park map and tightly gripped the sleeve of her mother. But when she looked up, the sleeve she held wasn't her mother's after all.

Little Tori stumbled backward from the line and began calling her mother's name. Back and forth along the line, then back to the bench to see if her Dad was waiting.

No Dad.

She squinted at the sun.

She was alone in a crowd. She studied the people walking hand in hand and others eating ice cream.

How will they find me?

Have they left me?

Was this the plan all along?

Tori felt for the bulge in her pocket, the silver flip-open lighter that her Dad let her carry for him. He'd even showed her how to use it.

She could get their attention.

She walked to a large trash bin, casually lit the paper map in her hand and tossed it into the open trash container.

In a few moments there were screams of "Fire!" Park visitors scattered. A man in a uniform grabbed her by the arm; another wielded a fire extinguisher.

The man released her arm and knelt to eye level. "What are you doing?"

"I don't know where my mommy is."

Later, after she'd been taken to what she forever after thought of as the lost-and-found building, she saw her parents through the window in the door to the small room where she'd been waiting. Her mother talked with a uniformed man, covered her mouth with her hand, and cried. Tori remembered hearing her father's comment, "We should have expected something like this."

Her parents escorted her from the park.

Tori cleared her throat and looked at the psychiatrist.

"Wow," Dr. Jaworski responded. "What did you feel? Scared?"

"I don't remember."

"Did you cry?"

"My mother cried." Tori looked at her hands. Her knuckles had whitened as she gripped the edge of the recliner. "I remember how she looked at me. Not like she was glad to see me, but like she pitied me." She shook her head. "I didn't cry," she responded, her voice just above a whisper.

"Come on, all lost little girls cry."

Tori shrugged. "Not me," she said. "Not me."

25

Christian Mitchell was a favorite of his little patients and their parents. His ability to explain problems in plain language as well as to empathize with their misery, even through shedding his own tears, endeared him to them as a caring and competent physician.

Unfortunately, his superiors didn't appreciate his emotional connections. As a consequence, Christian was scrutinized. He was often given assignments others didn't want. When a program to give interns a taste of the life to come was instituted, his chief resident assigned other interns to assist in the private practices around the Baltimore suburbs and routed Christian to the downtown free clinic where the poor and uninsured clogged the system with trouble.

After a morning of seeing a dozen kids with flu symptoms, Christian spent thirty minutes following up with a child who suffered from terminal recurrent retinoblastoma, a cancer that had begun in the patient's eye. His patient, Dale Walker, had undergone surgery to remove his right eye, as well as chemotherapy and radiation. Unfortunately, the cancer had recurred, and after three more rounds of an experimental regimen of chemo, his oncologists had told the Walkers that Dale's condition was ultimately terminal. It was time for comfort measures only.

Christian had reviewed the latest MRI scans and made a referral to palliative care. He was sitting down to eat a ham-and-cheese sandwich when Clara Rivers, the clinic's director, opened the door to the small break room. She held a prescription in her hand. "What's the meaning of this?" she asked.

Christian looked at the prescription. "It's a prescription for oxycodone for my terminal patient. Is there a problem?"

"Only with the amount."

Christian sighed. "Look, addiction isn't a concern here. The boy is going to die. My main concern is to get him pain relief."

"You don't seem to understand. I'm not critical that you provided too much medicine. I want you to give him more."

"I prescribed thirty tablets and referred him to palliative care. They should be able to take care of him."

The director pushed a strand of graying blonde hair behind her ear and took a deep breath, her expression conveying clear annoyance. "This family can't afford the palliative team. You need to provide him more medicine."

"Okay," Christian said. "Sure."

She shoved a new prescription in front of him. "I take care of the palliative treatment for the clinic patients. Just sign the script, and I'll fill out the details."

"But it's a controlled substance, a powerful narcotic. I'd like to know what's being done in my name."

"Just sign this. Dr. James oversees everything anyway." ·

Christian shrugged. Dr. James was his department chair. It wouldn't do for him to think that Christian was rocking the boat. He signed the prescription.

"Would you mind signing a few more?" she asked. "I'll only use them for the palliative cases."

Christian studied her for a moment. She appeared tired, and even a heavy coat of foundation couldn't hide the crow's-feet extending from the corners of her eyes. "Actually," he said, "I do mind. Let's keep this to a case-by-case basis, shall we?"

She straightened and sighed. "Well," she said, smoothing the front of her white lab coat.

He thought some other comment was forthcoming, but she turned and stomped out, clicking her heels on the spotted linoleum floor.

He watched her disappear as the door closed and shook his head. *Weird.*

He turned his attention back to his brown bag, but his mind was far from lunch. His eyes had fallen to a small framed photograph on the wall. It was of Clara Rivers receiving some sort of civic award. He squinted at the photograph. Shaking her hand was his chairman, Dr. James. *Great, that's all I need. She's in with my boss.*

He looked at his sandwich, suddenly not hungry. He stuffed it into the bag again and tossed the bag into the corner trash can.

Sighing, he left the break room in search of his next patient.

Tori talked for two hours about growing up in Richmond, Virginia. First memories. Biggest fears. A childhood without tears.

She wearied of the questions. She'd told all she could remember and felt spent. Dried up. She sat. She paced. She consumed a liter of bottled water, and still Dr. Jaworski questioned, probed, and pried.

When time came for a trance induction, she welcomed it. Anything to stop the conscious searching of every little recollection. For her, the time during the trance passed without consciousness.

When she awoke, she heard her name being called, as if at the end of a tunnel. And for the first time since her heart transplant, she had the sensation of heart pounding. A horse race in her chest.

Sweat stung her eyes.

"Tori, Tori!" A voice sharpened with urgency. "You're okay. No one is hurting you."

Images of fire, falling, and pain fled from the edges of consciousness.

A man? Screams? I'm burning!

Tori reached up to touch the face in front of her. *The psychiatrist.* She wiped sweat from her eyes. *Was I crying?*

She looked into the searching face of Mary Jaworski. "You're okay, Tori. You're in your home. You're safe."

Tori shook her head and tried to dispel the sense of fear. She couldn't speak. She took inventory of her emotions. There was something besides fear.

Anger! White-hot. A tiger ready to defend or attack.

When she finally found her voice, it came as one finding air upon breaking the surface of the ocean. She gasped. "What did I say?"

Dr. Jaworski returned to her laptop and typed for a moment.

Tori pressed. "Did I reveal something important? Did I tell you who killed my donor?"

"Oh, Tori," she said, "I really need to go over the tape." She closed her laptop and folded her hands and let them rest on the surface of her denim skirt. "Are you hungry? You've been working so hard."

She shook her head. "I'm not hungry. I want to know what I said."

"You don't remember?"

Tori concentrated. "No. Everything's gone."

The psychiatrist smiled in a smug sort of way that irritated Tori.

"Tell me what I said," Tori said, standing, still feeling the fear and anger that had greeted her when she surfaced from the trance. "I have a right to know."

Mary Jaworski stood and backed away from Tori, her face showing a hint of fear. "Not now," she said, lifting her hand. "I want to reveal the information to you in a controlled setting. I'm concerned for your well-being."

Tori huffed and shook her head. "You think I can't handle this? The memories can't hurt me. They belong—" she touched the front of her blouse—"to Dakota Jones."

"Your case is complicated, Tori. Give me a few days to make some sense of this and make a report for the captain."

"Give me a clue."

"We made real progress."

Mary Jaworski slipped her laptop into a leather satchel and lifted the video camera from a tripod. She folded the tripod, lifted the satchel, and collected her notes.

As Dr. Jaworski prepared her belongings, Tori protested. "I'm your patient. You're obligated to me."

"Well, not exactly. I was hired to interview you as a potential witness to a crime, not as a patient," she said. "Baltimore PD is paying my salary. I'll make my report, and we can talk next week." The psychiatrist headed to the front door.

Tori wanted to scream. This didn't seem fair. She was so close, yet so far from the information she wanted.

At the open door, the psychiatrist stopped. "Call my office and make an appointment. We can talk once I've had a chance to process the information on the tape and go over my notes."

"Was I able to give you any more information?"

Jaworski put her hand to her lip and sighed before speaking. "Yes."

"So what did I say?"

The doctor held up her hand and stepped onto the front porch. "Later, Tori. We'll have a chance to figure this all out."

"Later," Tori muttered.

Tori watched as Mary Jaworski plodded across the lawn to the driveway and her BMW sedan. She thought for a moment about wrestling the video-camera case from the psychiatrist, but she let the feeling pass. Instead, she just nodded and looked at the sky, feeling a sudden strange urge to pray.

"Help me, God." She touched the front of her blouse. "Why was Dakota so angry?"

Confused and still a bit angry, she closed the door. As she did, her cell phone sounded. She found it on the recliner in the den. "Hello."

Heavy breathing and a man's voice.

It was as if the call uncapped her anger again. "Who is this?"

"I thought I'd made myself clear."

"Clear? You're a coward. Tell me who you are!"

She ran to the front room and stood behind her front door before stealing a glance through a window bordering the door.

"I told you to stop. Now someone is going to get hurt."

There was no one on the street. Mary Jaworski's car was gone. *Was someone watching me?*

Who knew about this?

She repeated her question, but her voice had weakened, betraying her fear. "Who—who is this?"

But the line was dead. She looked at her phone. The call had ended.

26

A duo of Richmond police officers responded to Tori's urgent call for help.

After an interview and a careful search of Tori's property, the officers seemed unimpressed. To make things more difficult, Tori was reluctant to explain all the details of her transplanted memories, unwilling to risk more ridicule. So she told them only about her threatening phone call.

Hands on hips, she glanced toward the front windows, now dark since the sun had long set. "So what am I to do? Someone is threatening me."

The older and heavier of the two officers sighed. "You said the caller said someone would be hurt. How do you know that someone is you?"

"Who else would it be?"

"Don't know, ma'am," he said. "We just don't have enough information, do we?"

"Could you at least watch my house?"

She watched as the pair exchanged a look. *They think I'm crazy.*

"We can drive through the neighborhood a few times during the night. Do you have a security system?"

She nodded. "Doesn't everybody?"

"Is there any place you can go? A friend's place you can crash for a night?"

She thought about Phin. She hadn't left things on a very open note there. She didn't want to bother Charlotte. Besides, Charlotte would worry, and she had warned Tori to stop looking into her donor's death.

Tori looked up. "I'll go to a hotel. Could you stay to give me time to collect a few things?"

The older officer nodded. "Sure."

A few minutes later, she left her neighborhood in her Mazda. She circled her neighborhood, frequently checking the rearview mirror. Twice, when headlights appeared in the mirror, she pulled to the side, pretending to park, forcing the other vehicle to pass.

She drove downtown, occasionally doubling back, turning left three times in order to go right, and timing the traffic lights so that she could just scoot through on yellow. Finally, after thirty minutes, she pulled into the Jefferson and used the valet to park.

She paid with a credit card and settled into a room on the fourth floor. There, she took a long shower, hoping the water would not only cleanse her body but also soothe her troubled soul. She adjusted the showerhead to pulsate its delivery.

As the water pounded her back, she took inventory.

No job.

No boyfriend.

Do I have any real friends beyond Charlotte? Has my professional distance completely sabotaged my relationships?

No peace of mind.

A mystery I can't seem to solve.

Threats to my life.

The water did little to wash her fears away. If anything, she saw with more clarity the foundation of sand upon which she had built her self-confidence. She stayed under the stream until her skin started to wrinkle. She toweled off and slipped into a thick terry-cloth robe.

Back in the other room, she frowned at the clock. 12:40 a.m. With no sleep in her foreseeable future, she channel surfed the selection of digital drivel. She paced the room and stared out at the Richmond skyline, listening to the warble of an ambulance siren. Up the hill from her hotel, the medical school hospital campus would be in full swing, accepting the night's offering of trauma. She felt a profound sense of loss. She used to thrill at the challenge of an emergency case, but now, the work went on without her, the towering hospital apparently oblivious to her absence.

Without my career, who am I?

In the absence of friends, who would care if I lived or died?

What is the center of my identity?

How much have I changed because I have a new heart?

Tori opened the drawer to a small nightstand. It was empty except for the presence of one book. A Bible.

She shut the drawer. Stopped. Opened it again, looking at the book. She thought about Phin's love for the Bible. *But that's so not me.*

Maybe I should see for myself.

She thought for a moment of the way she was changing, and even as she lifted the Bible from the drawer, she felt incredulous. *If Charlotte could see me now.*

She opened the cover and examined the first few pages. In the front was a section for those unfamiliar with the Bible: "Where to Find Help." She scanned the categories and found a section referring to lack of peace of mind. *Bingo. That pretty much describes me.*

She sat on the bed with the book in her lap and was soon absorbed in a search. For years Charlotte had tried to interest Tori in the Bible. For years Tori had resisted, preferring her own science-rules philosophy.

She talked to herself: "So how's that life philosophy working out for ya? Not so good, huh?"

The directory sent her to a particular page where she read from the words of Jesus. *"Come to me, all who labor and are heavy laden, and I will give you rest. Take my yoke upon you, and learn from me, for I am gentle and lowly in heart, and you will find rest for your souls. For my yoke is easy, and my burden is light."*

Somehow, strangely, her heart warmed at the thought.

A yoke doesn't sound easy to me.

She followed a trail from one verse to another, directed by the page numbers provided in the guide. There she read silently. *"Casting all your anxieties on him, because he cares for you."*

She thought about Dakota Jones, and again, almost instinctively, her hand clutched the robe in front of her chest. "God," she whispered, "did Dakota Jones love you?"

Dakota must have been a follower of Jesus. Why else would Tori be feeling so drawn by the words of the Bible?

Could it be that Charlotte and Phin are right after all?

Does God really care for me?

Tori thought back to a conversation she'd had with Charlotte about the mysterious number that seemed tattooed into her memory after her transplant: 316. Charlotte had suggested that it might have been a message intended for Tori, a message of the famous verse Tori had been able to recall: *For God so loved the world.*

Was I able to quote the verse because Dakota loved it too?

Or just because I'd heard it from Charlotte so many times?

Tori looked at the Bible in her hand. She hardly knew what to think. *Here I am in distress, and in my old life the last place I would have turned was to this book. But now, I have a compulsion to read these words. Is this crazy?*

She weighed the book, moving it up and down in her hand.

What has happened to me? Am I Dakota? Or Tori?

"I'm Tori Taylor," she whispered. "But I am not the same Tori Taylor, am I?"

She turned to the back of the Bible and read about the steps to becoming a Christian.

Am I really separated from God because of sin?

She'd always considered herself a "good person." She worked hard in her job to do her best.

But in my quest for perfection, I managed to alienate my coworkers and ended up jeopardizing the one job I love.

I am a sinner.

Really?

Tori sensed a nervous energy and stood. She paced the room, considering the gravity of the decision in front of her. She'd been a scientist all her adult life. She lived for the power of her position as a surgeon. She loved the control and had rested comfortably in her own competence.

She touched the front of her robe over her new heart. She'd lost control, and it was obvious that her professional abilities were not the key to unlock faith.

This new heart has changed me. I want to believe.

Did my donor love Christ?

So what do I do? How do I learn to follow the leading of my new heart?

She slipped her hand under her robe and felt the pulsing of her heart beneath her fingers, amazed that her heart transplant had meant so much more than the physical healing it had brought her. She had opened up emotionally and spiritually as well. She wondered about Dakota Jones, her life experiences, relationships, and loves. She imagined the timelines of her life and the life of Dakota Jones from birth streaking toward an intersection on the day of her transplant. What had her donor experienced, felt, or feared that could be affecting Tori now? Were there significant events of happiness or sorrow? Worship or wonder? Faith or doubt?

"God," she whispered, "I'm not doing so well on my own."

She wondered about the proper posture for prayer. She knew that Charlotte prayed anytime, often even while driving, so she understood that there wasn't an exact formula. But for now, it seemed right to bow. Slowly she knelt by her bed and laid the Bible open in front of her.

Alone, she began to cry. She allowed the burden her life had become, her fears for her life, her failures at her career and relationships to be expressed in a flood of tears. Sobbing, she lowered her head to the bed.

I'm so lost.

She rubbed her eyes and read through the steps again. A prayer was written out for her to follow. She shook her head, amazed. Here she was, an educated, intelligent, beautiful woman, and she was contemplating her utter depravity before God.

"Dear Father," she whispered. "I know I am a sinner. I believe you died for me...."

I love you.

She looked up. Where had that come from? Another unwanted memory from Dakota Jones?

Tori read the prayer haltingly, unsure what to expect. She wanted to believe that God loved her and gave his Son to pay a penalty on her behalf.

Does simply praying a prayer mean that I'm in?

But what if I doubt? What if I think it sounds too good to be true?

She closed the book and wiped a tear from her cheek. Something was different. Not only did she want to believe, she *did* believe.

A sense of gratitude settled on her soul.

What had changed?

Her circumstances were still dreary. No job. No boyfriend. Someone was still threatening her life.

But I have peace.

Everything is crazy in my life ... but things are okay with God.

Knowledge of love enveloped her. Little mattered in that moment except the fact that she knew she was loved. Warmth. Peace. Joy. *How can I describe what I feel?*

A presence.

Glory!

She wanted to speak, to shout, to express her thanks, but her throat tightened. Trembling, she lifted her right hand into the air. There, kneeling on the floor of the Jefferson Hotel, Tori Taylor wept.

She wept for her own selfishness. She wept for the pride that had kept her running her own life for so long in spite of Charlotte's urging. And now, she wept for the joy of knowing her sins were forgiven.

Time disappeared. She felt only the embrace of her Savior, caressing her heart. She sniffed and looked at the clock. 1:45 a.m.

She took off the robe and dressed for bed. Slipping beneath the sheets, she whispered another prayer to God, something that, regardless of how alien it would have felt to her just a few days ago, now seemed to come as naturally as hunger or thirst. "Thanks, Father. Thanks."

27

The next morning, Tori enjoyed the delicious rarity of sleeping in. She awoke, stretched, and in her first moments of consciousness, thought back over the events of the night before. She looked at the Bible on the bedside table and breathed deeply, collecting her thoughts. *Yes,* she thought with a smile, *peace is here.*

She rose and decided that an extended stay at the Jefferson Hotel would be perfect. She stopped at the desk and requested to keep her room for a week.

In that time, she would do three things: find out about God, find out as much as she could about Dakota Jones, and try to discover who was threatening her.

She started her day by walking to a downtown bookshop. The Asian man behind the counter said, "May I help you?"

"I'm looking for a Bible," she said quietly.

He led her to a section marked "Religion." She looked through the options and selected something called a parallel Bible, with the New International Version on one side and a contemporary version called *The Message* on the other. It was real leather and smelled like an expensive handbag. The salesman explained that the NIV was a translation and that *The Message* was a modern paraphrase that might help her understand a bit easier.

She hurried back to the hotel, holding her purchase in her hand like a treasure.

"Okay, God," she whispered in her room, "show me who you are."

She began paging forward, yellow highlighter in hand, anxious to color the verses that meant something special to her. She wanted to personalize her Bible as Phin and Charlotte had theirs.

She scanned from book to book, trying to understand the big picture. Along the way, she thrilled to read metaphorical language in *The Message*, particularly when the words used were ones she could relate to as a surgeon. In Romans 8 she read, "God went for the jugular when he sent his own Son." In Hebrews 12 she read, "When you find yourselves flagging in your faith, go over that story again, item by item, that long litany of hostility he plowed through. *That* will shoot adrenaline into your souls!"

After two hours, she took her immunosuppressive meds and lay down for a nap.

In the afternoon, she called Phin MacGrath. He answered after two rings.

"Hi," she said.

Slight hesitation. "Tori."

"You sound surprised to hear from me."

"Honestly, I am. I didn't think I'd be on your list of favorite people just now."

"I didn't say you were on my favorite-people list, Phin." She paused and weighed her words. "I didn't call to ask you out. I need a favor."

"What's up?"

"You mentioned that you had a friend, an ex-cop who had a heart transplant. You had him look into a few things for me. I'd like his contact information."

"Okay," he said.

She listened to noises of paper shuffling.

"Say," Phin said, "did you ever talk to that psychiatrist?"

"Yeah. Let's just say I must have spilled some information, but her allegiance is to the Baltimore PD. She says she needs to process the data before she talks to me." Tori sighed. "So I'd like to do a little more digging on my own. That's why I need this contact."

"Sure. Here it is. Gus Peterson." He read off the phone number. "He'll remember."

"Okay. Got it. Thanks, Phin. Bye."

She had deliberately avoided letting things get too personal in the call. It was so much easier to retreat to a professional level, rather than deal with how hurt she'd been by the way they'd left things after their dinner.

She imagined Phin's confusion. *Let him stew. I've got little patience for a man willing to send me such mixed-up signals.*

She dialed Gus Peterson.

"Hello." His voice was baritone and cheerful.

"Mr. Peterson, my name is Tori Taylor."

"Yes, Dr. Taylor, I know of you."

"I'm calling to see if I can get you to do a little snooping for me."

"Well, well. I understand you're looking for your heart donor."

"Not exactly. But I should thank you for the work you did for Phin MacGrath. I've identified my donor, but I think she died under suspicious circumstances."

"Phin told me about that."

"He told me you had a heart transplant. Did you experience any changes afterward?"

He laughed. Tori smiled—he sounded like Santa Claus. "My wife and I joke about it. Didn't even know anyone else was experiencing stuff like this. Two things. Ever since my transplant, I've become a hugger. I never used to be like that."

"And the other?"

"I never liked beer before. Turns out my donor was Irish. When I mentioned a new taste for Guinness, my donor's wife just burst out crying. She said her husband never missed an evening without a pint."

"Wow."

"So what's on your mind?"

"My donor's name was Dakota Jones. Probably about thirty years old. Lived in a project downtown. The newspaper says she jumped from the fifth floor to avoid a fire. She was with a man, Christian Mitchell, a doctor I think she met at a free clinic downtown. He jumped with her."

"And you think there's something fishy about the way she died?"

"Exactly. It started with vivid new memories. Fire. A man screaming. Falling."

"But you said your donor jumped to escape a fire. You might expect that sort of thing."

"But there's more. Most of what I remember is images. The face of a man who has bad teeth. I remember pain in my ankle, my foot facing in the wrong direction. I distinctly remember a woman with green eyes and a little tattoo of hearts, and the number three one six. In the memory, the woman gave me the number and told me to remember because she wanted to make—" she held up her fingers and made quotation marks in the air—"that bastard pay."

"Okay, that's pretty weird. This is beyond anything I've read on transplanted memories."

"I researched and found one other case of memory transplantation that resulted in solving a murder. I think mine will be number two."

"Wow." Gus Peterson had stopped laughing.

"There's more, something that makes this a bit more tense. Since I've been looking into this, I've been getting threatening phone calls warning me to back off. Someone's unhappy about this."

"I'll poke around, see what I can find." Then Gus cleared his throat and paused, but seemed on the verge of saying something.

Silence hung between them for a moment before Tori asked, "What is it?"

"I'm not well off, Doc. I can barely pay my monthly prescription costs."

"I can pay for your services."

"Did you call me from the phone that received the threats?"

"Yes."

"Were you able to see what number the caller used?"

"No. It was some sort of unrecognized caller."

"Let me do some snooping. I'll find out something."

"Thanks, Gus. Call me soon."

Her phone rang just as she ended the call. "Hello."

"Ms. Taylor?"

"Yes."

"I'm calling from Home Security Systems. Are you at home?"

"No, I'm out."

"We've just received input from your alarm system. There is a possible break-in in progress. The police have been called."

"Break-in?"

"Someone just unlocked your front door."

Mary Jaworski spent the morning in her office sipping spiced African chai and studying Tori Taylor's interview tape.

The more she watched, the more concerned she became. Something was amiss about the death of Dakota Jones. But extracting information across transplanted memories was new territory for her. Several things were clear, yet several other things remained cloudy.

In the early afternoon, she managed to get Captain Ellis on his private line. His greeting was gruff and straightforward, spoken with a voice that betrayed years of cigarette abuse. "Ellis."

"Captain, this is Dr. Jaworski."

"Yes, yes, glad you called. Have you been in touch with our little witness in the Dakota Jones case?"

"Indeed I have."

"What can you tell me?"

"This is a very complicated case. Not only are Tori Taylor's memories vivid and revealing, but the way she relays them may be mixed up with her own personal life."

"What do you mean?"

Mary sipped tea and formulated a careful response. "Tori is a remarkable woman. Very smart. But in some ways, she's just so closed emotionally. At least she used to be."

"Used to be?"

"Before her transplant." Mary looked at her unpolished nails. Cut short and without glamour, they reflected Mary's personal approach to hygiene and life in general: less is better, practical rules over beauty. "Tori is or was a scientist. Even as a child, she was very calculating and detached."

"So?"

"So it gives me an anchor to distinguish the donor's memories. The donor was evidently quite passionate."

"Okay, okay," he said. "Get to the point. Do you think this girl was murdered?"

"Hold your horses, Captain. I'll show you the tape. But be aware, there are some real oddities. Tori's memories from Dakota Jones are all third person. It's as if she sees things from outside her own body. The only thing I can figure is that somehow Tori's inner psyche has dealt with these transplanted memories as if they are indeed foreign. It's as if Dakota speaks to her from the outside. She doesn't always experience Dakota from the first person. It's like she sees her in action from someone else's eyes."

"I'm not sure I'm following. Do we have evidence of a crime?"

"Oh, yes. But it's not the kind of thing I want to discuss over the phone. I need to show you this stuff in private."

"Give me a clue. Why the secrecy?"

"You'll understand when I show you the tape. My report could be damaging."

"To who?"

"To Dakota Jones, among others." She hesitated, wondering how much to say. "Maybe the police."

"Bring me the video."

Mary sighed. "Look, I'm not sure who this Dakota woman really was. There are memories of abuses from people in authority over her, a father or an employer perhaps. I want to study this a bit more before I point my fingers at anyone who may have wanted to harm Dakota."

"Can you say who?"

"Dakota wanted to hurt someone."

"What?" The captain's tone suggested his growing frustration at the conversation.

"I'll bring you the tape and let you see." She paused. "Let's just say that I think Dakota Jones started that fire."

28

By the time Tori arrived at her suburban Richmond home, a Richmond PD vehicle sat in her driveway. She recognized the officer duo who had investigated her complaint from the evening before. She parked her Mazda on the street and walked up to the older officer.

He held out his hand. "Officer Campbell. We met last evening."

"What's going on? Did someone break in?"

He tilted his head toward her front door. "Punched a hole in the window in the entrance, then reached in and unlocked the door."

"Robbery?"

"Not sure. Need to go through the house with you."

The younger cop sat in the passenger seat of the patrol car, talking on the radio. "What's he doing?" Tori asked.

"We're calling for a technician. We want to dust for prints, photograph anything inside that may be in disarray."

She nodded. "Let's go."

"Don't touch the doorknob."

The door was ajar. She pushed it open with the back of her hand. Other than glass on the hardwood floor, the entryway was normal.

She scanned the front room, looking at photographs and books. "I don't notice anything missing or out of place."

"Do you keep valuables in the house?"

"I have a small safe, but only for important documents, my passport, that type of thing. It's in the bedroom closet."

"Jewelry? Cash?"

"Nothing much. My tastes are pretty simple."

They did a room-by-room inventory. In each room, she tried to imagine the impact of losing the contents. A vase that had been a gift from her mother. A seascape picture painted by a patient. A trophy from a high school track meet.

In her office, she looked at her ego wall, where her diplomas and awards were on display. This was the personal shrine she'd built. *What kind of life have I built? Would I miss anything I own if it all were taken away?*

In her bedroom, she opened the top drawer of her dresser and slipped a small wad of cash from the inside of a sock. She checked her small jewelry box and then knelt over the safe in her closet. Peering inside, she said, "Everything is here. I can't tell that anything has been bothered. Maybe it wasn't robbery. Maybe it was meant to scare me into stopping my search into my heart donor's death."

"And maybe your alarm scared off a potential burglar who didn't have a chance to take anything."

"That doesn't feel right. There has to be a connection with the threats. I've never been a target of burglary before. The timing of this break-in is too close to the phone calls to be coincidence."

The officer made a note.

"Could you at least talk to Captain Ellis of the Baltimore PD? He's in charge of the investigation into my donor's death."

The officer rubbed at a small stain on the front of his uniform. It looked like powdered sugar. "Sure."

When they walked back out to the foyer, a technician was dusting the doorknob for fingerprints. "Hey, George," the man said, "this has been wiped clean. Nothing here."

"No surprise."

Tori stayed quiet, watched, and paced around the front room.

After a few minutes, Officer Campbell took a step toward her. "Are you okay?"

She offered a smile. "I was just thinking about all this stuff. None of it really means that much to me beyond a few photographs."

"That's pretty typical, isn't it? It takes a crisis to let us know that family and friends are the only things that matter."

Tori nodded silently and felt alone. She hadn't invested much in friendships, and without family, she was acutely aware of her isolation. She looked at him. "Can I fix you some coffee?"

He nodded. "Sure."

The menial task brought her some sense of comfort in the presence of yet another stressor. It seemed somehow the right thing to do to care for someone else. And when it came to life outside the operating rooms, she'd never been very good at that sort of thing. Sure, she could take out pancreatic cancer, but could she do the minor things? Could she offer a cup of cold water on a hot day? The thought nailed her conscience. She'd spent the majority of her adult life being cared for by others in orbit around her.

When she handed the officer a mug of steaming black coffee, she said, "Someone's trying to scare me, aren't they?"

"Appears so." He shrugged. "Can you think of anyone who might want to scare you? A mad family member of a patient with a bad outcome?"

She thought back over the last few months. As a cancer surgeon, she often dealt with patient deaths, but she didn't recall any unbalanced or angry family members. "No."

"Boyfriend? Jilted lover? A married man?"

"No, no!"

"Just askin', ma'am. It's part of the job."

"I can assure you, until my heart transplant, my life was appropriately boring." She gripped her coffee mug as if it might escape. "What about you, Officer Campbell? You have family and friends to make your life meaningful?"

"Just my wife at home now. My son is deployed in Afghanistan."

The technician called from the foyer. "All finished here, George."

The officer took another swig of the coffee and set the mug on the island. "Thanks. You should try and get that glass fixed or at least put up some temporary barrier."

"Sure."

The officers left, and Tori swept up the fragments of glass. Being in the house alone was giving her a creepy feeling. She packed a few additional clothing items in a suitcase and put duct tape over the window.

She took a Coke Zero from the fridge and stopped to pull the 316 note from under a magnet on the door. She shoved it in her pocket. *This will make the perfect bookmark in my new Bible. I'll put it right at John 3:16.*

On the way to her car, she stopped at the mailbox where she found two Kohl's flyers and a package. It was a brown package about six by eight inches, postmarked in downtown Richmond the day before.

She studied it a moment. No return address. Must weigh two or three pounds. *I don't remember ordering anything.* There was no Amazon symbol.

She took it back into the house where she loosened the paper wrapping with a knife. Inside, at first, she saw only Styrofoam packing peanuts. She brushed them aside to find a plastic Ziploc bag. She lifted it from the container and screamed.

Stepping back, she let the bag and its contents fall to the floor.

Inside, the red-brown flesh was easily recognizable to the surgeon.

She stared at it in disbelief, fighting back a wave of nausea.

A human heart!

29

Emily Greene approached the pharmacy counter and showed her badge to the clerk. "Baltimore PD. I called earlier and spoke to a pharmacist, Mr. John Bell. Is he available?"

The young woman seemed barely old enough to be out of high school. "He's expecting you. He's in the office." She motioned Emily to follow around the end of the counter. "This way."

She walked past several rows of shelving stocked with drugs. In a small office, she saw a man staring into a computer screen. His hair was dark and curly, falling to the top of his white coat. He was clean-shaven and wore one of those pink ribbon pins on his lapel, the kind that identified his support of breast-cancer research.

"Mr. Bell? I'm Emily Greene with Baltimore PD. We spoke on the phone."

"Yes, yes. Thanks for coming over." He motioned toward a chair on the opposite side of his desk. "I'll get right to the point. I'm seeing a shift in some of the prescribing patterns. I haven't checked with other pharmacies, but from what I see, the downtown free clinic is starting to prescribe a ton of narcotics."

"What pills exactly?"

"Mostly OxyContin. Some Percocet and Tylox."

"We've been seeing a lot of OxyContin on the street. In fact, that's why I'm looking into this. Someone has found a new source. A forty-milligram tablet can be sold for up to forty bucks a pop in the suburban high schools."

"I get that. Now, nothing here is illegal. I just wanted you to be aware of a trend." He held up a stack of prescriptions. "Look at these. I called the clinic on a few of them, but the story is always the same. They are seeing more and more terminal patients due to problems with the poor not being able to see home health hospice."

She took the stack and peeled her finger across the edge. "Whoa." She shuffled through the top ten or so and read the names of the prescribing doctors. The name on the third prescription caught her eye. Christian Mitchell.

She lifted the prescription. "This guy," she asked. "Are you seeing a lot from the same prescribers?"

"The same five or six doctors man the free clinic, so I see a fair number of repeats. I've also seen the same trend with a few of the home health hospice programs."

"This is for one hundred tablets. Who could possibly need that many pain pills?"

"I asked the clinic the same question."

"And they said?"

"These are for terminally ill patients, and many of them have built up a tolerance."

"Did you look back? Have the same patients been receiving narcotics in a slowly rising trend?"

He shook his head. "That's just it. I'm seeing more and more first-time prescriptions for this amount."

"Can I have copies of these prescriptions? If these are terminal patients, I would expect you'd be getting prescriptions for just a month or two. I'll cross-reference this to the obituaries."

"I'm not supposed to give out patient names. Can you get a warrant?"

"Not sure. Let's follow the trend for a little while and if it worsens, I'll sweet-talk the magistrate into giving me a warrant."

"Okay."

"In the meantime, maybe I can figure out a way to get into that clinic to do some snooping." She looked back at the prescriptions and frowned.

"Something bothering you?"

"This name … I wonder if it could be the same guy I knew."

"You bust him before?"

"Nothing like that." She set the papers on his desk. "Just someone from a former life, that's all."

She touched the edge of a prescription with Christian Mitchell's name and remembered....

Thirty minutes after Officers Campbell and Moore left Tori's suburban Richmond home, they were back, this time to investigate the package she'd received in the mail.

"It's in there," she said, pointing toward the kitchen.

She followed the duo.

Officer Campbell put on a latex glove and lifted the bag from one corner. He twisted his mouth as if tasting something sour. "You're sure this is human?"

She nodded silently.

He squinted at the package. "Could be a deer, maybe a bear. I saw a deer heart when I went hunting with my cousin."

"It's human," Tori said. "I should know."

"Looks like it's been opened, maybe stabbed."

The younger officer looked on. "We need to talk to homicide."

Officer Campbell gestured with his head. "Open that evidence bag." He then carefully placed the Ziploc into a second bag that he sealed for evidence.

Tori pointed to the box on the island. "It was in there."

Campbell frowned. "Postmarked Richmond."

"So now I guess everyone will agree. Someone is threatening me."

"No doubt about that."

"I need to explain something," she said. She launched into the explanation about cellular memory and her concern that she'd received transplanted memories, clues to how her donor had died.

Officer Campbell sighed. "Why didn't you tell me this in the beginning?"

"I was afraid you'd react like everyone else. No one seems to believe this."

"I'll get our team to evaluate the package and the contents, see if they can find fingerprints and confirm your suspicions that it's human."

"Oh, it's human."

"Okay," he said, holding up his hand. "We just need to confirm."

The younger officer shook his head. "Whoever did this wants us to know exactly what he's capable of. That's sick."

"Are you done?" Tori backed away. "I want to get out of here. I'm staying at the Jefferson downtown if you need me. You have my cell."

He nodded and handed her a card. "My cell number is here. Call me if you get any more threats."

Tori escorted the officers to their patrol car. The sky was overcast, threatening rain, adding to the eerie mood and Tori's anxiety. She looked down the street, wondering if someone watched. Everything was quiet except for the chattering of leaves responding to the wind.

She locked the house and jogged to her car, nearly stumbling over a flower bed. Once inside, she pressed the door lock, checked the backseat, and slowly pulled out. She circled the neighborhood three times watching her rearview mirror. The rain started just as she saw headlights in the mirror.

She followed a crazy route through town, dashing forward through yellow lights, making U-turns, and even circling the med-school employee parking deck before handing her keys to a valet at the Jefferson. If she'd been followed, she hadn't detected it.

As she wheeled her suitcase past the front desk, a hotel employee, a young man of college age, called her name from behind the counter. "Dr. Taylor?"

She looked over.

"Good," he said, his eyes bright. "I thought that was you." He smiled. "You got a delivery."

264 · HARRY KRAUS

Immediately, her chest tightened. *Not here. No one knows I'm here.*

He disappeared momentarily into an office behind the counter and returned a few seconds later holding a vase of red roses.

Mentally, she ran a short list of men who might send her flowers. It was a very short list. *Phin? Jarrod? Who knows I'm here?*

She reached for the flowers and plucked a small envelope from a clear plastic holder. She slipped out the card. Inside there were only two words.

"You're next."

30

Trembling, Tori looked up. "Who delivered these? What florist did they come from?"

The young hotel clerk smiled flirtatiously. "Why?" His voice had a singsong quality. "Secret admirer?"

"It's not funny. Someone is threatening me."

An older brunette woman stepped up next to the young man. "Nice way to be threatened."

Tori looked up at the woman. Tori estimated fifty, dyed hair, gray roots. "Did anyone ask for me? Visit my room?"

"We don't give out room numbers."

"Did anyone ask?"

The clerks looked at each other and shook their heads. "No one."

"I ... I need to check out."

The woman tapped the computer keyboard. "We have you in until the end of the week."

"You don't understand. I can't stay here. Someone knows I'm here. Someone is threatening me."

The male clerk looked at his coworker. "The cancellation policy—"

The woman interrupted. "I'm handling this, Stan." Her voice was firm and silenced the young man.

"I'll need a minute to collect my things."

"Certainly."

Tori looked at the man. "Can you come with me?"

He looked at his coworker and raised his eyebrows.

The female clerk said, "Go. I'll cover the desk."

Tori led the man to the elevator and then down the hall to her room. Once there, she let him enter first. She stood in the hall. "Anyone in there?"

"No."

She entered and scanned the room. She emptied the closet, grabbed her toiletries and her new Bible, stuffing them into her suitcase. "Let's go."

"You can take the shampoo," he said. "It's from Redken, but they make it special for our patrons."

Tori wanted to roll her eyes. "Keep it."

She stomped back to the elevator, hiding her fear, pushing back a sudden urge to cry. *Who wants me dead?*

Where do I go?

Not home.

Not here.

In the lobby, she left her bags with a bell captain, who promised to have the valet retrieve her car. Then she paced the spacious public areas, trying to spot anyone who may have been watching her. But no one seemed to care. The statue of Thomas Jefferson was marvelous, but indifferent. The pool in the Palm Court, long ago the home of live alligators, was still. She opened her cell and dialed Officer Campbell. She got his voicemail.

She spoke quietly, facing a massive marble column. "Officer Campbell, this is Tori Taylor. I've been staying at the Jefferson Hotel downtown. Someone delivered some flowers with a note saying 'You're next.' I left the flowers at the desk. I'm scared. I'm leaving town." She closed the phone.

She was leaning against the column when the bell captain called, "Dr. Taylor, we have your vehicle."

She watched as the valet put her luggage in the trunk. She handed him a tip and sat behind the wheel. *Now what?*

She pulled into traffic and tried to come up with a plan.

She flipped open her phone and punched in a number.

"Phin MacGrath."

"It's Tori."

How to begin?

She took a deep breath. "I need your help. Can you meet me in the employee parking structure?" She waited for a response. She heard papers being shuffled and a squeak of his chair. "Now?" she added.

He sighed. "What's this about?"

"I don't have time to explain. But I'm in trouble, Phin. Someone's really upset with me looking into Dakota's death." She felt her voice thickening. "Someone's trying to kill me."

"Okay. Try to calm down. I'll come to the deck. My Accord is on the second level."

"I'll be there in five."

Tori drove up the hill toward the VCU Medical Center complex, frequently checking her rearview mirror. There was so much traffic, she couldn't tell if she was being tailed. Her only comfort was that the entrance into the parking deck required an employee ID badge.

Once in the deck, she circled the second level and found an open spot a few spaces from Phin's Honda. He arrived two minutes later. She transferred her luggage and got into the backseat.

As he pulled out, she quickly slipped forward off the seat and pressed herself toward the floor.

"What's going on, Tori?"

"If you talk to me, raise your phone to your face," she whispered. Quietly and urgently, she summarized the terrifying events from the last few days.

She listened as Phin flipped open his phone. "This is crazy. Have you talked to the police?"

"Of course. They have the heart. They advised me not to stay at home. But whoever it is was able to follow me. Trading cars in the employee deck was my idea to throw them off. Hopefully they won't recognize your car."

He sighed. "Why me? I thought we were kind of—" He halted. "Off."

She took a deep breath. "I didn't know who else to call."

She felt the car turn left, accelerate, slow, and turn again. "I'm pulling into Popeyes Fried Chicken. No one followed me. Why don't you come up here?"

When the car stopped, she quickly got up and out, then back in on the front-passenger side. After smoothing her hair with her hand, she looked over and smiled. "Thanks."

He shook his head. "You make me crazy. What have you gotten into?"

"I don't know."

"What's your next move?"

"I need to talk to that psychiatrist. She interviewed me under hypnosis but wouldn't reveal what I said, only that she needed to process the information. I think my interview must hold the key to why someone wanted Dakota dead."

"Have you talked to the Baltimore PD, told them about the threats?"

"I asked Officer Campbell with Richmond PD to talk to them. Hopefully they can come up with something together."

"You talked to Gus Peterson?"

"Yep. He's looking into finding out what he can on Dakota Jones."

"Okay, let's go back to my place to regroup."

She looked at him. It felt better to have someone else in on her misery. "Thanks."

"Have you eaten?"

She thought back over her day. It seemed like another life ago when she'd ventured out from the Jefferson and bought a new Bible. "Coffee this morning."

"Hey, I know what kind of medicine regimen you must be on. You have to eat."

"I know. Time got away from me today."

On the way home, he stopped at a Ukrop's grocery store. She stayed in the car, relaxing for the first time in hours. She closed her eyes after he locked her in.

She awoke about fifteen minutes later when he unlocked the doors.

Phin lived in a three-story townhouse in Henrico County, north of downtown. He carried her suitcase and two bags of groceries. She carried a two-liter bottle of Coke Zero. At least he had good taste in diet drinks.

His townhouse had bamboo floors, taupe walls with white trim. They were covered with modern-art reproductions, neatly framed and spotlighted. The kitchen had cabinets with wormwood doors of green, yellow, and cranberry, a happy Caribbean-island style. Tori relaxed a notch just walking in. A reproduction of a Calder mobile hung over an oak kitchen table. There were two complete arched window-like openings through the wall between the kitchen and great room. Each contained some sort of modern sculpture accented by recessed lighting in the tops of the cutouts.

He smiled at her inspection. "I did that," he said. "The room needed some character. Cutting those in the wall did the trick." He pointed at a pale-green painting. In the center, outlined in a prominent blue circle, was a green-brown sphere. "This is my favorite. It's called 'Burst' by Dalia Rubin. She's an artist from Israel. Her art is all about nature and creation."

"It's perfect."

He emptied his grocery bags onto a granite island. "I picked up a rotisserie chicken. Give me a minute to throw together a salad."

She helped, washing baby spinach leaves and watching him sprinkle in Craisins, walnuts, and crumbled blue cheese.

"Not quite up to your gourmet standards," he said.

"It looks great. Besides, my gourmet tastes are relatively newly acquired."

He shook his head. "A lot about you seems to be newly acquired."

She smiled.

"I want to heat this up a little," he said, sliding the chicken in the oven. "I'm going to call Gus and see if he's found out anything."

"Okay, I'll call Mary Jaworski." She fished a business card out of her purse.

She reached the psychiatrist's voicemail. She didn't want to leave a message.

She listened to Phin's half of his conversation with Gus.

Phin closed his cell phone. "That's weird. He wonders if Dakota was a nickname. He can't find anything on a Dakota Jones. No driver's license, no credit history, no criminal history, nothing."

"What's that mean?"

"He's seen it before. Either we have the wrong name, or ..."

"What?"

"He thinks Dakota Jones may have been an alias."

"What?"

"He thinks Dakota Jones was hiding her true identity."

31

Christian Mitchell had started actually looking forward to working at the Sixth Street free clinic. The patients weren't as demanding as the ones in the university clinic, and the parents said thank you. The only thing Christian didn't like was dealing with the clinic's director, Clara Rivers.

It was a sunny Tuesday afternoon and Christian was finishing up with a young patient with an ear infection. "I think we have some samples that will work," he said to the patient's mother.

She balanced the fussy toddler on her hip and sighed. "I hope so. I can't take another night of crying."

He studied the bags under her eyes, wondering if he should ask her a few questions about how she might be dealing with her frustrations. She was a single mom with a history of alcohol abuse. The child may have been at risk for physical abuse, but Christian had seen no signs of bruising. He decided to let it pass. "I'll be right back."

He went to the large walk-in closet where the clinic kept a supply of donated samples. In the center sat a large rolling multidrawer station, much like a mechanic might use for his tools. It was the clinic's controlled-substance locker. He noticed that the lock wasn't secure. He thought about closing it but went ahead and opened the top drawer for a quick look.

"Whoa," he muttered to himself. The top drawer contained vials of morphine, fentanyl, and Demerol. He closed it and opened the lowest and largest of the drawers. There, inside several large paper bags, were pharmacy bottles already labeled with patient information. He lifted a bottle to read.

"What are you doing?"

He looked up to see Carla, red-faced and glaring from below gray-streaked bangs.

"Just looking for an antibiotic."

"We don't keep them locked," she said, lifting the bottle from his hand. She dropped it back in the bag, shut the drawer, and secured the lock.

"Why do we have prescription narcotics already labeled with patient names?"

"Palliative care brings over deceased patients' medicines."

"You dispense used meds?"

"They are not used. They are perfectly good. The clinic runs on a shoestring budget. You should know that by now." She put her hands on her ample hips. "I'll do what I need to do to help this clinic survive."

Christian wondered about the ethics of reissuing meds that had gone out to other patients. He knew that it had to violate pharmacy standards. From what he'd seen in the bottom drawer, most of the bottles seemed to be nearly full.

He was about to protest but knew it wouldn't get him anywhere. He decided he'd ask the pharmacist back at Johns Hopkins. He turned his attention to the shelves of antibiotic samples and ignored the director. He selected a supply of amoxicillin.

The director seemed to be watching him and didn't care to make it subtle. "You've got your medicine," she said. "Now run along and get back to work. The waiting room is overflowing."

He returned to his patient and handed the medicine to the mother. "Use this three times a day. Bring him back in ten days and we'll take another look."

Christian moved to the next room. He lifted a chart from the rack on the door. The chief complaint was listed as 'leg pain.'" He entered the small exam room to see two adult women, one white and one black, and a young black male. He looked at the young man. "You must be Mike," he said, extending his hand. "I'm Dr. Mitchell."

The African-American woman spoke. "I'm Kesha, Mike's mother. This here's my friend Dakota."

He looked at the second woman, a slender female with short dark hair, multiple ear piercings, and a right nose stud. She wore sunglasses. A druggie. A gray sweatshirt covered her arms.

There was something familiar about her. *Dakota?*

"What brings you to the doctor, Mike?"

"We took the bus."

Christian smiled. "What I mean is, why did you come?"

"My leg," he said, pulling up a pair of baggy Nike shorts. "It's been sore for a while. Then I noticed this lump."

"How long is a while? A month? A week?"

"Longer. Since Christmas."

"Did you ever get hit in that area?"

Kesha shook her head. "Ain' no one beatin' this child."

"How about accidentally? Maybe during a football game or something?"

"No," Mike said.

"Is it changing? Getting bigger?"

"Seems to be growing."

"Are you on any medicines? Do you have any other illnesses?"

"No."

Christian touched the top of the exam table paper. "Okay, could you hop up here for me?"

Mike moved to the exam table.

"Lie down." Christian reached out his hand. "I'm going to examine you."

Mass deep anterior quadriceps. Fixed. Rock hard. Mildly tender. Four by six centimeters.

He felt over his left femoral area. *No lymphadenopathy.*

Christian started down a list of things that felt like that. The short list began and ended with rare cancers. "I'd like to order a few tests. A blood count. A chest X-ray."

Kesha shook her head. "His chest is fine. It's his leg."

Christian didn't want to explain that he was looking for spread of cancer to the lungs. Metastasis. Instead, he just said, "It's routine." He scribbled an order and filled out an X-ray request. "We don't have an X-ray unit here, but if you take this to City Hospital, they have an agreement with us. Can you bring Mike back here to see me on Friday after the X-ray?"

Kesha looked at her friend. "Can you come with us?"

She nodded without speaking.

Christian studied her face. *Could it be? It's been more than a dozen years. The hair color is wrong. I want to see your eyes.*

He reached out his hand. She looked at it and kept her head down. She didn't accept his hand. "I didn't catch your name."

"Dakota Jones."

That voice.

Kesha took the hand that Christian still held out toward Dakota. "Thanks, Doc. We'll see you on Friday."

He smiled. "Sure. Just stop at the desk on your way out to make an appointment.

He watched them go. *That's crazy.* He shook his head. *She must be Emily Greene's twin. Separated at birth.*

The height is right. Her build and shape are the same.

He thought for a few minutes but couldn't seem to shake the feeling that he knew her. He walked back to the waiting room, but they were already gone. He exited the front door and squinted at the sun. He looked across the parking lot to a bus stop just down the sidewalk. A bus was pulling up. The door opened.

He shouted after her, "Emily!"

He watched as she turned her head toward him. *Recognition.*

He took a step toward the bus.

She shook her head, turned, and leaped onto the bus.

He jogged a few steps, but the bus pulled away.

He thought about her sweatshirt, the sunglasses, and the piercings. *She definitely looked when I called her name. Oh, Emily—what has happened to you?*

Tori ate. And ate. In fact, she couldn't remember when her appetite had been better.

When she looked across at Phin, he raised his eyebrows.

"What?" she said, licking her fingers. "Haven't you ever seen someone enjoying your cooking before?"

He shrugged, smiling. "I just thought that with all the stress, well, I didn't expect you to be hungry." He shook his head. "Someone threatens your life, sends you a heart in the mail—that kind of stuff can mess with your appetite."

She offered a smile and wiped her mouth. "Maybe things are different now."

He looked at her, waiting for an explanation.

She took a sip of iced tea. "After the phone call the other night, I'll admit, I was scared. Really scared. But I didn't want to call you." She halted and looked up to see the hurt register on his face. "Sorry," she whispered.

She took another bite of chicken. And more salad. Then she continued. "The way I see it, I was petrified because I was in charge."

He squinted at her. He didn't understand. "Was?"

She nodded. "I raced around town, running through yellow lights, making sudden turns, convinced someone was following me. I checked in at the Jefferson downtown. I couldn't sleep."

She paused to eat again. When she stabbed another bite of chicken, Phin's hand came down on hers. "Oh no you don't. Not until you tell me what's going on."

"Okay." She set down the fork. "It's not really so complicated. I started reading a Bible I found in the nightstand. There was a little directory to tell you what verses to read if you needed peace. I read,

'Come unto me all you who are weary and heavy laden, and I will give you rest.'" She looked into Phin's face. "You don't understand how much those verses impacted me. I felt *drawn*. I wanted what Jesus was offering. I knew I was doing a bad job at running my life. I mean, look at me. Sure, I'm a good surgeon, but I've alienated everyone I've worked with." She paused before adding, "And managed to run off most of the people I care about." Their eyes met for a moment before she looked away.

She went on. "Phin, before my transplant and all this trouble, I never wanted to believe. But lately, that's changed. I knew in my heart that I wanted to believe that God could love me more than anything else." She sighed. "Maybe Charlotte was right about the 316 message. Maybe I needed to believe 'for God so loved the world.'

"So," she said, "I found a prayer printed in the back of that Bible and I prayed it. Phin, I gave up control."

He smiled.

She wrinkled her nose. "I'm still a little scared. But not enough to kill my appetite." She laughed.

So did he. "That's obvious." He reached for her hand. "This is the best news ever. It's what I've been praying for."

She looked up. Phin was wiping his eyes. "Must be the pepper," he said.

"Don't start," she said, sniffing. "I won't be able to eat."

She remembered her purchase earlier that day. "I have something to show you," she said, standing up and heading toward the front door where Phin had placed her suitcase. Inside was her new Bible. She wanted Phin's approval of her choice. She hesitated and stole a glance through the front window.

An SUV with tinted windows was parked at the edge of the next block across the street. "Phin, I think I recognize that car. It followed me out of my neighborhood last night."

He came to her side. "I haven't seen it before."

"Is there another way out of here? We can't stay here."

"There's a back door from the basement, up the stairs into the backyard. But my car is parked out front."

"There's a bus stop on the next street over. We can take a bus back into town and rent a car."

"Then where?"

"Baltimore. I've got to see the tape of my interview."

Tori followed his eyes as Phin looked back at the kitchen. "I'll do the dishes. We'll leave the lights on. Go pack a bag."

He took a step toward the stairs. "Wait, what did you want to show me?"

She waved him off. "Just a little purchase I made today. I'll show you later." She glared at him. "Now go!"

32

They waited for dark before closing the front curtains and turning on the bedroom lights and closing the blinds. Before leaving, Tori again watched the SUV from a darkened upstairs bedroom. For a few seconds, the face of someone in the front seat lit up with the flicker of a cigarette lighter. Indeed, someone was waiting in the car. Waiting and watching.

They exited the back basement door and crept across the lawn to an alley behind the townhouses facing the next street. They stood in the shadow of a maple until they saw an approaching bus and then ran to the stop to enter.

It was two miles to an Enterprise car rental; Phin had called ahead and reserved a midsize car. Inside, he was given the keys to a blue Honda Accord. He hoisted their luggage into the backseat. In a few minutes, they were on Interstate 95 North.

A few minutes into the ride, Tori closed her eyes.

She awoke as Phin was exiting the interstate.

"Where are we?"

"Fredericksburg. I need to either stop for the night or get coffee."

Tori yawned. "Let's stop. We can easily drive the rest of the way in the morning."

They found two rooms at a Holiday Inn Express on Warrenton Road just off the freeway. Phin carried her suitcase to her door, next to his. He put the suitcase on the floor inside and politely said, "Good night." He paused. "Want to sleep in?"

"Not sure I can."

He nodded. "Just call me when you're up. They have breakfast in the lobby."

She didn't know what to say. They'd been so busy talking about her crisis. *We never talked about us.*

If there is an "us."

She closed the door, leaned toward the peephole, and watched Phin. The view was a small circle, distorted at the edges. Phin was in the center for a moment and then disappeared down the hall.

She thought about the dinner she'd made him at her home, the way they'd kissed, and the fire she'd sensed between them.

But he pulled away so quickly. She remembered his words and how they hurt her even now: "I can't do this."

Maybe it's not meant to be.

She thought about her new Bible and her new life. *I can only handle so much newness in my life at a time anyway.*

She walked to the bathroom and looked at her reflection. She thought again of their last kiss and made a promise not to be the first to initiate a kiss with Phin again. *If he wants me, he'll have to prove it.*

This is crazy. I'm on the run, perhaps with a killer on my heels, and yet my head is filled with these schoolgirl romantic ideas!

She showered, prepared for bed, and opened her new favorite book, enjoying the feel and smell of the leather.

After a few minutes, she whispered, "Good night, Father," and turned out the light. Sleep was calling hard, and she couldn't resist.

Her mother screamed. "I want you out!"

A man's voice. Cursing.

A slap.

Crying.

Images appeared, a view into the back bedroom from behind the couch, looking through the doorway. The man had a knife. Her mother screamed again.

She didn't want to hear. She shoved her hands over her ears and crouched low, hidden by the furniture.

Bumping noises. Another scream, gurgling sounds, a heavy thud.

She waited for a long time after the screaming stopped before going to find her mommy.

She saw her on the floor. Still, like a doll in a crib. But something was wrong. The carpet was red.

The man was there too, stretched out on the bed. Snoring and smelling like he did when he drank too much.

He always drank too much.

When he wakes, he will come for me, tell me I'm the one he wants.

He hurts me.

Hurts my mommy.

The bad man has to die.

Smoke. Fire licking the ceiling.

My arm is on fire!

The dream evaporated, but as soon as it faded, another took its place.

A sense of urgency. Fear.

Someone is coming.

Blue uniform. Help?

A cop?

316! Remember this!

Pain in my head. Blurred vision. Pushed against the wall.

Being tossed against the window.

A crash. I'm falling!

Tori sat up in bed, breathing hard. She touched her forehead and wiped away the sweat.

She felt like vomiting. She lifted her hand to her mouth and took slow breaths until the urge faded.

The images had broken through her dreams.

She pulled on a silk robe and paced the hotel room, trying to quell the panic, telling herself it was only a dream.

She grabbed her room key and walked down the hallway to the next door, rapping softly at first and then with enough vigor to wake her friend.

When he opened the door, he was shirtless, wearing a pair of jeans he'd evidently pulled on to answer. "Tori? What's wrong?" He motioned for her to enter. "Did you get another phone call?"

She shook her head. "Phin, it was horrible. I had a nightmare." She paused as he opened his arms.

She stepped forward. "I think I know what's on that interview tape."

He reached for her face and brushed away a tear before closing his arms around her. "Hey, it's okay. I'm here."

When Tori awoke, it took a few minutes to realize exactly where she was. She was in a hotel room. But when she went to the bathroom, the toiletry items weren't hers. They were a man's.

She walked back into the room as the realization dawned. *I slept in Phin's room.*

She remembered finding comfort in his arms. He'd held her, whispering comfort. She must have fallen asleep, and he covered her *in his bed.*

Did anything else happen?

She smiled at the thought but knew the answer. She would have remembered that.

So where's Phin?

She walked back into the bathroom and thought about using his toothbrush. *I don't know him well enough for that.*

She walked next door, clutching her robe around her pajamas. Knocking, she said, "Phin?"

After a few moments, he answered the door. She smiled. "So what's this called? Musical rooms?"

He chuckled. "Exactly."

"I need my own bathroom."

"Fine," he groaned, rubbing sleep from his eyes. "I'll go back to my room."

They swapped keys.

He yawned. "Would you like some breakfast?"

"Give me a few minutes. I'm going to freshen up."

He nodded but didn't move toward his room. Instead, he spoke again. "I lay awake for a long time last night thinking about the dream you told me about. Something bothers me about it."

"What?"

"I'm not sure, Tori. The dreams don't seem to match."

She touched his arm. "But, Phin, we're getting closer."

"Yeah," he said. "Almost there."

33

Officer George Campbell had worked with Richmond PD for twenty-two years. Over the years he had heard plenty of stories, but none quite like Tori Taylor's. He'd certainly never heard of a heart recipient being a witness to the murder of the heart donor. That said, he'd seen evidence of the break-in at her house and he'd seen all he cared to see of the heart some weirdo had sent her. So someone was playing a game with her. But just why, he wasn't sure. Could she be right? Was she being targeted because of memories she'd inherited from her heart donor?

He sighed and sipped a cup of lukewarm black coffee as he called the office to listen to his voicemail.

"Officer Campbell, this is Tori Taylor. I was staying at the Jefferson Hotel downtown. Someone delivered some flowers with a note saying 'You're next.' I left the flowers at the desk. I'm scared. I'm leaving town."

The call had come in late the afternoon before.

He cursed. Why hadn't he been told that she called?

His first move was to call the Jefferson. The desk clerk assured him the flowers were still there, being held for Dr. Taylor.

His second call was to Captain Ellis, Baltimore PD.

After speaking to several officers, he mentioned Tori Taylor's name. He was immediately placed on hold, and thirty seconds later was talking to the captain.

"Captain Ellis."

Campbell launched into his story and wasn't halfway through before Captain Ellis began chuckling.

Campbell wasn't amused.

"George," Ellis said as if they were the best of friends, "I'm sorry you've gotten mixed up in all this. I'm afraid the woman you're calling about is certifiable. Crazy as a rabid fox. Maybe her heart medications are screwing with her smarts, know what I mean?" His words poured out in a rush.

George could hear the squeak of a chair and a heavy thump, as if the captain had leaned back and dropped his boots on the edge of his desk.

"For starters, think about it. Who has access to a heart like that?"

"Someone sick, I'd say. A killer without a conscience. Someone who could do something like that and—"

"Who else?" Ellis interrupted. "A surgeon, George! The woman probably went down to the hospital and took her own sick heart and mailed it to herself. Surgeons have access to the pathology lab. What do you think they did with the heart they took out?"

"Captain Ellis, with all due respect, she doesn't seem like the type to be playing such a joke."

"It's not a joke to her. She's sick. I sent a psychiatrist down there to interview her, and she confirmed everything I'm telling you. The memories must be made up. There's nothing to suggest she's a reliable witness to any murder. The woman is paranoid, plain and simple. Paranoid people invent threats. They like the attention."

"I don't know, sir. I've interviewed her myself and the memories she described seemed real."

"Well, whatever this doctor has been telling you, let me tell you that I'm sure of one thing: the memories didn't come from Dakota Jones."

"How can you be so sure?"

"Because Dakota Jones isn't a real person at all. She's an alias."

George Campbell almost choked on his coffee. "What?"

"Dakota Jones was working for Baltimore PD. She was undercover, working narcotics."

"Well, I'll be—"

"Exactly. Dakota Jones didn't have a past to remember."

"And you didn't tell this to Dr. Taylor?"

"Didn't think it was her business. Besides, when she told me she had Dakota Jones's memories, I pretty much knew she was a kook from the get-go." The chair squeaked again. "Anyway, when we lose one of our own, we always investigate. I had an officer on the scene very soon after that fire started, and he didn't detect any evidence of foul play."

"So what do you make of Tori Taylor's—"

"Look, George. I've got reliable information from one of my best officers and then I've got a crazy woman telling me she thinks Dakota Jones was murdered. Who would you believe?"

"I see what you're saying, sir."

"Do me a favor. If she calls you back, find out where she is. I'd like to bring her in for questioning again. My psychiatric consultant thinks she may be of some danger to herself or others. Better yet, tell her to come up here and ask for me."

George cleared his throat. *Dr. Taylor? Crazy?* "Okay, sir." He hesitated. "By the way, what was Dakota's real name?"

"Officer Emily Greene. One of Baltimore's finest."

Phin looked concerned. "What's wrong?"

Tori reached under the table to rub her leg. "My ankle has been bothering me. Something like a chronic sprain." She shrugged. "But I don't remember spraining it."

"I checked the GPS last night. We still have about a two-hour trip."

Tori looked at Mary Jaworski's business card. "We can put her office address into the GPS."

He nodded.

She watched him sip his coffee. "I hope it's okay you took off like this."

He raised his eyebrows. "You didn't give me a choice. You show up to my place, tell me your life is in danger … what's a man to do?"

"My knight in shining armor."

"Oh yeah, that's me."

"Seriously, Phin. I didn't know what else to do."

"I get it. You don't need to explain."

She looked around the room. There were a dozen other hotel guests eating from the free breakfast buffet. She wanted to talk to

Phin about their relationship, but somehow, in the middle of a crowd stabbing toaster waffles didn't seem to be the place. "Ready?"

He drained his coffee. "Let's go."

They checked out and headed north on I-95. After nine, Tori tried calling Mary Jaworski again. "Still no answer. All I get is voicemail."

"Isn't there an office number?"

"I tried that, too. All I get is a recording. I hope her office isn't closed. She didn't mention going on vacation or anything."

"She's probably just busy. Hopefully she won't be too put off by us just showing up."

"I'll explain the threats. She'll understand. If anyone can help me make sense of all these dreams, she's the one."

They drove on, thankful for the sunshine. The traffic wasn't even too bad. The worst part was Phin's annoying tendency to change from radio station to radio station, searching for his favorite songs. Just as she was starting to enjoy a song, he'd change it. She hadn't noticed it in other areas, but when it came to listening to music with Phin, he was a diabetic kid in a candy store. Everything looked good at first but could only be sampled in small quantities.

"Musical ADD," she muttered.

They followed the mechanical female voice of the Garmin navigator. As they approached the final turn toward a professional building, they were surprised to find the building's parking lot blocked by four Baltimore PD squad cars and the front door ribboned off with yellow crime-scene tape. Blue lights on two cars at the edge of the parking lot strobed at a dizzying rate. Tori looked away.

She thought she recognized one face in the crowd of blue uniforms, a stocky, muscular officer.

They parked and walked across the lot toward the trio of officers. She looked for a name badge. It was him. "Officer Bundrick?"

He looked over, obviously surprised to see her. "Dr. Taylor? What are you doing here?"

"I was about to ask you the same question."

"You go first."

"I came to see the psychiatrist, Dr. Jaworski."

"You did? You have business with her?"

"You might say that."

"Would you recognize her?"

"Of course."

He lifted a radio from his belt. "Ron?"

"Go ahead."

"I might have a lady here who can ID the body."

34

Christian slapped the CXR up on the view board and nodded. "This is good news, Ms. Dexter. The chest is clear."

Kesha shifted in her seat. "I still don't understand why you're looking at the chest. It's his leg."

Christian took a deep breath. "One of the possibilities is a rare type of cancer. Cancer can spread. The lungs are one place that cancer spreads. I wanted to look at the lungs to be sure that what is in Mike's leg hasn't spread there."

Her lip began to tremble. "You sayin' my boy has cancer?"

"No." Christian let his hand rest on Kesha's arm. "But it's one possibility. We still need to do a few more tests. I'd like to schedule Mike for an MRI of his leg and then consult a surgeon for a biopsy."

"Is it serious?"

"Sometimes a mass like this is serious. Sometimes it's just a benign growth and not serious at all."

She sat quiet and unmoving.

"Do you understand what I am saying? Is there anyone else I should talk to? How about your friend Dakota?"

"She didn't come with me today."

Christian opened the chart and scanned for Kesha's address. "Does Dakota live near you?"

Kesha seemed to squint at him in question. "She's my neighbor." She straightened. "Why do you ask about her?"

Christian couldn't look up and meet her eyes. "She reminded me of an old friend, that's all."

He made a note in the chart and handed Kesha another X-ray request slip. "This is for an MRI. I'll ask the front office to schedule it right away. Then I'll need to see Mike again, okay?"

She nodded.

When he stood, she didn't move.

"Is my boy gonna die?"

"I know you're scared. That's normal. But we don't know if it's cancer. Even if it is, there is good treatment available. It's way too premature to give up hope. Mike needs you to be strong."

She sniffed. "He's all I got left."

"Let's take it one test at a time. MRI first, then a biopsy. Then hopefully, I'll have good news for you."

She stood and nodded. "I'll bring him with me next week."

Tori's hand covered her mouth. "What are you saying? Is Dr. Jaworski dead?"

The muscular officer frowned. "I'm sorry, Dr. Taylor. At this point, all we can say is that we have a body."

"Where? In her office?"

"In one of the medical exam rooms." He hesitated. "If you knew her, perhaps you could give us a hand and ID the body."

Tori looked at Phin. She couldn't believe this. "Sure."

"Okay," he said. "I know you're a doctor so you're used to seeing all kinds of stuff." He shook his head. "But I have to warn you. It's a bloodbath in there."

"Who found the body? Who comes in on a Saturday?"

"A cleaning lady." He nodded at the duo. "This way, ma'am."

She looked at Phin, who shook his head. "I'm staying right here."

Tori stepped over the crime-scene tape and followed Officer Bundrick. He led her through a tastefully designed waiting room, one with actual art, not like the utilitarian one where Dr. Taylor's patients had to wait back at the university hospital. In the hallway beyond, they bypassed at least a dozen men and women in uniform. Photographs were being taken.

The door to the exam room stood open. There was blood on the floor, spilling from the exam table, blood on the wall, and blood saturating the chest of a body. She wouldn't have known it was a woman except that she wore a denim wraparound skirt. The body was pale, and the right arm hung over the side of the table.

Her eyes were drawn away from the blood to the yellow "Live Strong" band around the right wrist. *Just like Mary's.*

Tori forced herself to look at the body. A white blouse looked as if it had been dyed deep red. Jelly-like clots matted the front of her clothing. The face was pale, the eyes open. Her last seconds on earth could not have been pleasant.

She stepped back, fighting a wave of nausea. "It's her. It's Dr. Jaworski."

She stumbled back into the hall, seeking air. Before she entered the waiting room again, she turned and called back, "Officer Bundrick, I know this may sound strange, but I need to know something."

He walked down the hall to within a few feet of her. "What is it?"

"I need to know if her chest has been opened. Did someone steal her heart?"

His expression changed. Hardened. "Why would you ask me that? We have not released any of those details."

"So it's true?"

"I'm not at liberty to discuss—"

She turned. "That's all I wanted to know."

Halfway across the waiting room, she realized she was tracking blood. She looked down. "Ugh!"

"Don't worry about that," he said. He followed her outside where she quickly found her place at Phin's side. With his arms around her, she began to cry, deep sobs of pain.

A moment later, she pushed Phin to arm's length. "Don't you see it?" she whispered. "This woman was killed because of me. Someone wants me dead because of what I know about Dakota Jones. And because Mary Jaworski figured it out, they killed her first."

A few minutes later, Officer Bundrick walked over with an open cell phone. "Here," he said. "Could you talk to Captain Ellis?"

She sniffed and took the phone. "Captain, this is Tori."

"Dr. Taylor, what a coincidence we find you at a crime scene."

"I was coming to meet Dr. Jaworski to discuss my interview."

"Yes, yes. I've been in contact with an officer from the Richmond, Virginia, PD."

"Officer Campbell?"

"Yes. He told me all about the threats. The heart. Even the flowers. I think it's time you came on in to the department. I want to arrange to keep you in a safe place."

"You believe my story now?"

"I believe Dakota Jones was murdered, if that's what you mean. And I know from what the psychiatrist told me that Dakota must have had a very troubled past."

"I believe someone killed her mother, too."

"The interview suggests a very hard life of abuse." He paused. "You're an important witness for us in this homicide. Now that Dr. Jaworski is dead, you're the only one who can testify as one who carries the heart of the victim. This is a very unusual case, Dr. Taylor. I want you to come over to the station. I'm going to arrange transfer to a safe place for your protection."

She took a deep breath and mouthed the words of relief to Phin: *He believes me.* Then, into the phone, she said, "We'll come right over."

She handed the phone back to Officer Bundrick and recited her conversation with the captain back to Phin.

Once in their rental car, Tori took a deep breath. "I can't believe this."

"At least someone is taking you seriously and is going to keep you safe."

She nodded. "Can we stop for a cup of coffee?"

"Sure."

A few minutes later, they sat, sipping Kenyan coffee at the nearest Starbucks.

Tori's cell phone sounded. "Hello."

"Dr. Taylor, it's George Campbell."

"Officer Campbell, I'm so glad you called. I just got done speaking with Captain Ellis."

"You did?" He halted. "Look, Dr. Taylor, we don't all feel the same way about this."

"At least he believes me. I'm on my way in to see him now. He wants to put me in some sort of protective custody or something."

"What? Did he tell you about Dakota Jones?"

"Only that he believes she was murdered and that I'm a key witness."

There was silence on the other end.

"Mr. Campbell?"

"Dr. Taylor, when did your threatening phone calls start? How soon after your transplant?"

"Not until after I moved home."

"When was that?"

She sighed. "Why is this important?" She counted back. "It was right after I came to Baltimore the first time."

"After you told your story to Baltimore PD?"

"Yes. Why?"

"Something isn't right. Where are you?"

"Baltimore. I told you, I'm on my way to see Captain Ellis. He practically insisted."

"I'll bet." He cleared his throat. "I may be off base here, but humor me. Who else knew about your theories about transplanted memories?"

She thought about it. "A few surgical residents. Charlotte. Phin. The Baltimore PD. Some of my doctors on the transplant service knew I was having nightmares."

"Tori, Captain Ellis told me something I think you should know."

"I'm listening." She pushed her coffee away and straightened her posture.

"He told me that Dakota Jones was an alias. Her real name was Emily Greene and she worked for Baltimore PD as an undercover narcotics officer."

She shook her head. "What?"

"He told me you were crazy and that your psychiatric interview essentially proved it."

"Really?"

Tori tapped her fingers on the tabletop. *Is this guy playing me? Why would Captain Ellis say I'm crazy? Certainly the psychiatrist wouldn't have reported that!* She sighed. "And now, no one can dispute his words."

"Why is that?"

"I've just come from a crime scene at Dr. Jaworski's office. She was murdered."

"What!" She heard a door shut, and he lowered his voice. "You need to get out of there."

"I don't understand."

"Look, Dr. Taylor, I'm sorry about all this, but I think it may be best to come on home. I don't think I'd be walking right into the Baltimore PD just now."

"But—"

"Listen, the threats started *after* you talked to Baltimore PD. What if they are the ones trying to cover up the facts surrounding Emily Greene's death? Think about it. Why would Captain Ellis tell you and me entirely different stories unless he's trying to throw us all off track?"

She sighed. She wanted to scream. Just when she was beginning to think she was close to safety. Now she didn't know what or who to believe. Was she being played? By whom? "So who was Emily Greene?"

"I did a little checking. She'd been on the force for six years. Exemplary record. Grew up on the Eastern Shore. Her parents still live there."

"I can't come home. Whoever wants me dead is watching. They even followed me to my friend's house, Phin MacGrath. We snuck out the back and rented a car to come to Baltimore."

"I hope I'm wrong."

"So what's my next move?"

He sighed. "I don't know. But if you don't show and the captain calls, do not tell him where you are."

She looked at Phin. His face showed the distress and confusion of trying to discern what was going on from her half of the conversation.

"Dr. Taylor, I'd advise you to leave now. He'll have all of Baltimore PD looking for you."

"Okay."

She stared at her phone in disbelief. In two short minutes, her world had been reconfirmed as dangerous and crazy. She didn't know what to believe.

"There's one more thing, Dr. Taylor. Something Captain Ellis said to me prompted me to ask a few questions down at the university hospital's pathology lab."

He cleared his throat.

She was growing impatient. "What'd you find out?"

"The heart that was mailed to you." He paused. "It was yours."

An hour later, when Tori Taylor failed to show up at the Baltimore PD, Captain Ellis issued an APB for a couple driving a blue Honda Accord. Female around thirty-five, slender build, curly light-brown hair, wanted for questioning in the murder of Dr. Mary Jaworski. Suspect revealed facts about the murder that only the killer would have known.

35

Twenty minutes after hanging up with Officer Campbell, Tori and Phin were speeding out of Baltimore on their way to the Eastern Shore.

Phin opened the sunroof. The sun felt good on Tori's face. "You know," she said, "they have an island over on the Shore where wild horses roam free."

"Oh, so now this is a sightseeing tour?"

She shrugged and let her hand rest on his arm. He didn't pull away. "I'm just saying that if we have to hide out for a few days, it might not be the worst place around."

"You think Officer Campbell is right?"

"I'm not sure. But it kind of makes sense. I saw a cop in my dream. I'm not sure he came to help Dakota—er, Emily." She sighed. "This is so weird. All along I thought I had the heart of a druggie." She smiled. "Turns out, I've got the heart of a policewoman."

"That explains a lot."

"What's that supposed to mean?"

"You're all about solving crimes now. Ever thought of that?"

She didn't answer. Instead, she lifted her face to the sun.

"Maybe we should just hit the road, leave the state entirely. Go to Florida or something."

"I think you would know me better by now. I'm committed to seeing this through. I'm not running just because my life is in danger. I owe it to Emily. I owe it to her family."

"You think contacting her family is a good idea? Didn't Barb Stiles contact them and ask them whether they wanted to know you?"

"Yes, but circumstances have changed."

Phin shook his head. "The transplant program could get in pretty hot water if they find out the information came from within the program."

"But it didn't really. If anyone gets in trouble, it should be me. I'm the one who figured this out. No one really came out and said it. I just guessed, and the resident confirmed it."

"There's another reason to be careful, Tori. If you really think Emily was murdered, what if her family was involved?"

She thought quietly for a moment. "I guess it's possible. But, well—it just doesn't feel that way to me."

"So what's your play?"

"Tell 'em the truth. Tell them I'm in trouble. Ask them if they knew anything about what Emily was doing. It's not like we can just ask Baltimore PD. We don't know who might be involved."

"Maybe we should go to the FBI. Who polices dirty cops?"

"Some departments have internal-affairs divisions, don't they?"

"Hey, I'm a social worker. What do I know about busting crooked cops?"

"Do you have a gun?"

He glared at her. "No!"

She slid down in her seat and muttered. "I wish you did."

Phin tapped the steering wheel. "We need gas."

They stopped at an Exxon with a Quick-Mart. "Use my credit card," she said. "It's the least I can do."

She went inside to use the restroom and bought some snacks and soda for the road.

When she came out, Phin recommended calling Gus Peterson.

Tori nodded. "I think he can be trusted."

As they pulled out, she called Gus and told him about Officer Campbell's fears that someone in the Baltimore PD might be involved in Emily's death.

Through the conversation, Gus got louder, expressing his frustration and concern. With a voice etched with urgency, he pled, "Come back to Richmond. The PD here will help you."

"Been there," she said. "I'm afraid." She hesitated. "And I don't know who I can trust."

"But that was before they knew how serious this is."

She moved on. "I want to go to the Eastern Shore and find Emily's parents. Maybe they know what she was working on. Can you help figure out who and where they are?"

She listened as Gus huffed into the phone. "Listen. You need to do a few things to avoid detection by the Baltimore PD. When you don't show up, they'll come after you with every resource available."

Her gut tightened. "So what do I do?"

"Stop using your cell phone, for one thing. They can triangulate your location from cell towers."

She looked at her phone and frowned.

"And never use your credit cards. They'll trace them and follow your trail. Do they know Phin's name?"

"I don't think so."

"So use his cards. Until they figure out that your car is a rental and trace it to Phin's name, using his card should be safe. It might be best just to get as much cash as you can with his ATM card and stop using cards altogether after that. They can't trace cash."

"I just used my credit card for gas."

"Well, change directions then."

"Okay."

"Turn off your phone and take out the battery, okay? Use Phin's phone from now on. I'll see what I can find out about the Greenes, and I'll call back on Phin's number." He paused. "Do you think they know what kind of car you're driving?"

"I'm pretty sure they would have seen it at Dr. Jaworski's office."

"Then you need to get a different car. Either park that car in a huge lot like at the BWI," he said, referring to the airport, "or take it back to an airport rental company and then use a different company to rent something else."

She was quiet.

"Are you getting this?"

"Yes."

"Good. Now get off the phone. We've talked too long. I don't want them to get a fix on your location. Move!"

Captain Ellis shook his head and looked at Officer Bundrick sitting across the captain's cluttered desk. "Where is this going to end? Now besides Greene's death, we have this psychiatrist to deal with."

"I don't like it. This Dr. Taylor is trouble."

"Agreed," he said, running his hand through his short crop of gray hair. "But apparently, she isn't doing what I asked."

Bundrick nodded. "She's running."

"Maybe she's smart."

The phone rang. Ellis picked up. "Good, thank you," he said. He looked up at Bundrick. "We just got a hit on Taylor's Visa card. An Exxon station south of town, on the exit after the Fort McHenry Tunnel."

Bundrick smiled. "Finally, a break. I'll send the boys."

"How much further?" Tori shifted in her seat and looked out the back window.

"Navigator says fourteen minutes." He smiled. "Maybe we should just bag the rental-car idea and catch a plane somewhere." He touched her hand. "Maybe Bermuda."

"Very funny." She turned her hand to accept his, palm to palm. "But I'll take a rain check. Sometime when I'm not running for my life and I can actually think." She traced her index finger around his palm. "We need to talk about us," she said.

She watched his eyebrows go up. "Us?"

"You haven't exactly explained why you left my house after dinner—"

"Uh-oh." Phin looked in the rearview mirror. "We've got company."

Tori turned to see the flashing blue lights. "Can we outrun him? We're almost to the airport exit."

"In this? No way."

The whoop-whoop of a siren sounded behind them.

"I've got to pull over."

"God, help us."

36

Christian Mitchell sat in his car watching the apartment building across the street. He checked the address he'd copied from his patient's chart. He squinted up at the old building. *Kesha and Mike live up there. She said Dakota was her neighbor. Does that mean in the same building? Or the building next to theirs?*

He didn't know any other way to find the mysterious woman. He'd convinced himself it was Emily. And if it was, she was in definite need of a rescue. She'd fallen far since he'd known her. Now she appeared to be road-weary, maybe an addict. *But will she remember me?*

Will she even care?

He thought romantically about the escapades of their youth. What a summer! Long walks, sweet strawberries from her farm, and oh-so-delicious kisses.

His approach wasn't well thought out. If anything, his plan was flawed by his own tendency to reach out to those who were hurting around him. He couldn't help it. He recognized their need in their faces, in their expressions. They might not verbalize their request for help, but he could see they needed it. And he couldn't stop himself from responding.

But will Emily want help?

Or will she resent me as an unwelcome reminder of her past?

He waited an hour, trying to redeem the time by alternating his visual scan of the area with reading a line or two from his pediatrics textbook. By six, his appetite called. There was a small grocery across the street. He left his car to get something to eat.

The store was a mom-and-pop operation. An Asian man smiled at him from behind the counter. Christian nodded and began to stroll the aisles. He selected some Combos and a soft drink, promising himself he'd eat something healthy that night.

The bell on the door of the grocery rang. He looked up to see her enter, along with Mike, his young patient. She didn't see him at first. In fact, because he ducked behind a stand of potato chips, she didn't see him until he was within arm's length behind her. He called her name tentatively. "Emily?"

She turned. *A reflex.*

Christian nodded at Mike. "Hey, sport."

"Hi, Doc."

Dakota Jones shook her head and backed away. "You must have me confused with someone else."

He squinted. The voice was Emily's.

Now he shook his head. "Emily, it's me, Christian."

"My name is Dakota." She took Mike's arm and led him down the aisle toward the frozen foods. Away from Christian.

"Okay, Dakota," he said, following her. "How are your parents? Do they still own a strawberry farm?"

She turned on him, glaring. She was a mother bear, fangs bared. "Get away from me, you creep."

He held up his hands. "Emily," he said softly. "I never forgot you. Even in Africa, I—"

"I don't know who you think I am, but I don't need you stalking me!"

The grocery-store owner approached. "Dakota," he said. "Is there a problem here?"

She placed one hand against Christian's chest and shoved. "Not if this guy backs off."

The green eyes. He would know them anywhere.

Christian took a step back. "What's going on?" he said. "We were close once."

"I don't know you!"

"Okay, okay," he said, backpedaling up the aisle. "You look just like someone I knew." But even as he spoke, he could see the recognition in her eyes. This was an act for Mike. For the grocer. For anyone else who didn't know who she really was.

He paid for his items and weaved among the cars stopped at a light to the other side of the road where he'd parked his car. There, instead of eating, he tossed the Combos in the passenger's seat and pulled out.

So much for finding my old lost love.

The officer torqued Tori's arm behind her back and slipped her into handcuffs. "Ow!" she gasped. "Is this really necessary?"

A minute later, she found herself with Phin in the backseat of a police cruiser.

"Where are you taking us?" Phin asked the officers sitting in the front seat.

"Downtown. It seems someone wants to question the lady about a murder."

"This is crazy. I didn't murder anyone. I'm a doctor."

She looked around the backseat. Trapped. No handle on the inside door. She was separated from the officers by a coarse metal sheet with diamond cutouts, almost like a thick chain-link fence.

Tori spoke again, a little louder to be heard over the racing engine. "I know Captain Ellis. He asked me to come in so that I could be protected as a witness."

"That's funny. An APB was issued by that very captain. Seems you knew too many details about a murder, stuff only the killer would know."

"What are you talking about?"

The officer glanced in the rearview mirror. "Save it for the captain."

It was awkward sitting with her hands behind her back. It put a stretching pressure on her chest. "What's going to happen to our car? I left my medications in my bag. I need them."

"What you need to do is stop talking."

Phin spoke up. "She had a heart transplant. She takes medicine to stay alive all the time."

Tori watched in the mirror as the officer rolled his eyes.

"And I asked for your opinion?"

"This position is painful. It puts pressure on my surgical wound. Can you at least cuff my hands in the front?"

"We're not going far, honey."

Tori and Phin exchanged looks. He looked frightened. In a moment, she watched as he closed his eyes. She understood. *He's praying.*

She nodded. She needed to pray. It felt like a natural impulse, but foreign at the same time. She had little practice, but an urgency in her soul prompted her. There wasn't time for wordiness. "Help us," she whispered. "Help."

Fifteen minutes later, the officers led them in to a small room, empty except for a table and one chair. Phin would have to stand.

The officers left. Tori stared at her reflection on the far wall. A one-way mirror, she imagined. Someone on the other side was cackling at her misfortune.

A minute later, Captain Ellis entered and closed the door. "Well, well," he said, reaching for her handcuffs and unlocking them. He did the same for Phin, who immediately started rubbing his wrists. "Sorry for all that over-the-top drama. It was the only way I knew to get my boys to really pay attention and bring you in."

"You mean it was all a game? I'm not really a murder suspect?"

He laughed. "Of course not. I told you to come in so we could get you to a safe place. You didn't seem to be coming in on your own, so I had to bring you in myself. I can't be responsible for your safety if you're running all over the country."

She looked at Phin. *What to believe?*

"Was Dakota Jones working for Baltimore PD?"

"What?"

"Answer the question," she said. "Dakota was really Emily Greene, wasn't she?"

He sighed. "Okay, sounds like you're figuring this out. I didn't believe your little story at first. I mean—" He hesitated. "I just found it so incredible that I wasn't sure if you were crazy or what." He raised his face to look in her eyes. His expression was one of pure sincerity. "I'm sorry I didn't believe you. But once I saw Dr. Jaworski's interview, I knew that Emily's heart was talking to us from beyond the grave." He stood and clasped his hands together. "I became convinced that the knowledge you have could only be from our Emily. She was onto something big, about to break a real drug ring that involved the free clinic and a handful of palliative-care nurses and maybe even a dirty cop."

Tori took a breath. A deep cleansing breath of relief. "So you know about a dirty cop?"

"We have our suspicions. I've had internal affairs working on this for some time." He shook his head. "But Emily knew something that put her life in jeopardy. Since seeing your interview, we think someone may have started the fire to make it look like Emily had a reason to jump."

"But she was thrown out, wasn't she?"

His expression was sorrowful. His voice was soft. "We think so." He unclasped his hands and made a ceremonial clap. "So where does that leave us? I have a dead psychiatrist, the only person who knew the truth about what Emily knew." He paused. "And I have you."

Phin spoke up. "In other words, she's your whole case."

He nodded. "I need you to tell me what you can about this number 316. Could it be an address? A combination? A locker number or something? When Emily found out that the drug ring involved someone inside the police department, she wouldn't have known who she could trust. I think she hid information in order to keep the police from finding out."

"I think you're right," Tori said, her voice lifting with excitement. "I've always had the impression that the number was a location— a drawer, a combination, or a locker. I'm not sure why. What was revealed on the tape?"

"Only Emily telling you to memorize this number, that it was the proof to make a bad person pay."

"Only she didn't say 'bad person.'"

"I'm only being polite," he said, smiling.

"I'm afraid I don't remember anything else."

"Okay," he said. "I'm going to have Officer Bundrick take you to a remote safe place."

"I need my luggage from the car. It has my medicine."

"Your car has been brought to our lot here. You can collect your things on the way out."

Outside, Officer Bundrick helped them put their luggage in the back of a white police van. Tori looked at the seats in the back of the van, and her relief balloon started a slow leak. "We have to ride back there?"

Bundrick nodded. "Afraid so."

Phin shook his head. "There are no windows."

"The captain wants us to institute something he calls protective ignorance. If you don't know where you're going, you can't give away your location."

The officer held out his hand. "I need your cell phones. You won't be able to use them where we are going."

"I can just switch it off," Phin said.

Bundrick shook his head. "It's part of the protocol."

Tori looked around the parking lot and flinched. In the last spot next to a chain-link fence sat a dark SUV with tinted windows. *Just like the one in front of Phin's house.*

She dismissed her apprehension. *There has to be a million of those.*

She followed Phin into the back of the van and buckled up. Immediately, a feeling of claustrophobia set in. She took Phin's arm. "I don't like this."

"I wish we could talk to Officer Campbell," Phin said. "None of this is making sense."

"What's your gut say?"

"You don't want to know."

"I'm scared." She tightened her grip on his arm. "I want to know."

"Ellis is too smooth. I think he's on the take."

"Phin, what's going on?"

"One of two things," he said, running his fingers through his hair. "If Ellis is telling the truth, then we're going to be fine and we're protected."

"If he's not?"

"Then he's getting rid of us like he got rid of Mary Jaworski and Emily Greene."

She looked at her watch. "Let's memorize our route. It feels like we're turning right."

"Okay," he said. "And we're in stop-and-go traffic."

A few minutes later, the van turned left and accelerated.

That's when Tori began to cry.

37

"Sixteen minutes in. The van is accelerating. This must be the inter-state." Tori rehearsed the turns that they had made.

Phin sighed.

"Are you feeling sick?"

"I don't like not being able to see out." He looked at Tori and brushed her bangs away from her forehead. "We used to have this schnauzer when I was growing up. Every time we were in the car, he hung his head out the window. And for a while when I was a kid, it seemed I was always getting carsick. My mom threatened to hang my head out the window like the dog."

Tori pounded on the wall behind the driver. "Hey, we're feeling sick back here."

No response. The van sped along.

Phin took deep breaths. "I'll be okay."

After forty minutes, they seemed to be getting off the inter-state. They came to a stop and then the travel was stop-and-go for a while.

By fifty minutes, they lurched to a stop. In a few moments, Officer Bundrick opened the back door. They exited into the moist air. Tori inhaled. There was seawater nearby. "Where is this place?"

Bundrick's eyes narrowed. "Nice try." He pointed at a gate in a high wooden fence. "You're staying in the guesthouse out back."

They walked around a massive and beautiful Cape Cod–style home with a broad wraparound porch. Fifty yards across a lush green lawn bordered by azalea beds sat a one-story guest facility. It too had a wraparound deck, connected to a pier that extended into what appeared to be a river or some sort of inland waterway. In different circumstances, it would be a place for a dream vacation, and Tori would have been excited about exploring. Instead, she gripped Phin's arm and walked toward the house.

After a few steps, she turned back to the van. "My luggage."

Bundrick smiled. "I'll bring it up later. Let's check out your new digs."

Inside, the guesthouse was clean, decorated like a typical beach house. A seascape hung over a stone fireplace. A large glass lamp was filled with seashells. Wooden lighthouses punctuated shelves containing an array of novels and biographies. A large leather couch sat in front of the fireplace. The wood floors looked like knotty pine. The wall closest to the water was dominated by glass, with an unobstructed view of the covered pier and the water beyond.

The floor plan was open. The great room was divided by a counter topped with a deep-gray speckled Corian. On the counter, a plate of cheeses and sliced apples sat next to two wine glasses, a bottle of Merlot, and an assortment of crackers.

"I called ahead, thinking you might be hungry. Enjoy the appetizer. I'll let the kitchen staff know you've arrived." Officer

Bundrick poured the Merlot, coloring each glass halfway to the top.

Tori exchanged glances with Phin. She wasn't sure whether to relax or be on guard.

Bundrick pointed to an open door leading to the master suite. "The bedroom is in there."

Tori looked around. "There's only one bed?"

The officer smiled. "There's a second one in the loft."

She followed his gaze to a loft above the kitchen, overlooking the great room. A wooden spiral staircase led to the overlook.

With that, Bundrick handed glasses to Phin and Tori and exited toward the main house.

Phin sipped the wine. "This all looks great," he said, shaking his head. "But I still don't trust him. I want my phone back."

Tori sampled the cheese and crackers and realized she was ravenous. She spoke between bites. "Mmm. This is wonderful."

"Let's check out the pier."

They walked to the water's edge. The lawn was bordered by a concrete bulkhead. On the water, a jet ski crisscrossed the wake of a larger craft. A ski boat rested on some sort of harness just above the water under the roof covering the pier.

"I'd love it if they'd let us use the boat. I'd have brought my bathing suit if I'd known," Tori said. But even as she said it, she touched the top of her sternal scar and wondered how hideous she would look to Phin in a bathing suit with a raised pink scar diving into her cleavage.

Phin sighed and moved next to her. The sky was beginning to color. It had been a long day since leaving their hotel.

Tori leaned in against him. "Do you think the captain was telling the truth about Emily Greene? Do you think she was about to bust a dirty cop involved in a drug ring?"

"It sounded like the truth." Phin put his arm around her shoulder. "But I don't understand the different message he gave to Richmond PD."

Tori yawned, suddenly aware of her fatigue. "Wow," she said. "This wine is potent. I can barely keep my eyes open."

"Me too," he said, lifting his glass to his lips again. "Maybe I'll crash on that couch before dinner."

"I'm claiming the master bedroom."

"Oh, so I get the loft?"

She giggled. Her lips were tingling.

They swayed, arms around each other, as they walked back up the pier to their new little hideaway.

"How long will we have to ss-sstay?" she said, but the words felt too heavy to spring from her tongue over lips that felt large and lazy.

Phin's image blurred. She leaned on him, and they stumbled forward.

Inside the house, Phin tried to remove his arm from around her shoulders but knocked her head as he disentangled himself.

Tori looked at him, aware of her lowered inhibitions. She wanted to kiss him and fought back the urge to push him onto the couch.

As it was, she didn't need to push. Phin fell onto the couch as his wine glass crashed to the floor. Tori managed to set her glass down before landing on the couch beside him.

The wine was drugged.

She wanted to tell him, but her voice wouldn't cooperate.

He looked at the mess on the floor. "Ooops." He then looked at Tori, but his eyes didn't seem to focus. "You're sssso beautiful."

She fought to stay awake.

Phin lifted a hand toward her face but dropped it onto the top of her head instead. He patted her like a dog. "Good girl," he said slowly.

They both laughed.

His expression changed to alarm. "Drugged," he said.

Tori nodded but couldn't seem to control her head. It rocked forward and back like one of those baseball bobblehead dolls. She tried to catch her head in her hands to slow down the wobbling, but her hands glanced off her forehead in an uncoordinated slap.

Everything around her slowed. *What is happening?*

She felt warm. Delightfully so. She had no inhibitions. And she knew it and didn't care.

She stared at Phin and tried to focus. Her head fell against the couch and remained still. She was aware that she had fallen partially on top of Phin, their legs tangled and her blouse pulled up. Rather than horror, she felt only amusement at the clumsy and provocative way they had fallen. If she were able to speak, she would have urged Phin forward. She wanted to kiss him, but she felt so tired.

She closed her eyes.

When she awoke, she watched a doctor plunge a needle into Phin's arm. *He isn't a doctor, is he? It's Bundrick.*

She watched helplessly as the officer dragged Phin across the floor to the railing of the spiral staircase and handcuffed him to a metal post.

Then Bundrick returned to her, lifting her upright on the couch. She felt only half conscious. Bundrick tugged at her blouse, lifting her toward him by her neckline. *Will he rape me?*

Tori fought back an image of a bad man reaching for her.

"The drugs will help you remember, Dr. Taylor." He gave her a light slap on the cheek. "Wake up. Tell me where Emily hid the information. Tell me about 316."

She shook her head. Even if she could remember, she would fight not to tell this monster.

"Well then, let's create an environment that will help you remember."

Officer Bundrick walked outside to the woodpile stacked in the corner of the wraparound deck. *Fire*, he thought. *Fire may be just what I need to trigger her memory.*

His cell phone sounded. He looked at the ID. Ellis. He flipped open his phone. "Hello."

"Talk to me. Are you getting any information?"

"Just starting." He looked up at the main house. "By the way, love the place."

"Look, I'm alone now, so I want you to start explaining. What did you do to Mary Jaworski?"

"I used the fentanyl my sister gave me from the clinic. One big syringe and she snored like a lumberjack."

"You're a sick man."

"Well, thanks to this sick man, you're a rich man, don't forget that."

"I don't like it. Things are getting too messy. Why did you have to mail the doctor her own heart?"

"It served a purpose, just like the phone calls. It freaked her out. I hoped she'd have sense enough to stop prying."

"Just find out what she knows. Then get rid of them. I want this to be over."

"I'm on it. Quit worrying."

Bundrick closed his phone, lifted an armload of kindling and wood from the stack, and walked back into the guesthouse.

He looked at Tori, sprawled on the couch with a glassy-eyed expression. "Hello, doc. I thought a fire might be romantic."

Tori watched as Officer Bundrick bent down at the fireplace and lit the base of a stack of kindling. In a few moments, the fire crackled, and he began to add split logs for fuel. He appeared to be in no hurry.

She kept looking at Phin, hoping his slumped body would begin to move, but he only snored.

Bundrick looked back at Tori. "Now isn't this romantic. You, me, a bottle of wine, a roaring fire …" He came back to her and grabbed the edge of her collar. Ripping it open, he sent her buttons bouncing across the wooden floor and exposed her brassiere. He tapped the scar and spoke directly to her chest. "Okay, Tori, or should I say, Emily? Talk to me." He traced his finger along her scar as a smile curled the edges of his mouth. "Where did you store the evidence?"

She moaned, unable to think.

"Emily," he said, "listen to the fire. Remember how the walls began to burn? Remember how it sounded that day? You and Christian about to die. What did you tell him? Think, Emily, think!"

"I ... I don't remember."

"What did you say on the tape? You talked about a man who hurt you, a man who killed your mother. You hid that during your background check at the academy, didn't you? Did you change your name, Emily? How did you fool us?"

Bundrick lifted a knife and pressed the point into her neck. Then, he traced it along her scar and let the blade come to rest under her bra. He lifted the blade and pulled the cups of her brassiere away from her skin.

"No!"

He let the bra snap back against her skin. He grabbed her by the back of the head, pulling her forward to the edge of the couch. "Emily, tell me about the numbers. Is it a storage unit? An address? A code?"

Tori thought about the numbers. *Memorize it! It's the proof.* She gasped. "It's a verse!"

"A verse?" Bundrick jerked her off the couch and pulled her across the floor toward the fire.

He shoved her forward, her face warm, then hot, from the flames. He pulled her back to safety. "Three one six!" he shouted. "What does it mean?"

"I don't know such a number."

"Where did you hide the evidence?"

He shoved her face toward the fire again.

She screamed and closed her eyes. Her world turned red as she sensed light through her eyelids. Then, in a moment, she was transported back. *Fire. My arm is burning. Run. Run to the hallway.*

Behind her, a man screamed.

Evil. An evil man.

I killed him.

He will not hurt me again.

Tori took a deep breath, inhaling hot air and smoke. She choked. "I ... I re-mem-ber."

Bundrick yanked her back again into the cooler air of the room. "A locker," she said. "My locker."

He pulled her back to the couch. Her cheeks were hot. She smelled the acrid odor of singed hair.

"Tell me about the locker."

But she couldn't. The room was turning from darkness to black.

She felt his hand tapping on her chest. "Talk to me. Remember."

She tried to answer, but her voice wouldn't cooperate. She listened as Bundrick cursed. She felt her body being lifted and then tossed aside onto the floor.

38

Her next conscious thought was of soft, billowy comfort. She opened her eyes and in the dim light could see the outline of her bed partner.

Suddenly aware that she wore only her undergarments, she quickly gathered a sheet around her. In doing so, she uncovered Phin, who lay next to her wearing only a pair of plaid boxers.

The scent of smoke was in the air. She nudged him, first gently, then with force. "Phin, wake up." She pushed down on his chest, pressing him into the mattress. "Phin!"

He groaned and opened his eyes. "Tori?"

"Phin! What are you doing here? What did you do to me?"

His hand explored his face. His lips smacked as if he awoke from a deep sleep.

"Phin! What did you do?"

"Me? Nothing?" He looked at his own body, apparently as confused as her. He slid from the bed, rolling clumsily onto the floor and pulling a blanket around his waist like a skirt. He wobbled to his feet, reaching for the foot of the bed. Once stable, he lifted his hands to the side of his head. "Whoa, I'm drunk."

The wine, she remembered. *The wine was drugged.* Tori took a deep breath and coughed. "Me too."

"I smell smoke."

She nodded. Her lips felt thick, her tongue fat and uncoordinated. "I remember Bundrick starting a fire in the fireplace. He used it to threaten me. He wanted me to tell him what Emily knew." She rubbed the back of her neck. "What did he give us?" she asked. "My head is throbbing."

"Not sure."

"How did we get here?"

He stretched. "Not sure of that either." He rubbed his eyes. "We need to get out of here." He paused. "Listen. He may still be here."

She felt anxiety rising. "Let's get out of here."

No sooner had she spoken than the piercing note of a smoke alarm began to sound.

"Now!" she said, looking for her clothes. *How did I get here?*

She remembered Bundrick jerking her from the couch, shoving her face toward the fire. *What did I tell him?*

"Get up," Phin said.

"Where are my clothes?"

"Can't worry … about … that now," he said. He stumbled toward the door. Halfway there, he tripped on the blanket he'd gathered around him, pitching his body forward against the door. "My legs won't work." He shook the door. "We're locked in."

He looked at a window, but it appeared to be covered by plywood. He crawled over and pounded his fists against the window before collapsing again.

The alarm continued to shriek, each note sharpening the knife of fear in her gut. She turned to the nightstand and lifted a phone from its cradle. She punched 911. "Ugh!" she said. "No dial tone."

Tori stood and coughed. The ceiling was dark, swirling. She felt light-headed and nauseated. The room began to spin.

Smoke poured from under the door. "Stay low," Phin said. "The smoke will rise."

She dropped to her belly. "What's going on?"

"Bundrick must have put us in the bed, then set the place on fire."

"He's killing us, Phin. He found out what he needed and now he's killing us, just like he did Emily Greene. Bundrick must have been the man in the dream."

"Think, Tori." He coughed.

She fought off the feeling that she would pass out. Phin crawled on his hands and knees beside her, his body shaking with violent spasms of coughing.

Tori reached for his back. "My head is already fuzzy. He handcuffed you."

"Handcuffed?" He rubbed his wrist. He shook his head and spoke haltingly. "I just remember walking on the pier. Feeling drunk."

"Not exactly drunk. Remember the wine and cheese."

"The w—" Phin coughed again. "Wine."

She could hear the noise of the fire beyond the door.

Where do we go? What can we do?

She tried to scream, but her voice was weak. "Help!"

Phin grabbed her wrist and started dragging her with him along the floor.

Smoke collected in a thick layer just above their heads. Phin coughed and crawled on, pulling her to the master bathroom. "We'll fill the tub," he said.

She looked for windows in the bathroom—there were none. She kicked the door closed, slamming it against the wooden frame behind them.

Phin turned on the water. "Get in. We'll soak the blanket and hide beneath it."

The water slowly rose around them. As soon as there was an inch in the bottom, they pushed the blanket down to saturate it with water. Tori splashed the water onto her face and hair. Phin did the same. For a few moments, their only communication was the fear they exchanged with their eyes. Then she reached for him and began to cry. Phin gripped her hand. "I'm with you."

The tub was big enough for two, one of those fancy ones with whirlpool jets like Tori had in her bathroom back home in Richmond. Once the water had risen over their legs, they covered themselves with the saturated blanket, making a small tent, but the air quickly ran out beneath it. When Tori pulled the blanket back from her face, she was greeted with smoke. The fire just beyond the door consumed the oxygen, leaving them gasping, coughing, and frantic.

They were not yet burning, but without air, the room seemed a certain tomb. "We're going to die if we stay here," she said. "We can break down the bedroom door."

But every time she lifted the blanket, the air seemed to vanish.

"Can't," he said. "We can't even walk."

Phin scooted around and encircled Tori with his arms, pressing his face next to hers. "I need to say—" He stopped in a spasm of coughing. "Something before I die."

"No," she cried, coughing against his face.

"I—" he coughed.

The room darkened, filling with smoke.

"Tori—" His voice was barely a whisper. The fire beyond the wall roared its sentence of death. "I ... lo—"

His eyes unfocused. She sensed him slipping away. Every breath brought another series of fitful spasms. The air was not friendly but deadly.

Tori took a shallow breath and held it until everything went black.

39

The sensation of being cold, hands beneath her armpits pulling her toward cool air, the scrape of her back against a shard of glass. Someone dropped her on the grass and disappeared again.

A minute later, she looked up to see a man dragging a large sack through a window. She shook her head. It wasn't a sack; it was a body, pulled along the ground and cast as a log beside her.

A man knelt to listen to the body's face. He placed a finger against his neck and then began chest compressions.

Slowly she emerged from a cloud of confusion, a world where images and words were slow and uncoordinated.

She looked at the body the man was working on. *Phin?*

No!

He wanted to tell me something!

She struggled to sit.

"God, please," she gasped.

The man doing compressions looked over. "Dr. Taylor."

She nodded.

Phin gasped and coughed.

She heard the warble of a siren somewhere in the night.

She moved so that she could see Phin's face. It was blackened by ash. She put her fingers against his neck and felt for a carotid pulse.

The man dropped his jacket around her shoulders. "Here," he said. "Cover up."

"He has a pulse," she said.

Her mysterious rescuer wiped his forehead. "Is there anyone else inside?"

She thought about Bundrick. "A policeman was there," she said. "I'm sure he's gone."

"Bundrick? He left thirty minutes ago."

"Who are you?"

"Gene Davis. I'm with the FBI."

She looked up to see a trio of rescue-squad personnel running toward them.

In minutes both Tori and Phin were on stretchers, wearing oxygen masks and covered in warm blankets.

"My back," she said.

A female paramedic nodded. "Roll over so I can see."

Tori cooperated.

"Ooh, you've got a nasty cut."

"My fault," the FBI agent said. "There was some glass left on that bedroom window."

Tori coughed. "No problem." When the coughing spasm passed, she reached for the agent's hand. "How did you find us? How did you know we were in trouble?"

"Gus Peterson called me this afternoon. We used to work together before I joined the Feds. He told me he'd tried to reach Phin's phone and how worried he was in light of the other threats and the death of the psychiatrist." He shrugged. "I owed Gus a favor. He took a bullet for me."

"Sounds like Gus."

"I followed the pings of Phin's cell phone as it communicated with the cell towers, so I knew the general direction you were moving. Meanwhile, Gus did some checking and found out that Captain Ellis had left a money trail. He thought his tracks were covered—he'd set up a dummy corporation and used an offshore account. But his corporation made a major real-estate purchase last spring, and the amount caught Gus's attention." He held up his hand toward the house. "You're looking at Ellis's beach house. Not in his name exactly, but his, nonetheless."

"Whoa. A police officer with a second home?"

The agent nodded. "Exactly." He paused. "This place was pretty well hidden from his staff back in Baltimore."

Tori understood. Ellis was no dummy.

The FBI agent pointed at the wooden fence. "I've had the house under observation from that vantage point for the past hour. I saw Bundrick leave. A few minutes later, I saw the smoke and realized what he had done."

Phin struggled up on one elbow. "Where are we?"

"A place called Gibson Island on the western shore of Chesapeake Bay."

Tori nodded and looked up to see firefighters dragging a large hose across the lawn.

Tori and Phin were placed in separate rescue vehicles and rushed toward the nearest hospital. On the way, Tori counted four additional fire trucks heading toward their little Gibson Island hideaway.

Once they were in the hospital emergency department, chest X-rays were taken and blood tests for carbon monoxide confirmed that the pair had significant smoke inhalation. They were admitted for high-dose supplemental oxygen.

A surgeon repaired Tori's back laceration.

Two hours after their ordeal in the bathtub, they were admitted to the same room on the second floor of Anne Arundel Medical Center.

Gene Davis entered their room with another man wearing a dark suit. Gene smiled. "Glad to see you two alive and breathing." He nodded at the man to his right. "This is Special Agent Andrew Lightner. He will be assisting in this investigation."

"Where are we?" Tori said.

"A hospital in Annapolis. For obvious reasons, we didn't want you taken back into Baltimore. I've talked to everyone involved in your care, including the rescue-squad personnel. You've been admitted under the names John and Jane Doe for your own protection."

Phin's eyes widened. "Okay."

"We're just at the beginning of an investigation of the Baltimore PD on the basis of our communications with Gus Peterson. I'm going to need your cooperation."

Feeling safe for the first time in days, Tori smiled. "Sure."

"First things first," Gene said. "You're dead."

"What?"

"Well, not actually dead, but pretend dead. We've talked to the fire department, and they are releasing a statement for the media that two bodies were found at the Gibson Island residential fire."

Phin frowned. "Two bodies, Tori and me?"

"Right," the agent said. "The bodies were described as charred beyond recognition. We want the police responsible for this to think their little plan worked. They will assume you're dead, so no reason to look for you. We think the corruption goes beyond just Officer Bundrick. Certainly it involves the captain, but beyond that, we don't know."

"Ellis told us that Emily Greene had uncovered a drug ring involving some free clinics, palliative-care nurses, and maybe a dirty cop."

"Perhaps his only honest statement, something he wouldn't have done unless he was sure you'd soon be out of the way." Gene took a deep breath. "So here's how we play it. We put Bundrick and Ellis under investigation and watch their movements carefully. They may get sloppy if they think everyone who can implicate them is dead."

"So what about us?"

"You stay here until you're recovered. Then we talk about you hiding out somewhere other than Baltimore or Richmond."

"You're not going to release our names to the media as dead, are you?"

"We don't have to. Bundrick and Ellis will be comfortable that you're dead based on the account we've given of finding the burned corpses."

"Okay."

"It's getting late. We'll need more information from you. We can do that tomorrow. There'll be a guard just outside the door."

The agents excused themselves, leaving Phin and Tori alone.

In a few minutes, Phin slipped off on the opposite side of his bed. He unlocked the wheels and rolled it up against Tori's. Then he crawled back into bed and rested his head on his pillow. "I thought we were dead," he said.

"Me too."

He smiled. "What a way to die." He laughed.

"It's not funny."

"It's kind of funny, knowing we didn't die."

"What do you mean?"

"I mean, isn't that every man's dream, to die in a Jacuzzi in the arms of a lovely woman?"

Tori giggled. "You're hopeless, you know that." She shook her head. "Bundrick must have wanted everyone to think that we died in bed together."

"What's the last thing you remember?"

She looked at him and felt her eyes brimming with tears. "I remember you putting your arms around me. I remember the smoke. I couldn't get my breath." She sniffed. "You tried to talk, but you couldn't."

"I wanted to say something before I died."

"Looks like you've got your second chance, cowboy."

He reached over the edge of his bed. She did the same, and they interlocked fingers.

She gazed in his eyes.

He took a deep breath, coughed once, and wiped his mouth. He touched his oxygen mask. "Look at us, both on life support," he said.

"This isn't exactly life support."

He smiled. "Whatever."

"What did you want to say?"

He brushed back a tear from his eye and looked above her head to a cardiac monitor that recorded the rhythm of her heart. It was steady *beep, beep, beep,* right at 80 times a minute. He squeezed her hand. "Tori Taylor, I love you."

The monitor verbalized her response. *Beep, beep, beep,* but now at a new rate, clipping happily along at 96.

40

Christian's encounter with Dakota in the small Asian grocery brought him both clarity and more questions.

Emily recognized me. She's putting on an act.

But why?

What has happened to the Emily Greene that I knew and loved?

His heart warmed to the memory of her. Was it possible that he had really known true love at such a young age?

No one else has stirred my heart like she did.

He lay on his bed in his small apartment, wishing for another chance. He needed to meet her alone, with no one to interfere.

In the grocery, she had seemed to be putting on an act, not for him, but for the few others in the store.

He looked at his clock and sighed. It was past midnight, and he had early rounds in the ICU in the morning.

Maybe in the afternoon, he'd try to find out her apartment number and visit with her alone.

Maybe she was just embarrassed because of how bad her life has turned. Maybe she didn't want me to recognize her. She didn't want the others to know.

Christian sighed and wished for sleep. When it remained elusive, he reached for the leather-bound book on his nightstand.

He flipped on the light and whispered a prayer. "God, help Emily Greene."

Two days after being dragged from a burning building, Tori met Gus Peterson face-to-face for the first time.

She let herself be enveloped in his strong arms, and for a moment, she rested her chest against his and wondered just what stories the heart of his donor was speaking.

"Your new rental car is in the B lot," he said. There are two suitcases there, one for Phin and one for you." He smiled. "Packed 'em myself."

Phin laughed. "This ought to be interesting."

He dropped a plastic Wal-Mart bag on the bed. "Here's some clothes for today."

Tori lifted a pair of jeans, a white blouse, and a pair of sandals. "Not bad, Gus."

"It was easy to find clothes for you," he said. "Your drawers are neat. Everything's folded. But this guy," he said, pointing at Phin. "Haven't you ever heard of actually folding your shirts?"

Phin protested. "I'm the only one who sees."

"Until now." Gus sat in a visitor's chair beside Tori's hospital bed. "So what's next?"

"We're going to the Eastern Shore. I want to see Emily's parents."

"Be careful," he said. "What does Gene think of that?"

"He's okay with it, as long as they understand that they can't tell anyone they've seen me alive."

He handed her a phone. "Use this. It's a pay-ahead cell that I picked up on the way. You can't use yours if you're dead, can you?"

They stood, and she hugged him again. "You think of everything."

Tori moved to the bathroom. "I'll change in here," she said. "I'll be glad to shed this hospital gown."

When she came out again, Phin had changed into jeans and a green polo.

"Let's go," Gus said. "I'll show you to your car. You'll have to drop me at the rental place so I can get mine."

It was nearing 1:00 p.m. as Tori used the rental car's navigator to search for seafood restaurants. They selected the Watermen's Inn in the small town of Crisfield, Maryland. It required a small detour, but Phin convinced Tori that Eastern Shore seafood wasn't to be missed.

He was right. She had she-crab soup followed by a hot crab dip served on French baguettes. Phin had shrimp-stuffed mushrooms followed by an oyster sandwich.

They had a relaxed meal overlooking a small inlet of the bay.

"Okay," she said. "Where has this food been all my life?"

"Right here," Phin said, sighing and wiping his mouth with a cloth napkin. They ate, talked about meeting Emily's family, and walked hand in hand toward the car.

Forty minutes later, they approached a gravel lane turning off to the right. The navigator spoke, "Arriving at destination. On right."

Tori flipped off the navigator. "Here we are."

She'd called the day before and kept her comments vague. "Would you be willing to talk to me about your daughter, Emily? I'm a doctor, and I am interested in finding out about her life and work."

Carolyn Greene had been pleasant and seemed surprised, but was open to a visit. "Could you come in the afternoon? My husband will be home then as well."

Tori looked out over the strawberry fields. "Wow, look at all those berries."

They approached the white farmhouse hand in hand. They were met at the door by an elderly couple. The man extended his hand. "I'm Billy Greene. This is Carolyn. We're Emily's parents."

"Tori Taylor," she said, taking his hand. "And this is my friend Phin MacGrath."

"Shall we sit on the porch? It's such a nice day."

They sat on wicker furniture, and Carolyn served Southern sweet tea. "You said you were interested in Emily's work. What's this about?"

"Actually, although we aren't law enforcement, we are assisting the FBI in an investigation. I'm, well, let's just say I'm considered a witness for a case against the Baltimore PD."

Tori watched for a reaction. Other than a few nods, there was no indication of hesitancy.

"We understand that Emily was working undercover as a police officer."

"Yes. We are quite proud of her."

"Before—". Tori hesitated. "Before the accident," she continued, "we think that Emily was working on busting up a drug ring and think she may have been collecting evidence that implicated members of her own police department. Did she tell you about her work?"

"Her undercover work was so secretive," Carolyn said. "She could speak about it only in vague terms."

Billy sipped his tea noisily. "She sent us a picture of herself from her phone. Didn't look a thing like her. Short hair. Dark."

Carolyn leaned forward. "And all those extra earrings."

"We saw her the weekend before the fire," Billy said. "She was troubled, only stopped in for a few minutes and said she'd have more time soon."

"It was odd," Carolyn said. "She wouldn't stay for lunch, and I had prepared a strawberry shortcake and everything."

"Did she have anyone else close to her that she may have confided in, a boyfriend perhaps?"

"No, no boyfriends, at least none recently."

"I need to tell you something. I don't want to upset you," Tori said. "But I really want to find out the truth for Emily's sake. She put a lot of effort into her work, and I wouldn't want to see it go to waste."

"Of course." Billy patted his wife's wrinkled hand.

"I don't believe the fire was an accident. I've come to believe that it was an attempt to cover up a murder."

"A murder?"

"I believe Emily may not have jumped that day. I believe she was pushed or thrown from the window, and the fire started to cover it up."

Billy cleared his throat. "We don't know much about that."

"Did you know the man who jumped with her?"

"Christian? Oh, yes. Chris and my Emily were high school sweethearts. The curious thing is, we hadn't heard she'd had any recent contact with him until after the fire and we heard about his death. It's so sad. Hopefully Emily will tell us someday what was going on."

Phin and Tori exchanged glances. She nodded. "Of course."

"Would you like to see her room? We've kept things much the same since she left for the academy."

"Sure."

Tori and Phin followed the couple through the front room and into a hallway to Emily's old room.

"She loved this room," Carolyn said. "Every time she came home, even the last time, when she stayed only a few minutes, she spent time here."

Tori looked at the collection of sports letters and photographs decorating the walls. A shelf of track ribbons and trophies sat above a small wooden desk. A picture of Emily in her blue police academy uniform hung on the wall by the door. Along the far wall was what appeared to be a series of gym lockers, one tall one in the center and three square ones on each side, each labeled with an initial, A through F. On the front of the long locker, beneath the number 91, was a sticker with what appeared to be a black-and-yellow hornet. On the emblem were the words *Northampton Yellow Jackets*. "Emily was quite an athlete, I see."

"The lockers were from her old high school before the renovation. They offered to give them to the varsity athletes. Just a keepsake."

Tori nodded. "Sweet."

"She loved to run." Carolyn wrapped her arms across her chest as if protecting a heart that had been broken by the loss of her daughter.

Somehow, being in this room, Tori felt warmed. Somewhere inside her, she felt *love* for Emily. Not just because she respected her work. It was something much deeper. It was just there. Almost tangible like something you could hold in your hand and treasure.

She *loved* Emily.

"I should tell you something else. She saved my life."

"What? Emily saved you? She was always downplaying her role. But we know in her police work, she helped a lot of people," Billy said.

"Not in her police work," Tori said. "By her heart."

She looked at Carolyn, who seemed to be struggling with understanding. Tori had felt it best to approach the subject of her heart transplant slowly. She reached for Carolyn's hand and pulled it toward her own chest. "Would you like to feel you daughter's heart again?"

Carolyn pulled her hand away. "What are you saying?" Her face was etched with alarm.

"Mrs. Greene, when your daughter died, she donated her heart to me."

Carolyn backed up a step, shaking her head. "Y-you … what are you saying? Is my daughter dead?"

"Surely you knew—" Tori locked eyes with Phin, and her hand covered her mouth. "Oh, Mrs. Greene, I'm so sorry. I thought you knew."

But Mr. Greene stepped forward and put his arm around his wife in support. "Now hold on. These things don't happen without people being told. Emily isn't dead. We'd *know* that. I saw her just Friday morning."

Now Tori stepped back. "I don't understand."

Billy shook his head. "Emily didn't die in that fire. She didn't even die jumping from that building. She's here on the Eastern Shore at Oyster Point Rehabilitation Hospital, just like she's been every day since her release from Baltimore City."

Tori slid down and sat on the bed. "Emily's alive?"

Phin stood silently, mouth agape.

Tori put her hand over her chest. "Then whose heart do I have?"

41

"Where should we go?" Phin asked, tapping his fingers against the steering wheel.

Tori shrugged. "Just drive. Let's take the Bay Bridge-Tunnel." The Chesapeake Bay Bridge-Tunnel was a marvel, with long sections of bridge extending over open water between man-made islands that served as the entry points to the underwater tunnels.

She opened her phone and scrolled through her contacts to the Virginia Commonwealth University Hospital operator and pressed "call."

She asked for Dr. Paul Griffin, a resident in surgery, to be paged.

After five minutes, she had him on the phone. "Paul, this is Dr. Tori Taylor."

"Dr. Taylor, how are you? Are you back at work?"

"Not exactly. Listen," she said. "I need some information. Remember the night we went down to Legend Brewing Company?"

"Boy, do I. We need to do that again. My treat this time."

"Thanks, but I'm not calling to suggest we grab a beer. You told me something that night that I've relied on, something that has turned out to be bad information."

"What are you talking about?"

"You knew I was trying to find the identity of my heart donor, right? And I asked you about a particular woman who had jumped from a window to escape a fire. I asked you if that was where my heart came from. And you said yes. But now I find out that the woman actually survived the jump. So what gives?"

"Dr. Taylor, you showed me an article from the *Baltimore Sun* about some jumpers who escaped a fire. You asked me if that was where your heart came from and I didn't lie. That is where your heart came from. But it wasn't from a woman. You got the heart of a young male."

The realization struck her like an ocean wave. *Dr. Christian Mitchell.*

Of course.

She mumbled a thank-you and closed her cell phone.

Phin touched her arm as she sat in stunned silence. "Well?"

"Christian Mitchell," she said. "I assumed when they indicated my heart came from the jumpers, that it had come from Dakota. But it came from Christian." She sat still except for nodding her head and occasionally murmuring. "Aha."

"What are you thinking?"

"Just that it's all starting to make sense. I saw the face of Emily Greene. It wasn't the face from a mirror. It was through Christian's eyes. The love I feel for Emily must be from Christian. He loved her. The number was something she must have given to him to memorize. My intuition about Mike's cancer diagnosis was because Christian treated him in the free clinic. He knew all about the cancer."

She opened her phone again.

"Who you calling now?"

"Gene Davis."

She called and explained what she had learned about her heart donor. Gene said "Hmm" about ten times through the conversation. Finally, she asked him what he was thinking.

"Obviously, Captain Ellis and his men don't know this. They took your word for it that Emily was dead." She heard a pen clicking against a hard surface. "We can use this to our advantage." He paused. "I've got an idea. Yes, this just might work. Yes, I like this," he said.

"What?"

"Let me check a few things out. Are you still in the area?"

"Going over to Norfolk tonight."

"Fine. Lay low another few days and this will all be over. I'll call you."

A few minutes later, she looked out over the expanse of water as it extended to the horizon from her vantage point on the Chesapeake Bay Bridge-Tunnel. Gingerly, she touched the front of her shirt, laying her hand over her heart. She needed time to process this new information. She didn't have Dakota's heart. She had the heart of Christian Mitchell.

So what was he like?

She rolled down her window and let her curls fly in the wind.

She exchanged glances with Phin. "You're quiet."

"Just thinking about Christian Mitchell. I'm trying to digest all this." She halted and inhaled the salt-laden air. "What was he like?"

Phin didn't answer.

After a few minutes of silence, she spoke again. "I like the idea that he was a pediatrician."

Phin nodded. "Someone who cared about children."

She nestled into her seat, comfortable with letting the silence hang between them. Finally, she squeezed his hand. "Let's go over to the Norfolk Omni. I'll treat you to dinner. We can go over to Virginia Beach and stroll the boardwalk."

"Wow," he said. "I could get used to life on the lam with you." He grabbed her hand. "Lucky my supervisor back at VCU is understanding."

Forty-five minutes later, they lifted their suitcases from the trunk and let the valet at the Omni Hotel park their rental car.

At the desk, they used Phin's card. When he asked for two rooms, he looked over at Tori. "I wouldn't trust myself in the same room with you," he whispered.

"Why?" she whispered back. "I trusted you in the bathtub, didn't I?"

He rolled his eyes. "Deadly smoke is such a turnoff."

She smiled.

They took the elevator to their floor. "Now let's see how Gus packed."

"Let's go over to the beach and walk," he said. "We have a few hours before dinner."

"Sounds great."

A few minutes later, Tori had changed into a pair of khaki shorts and shed the long jeans. She kept on the white blouse. She marveled that Gus had added some lipstick and mascara. *He must be married.*

When Phin joined her, he lifted the Gideon Bible from inside the dresser drawer. "Here," he said. "I found a verse for you." He turned to Ezekiel, paging over to chapter 36. "Here it is. Granted, I'm taking this out of context, but when I read this, I thought about how much you've changed, how new and open your heart is toward God. Look what he says here. 'And I will give you a new heart, and a new spirit I will put within you. And I will remove the heart of stone from your flesh and give you a heart of flesh.'"

She nodded, blinking back tears. "Yes, so much has changed. It's amazing my old heart of stone had any rhythm at all." She sniffed before starting to list some of her changes. "I cry a lot." Then she laughed. "And I am more open. To love," she added. "For God," she said. Then she turned and put her arms around his neck and added, "And you."

He kissed her gently and then eased away and caressed his finger against the top of her scar, sending chills down the back of her neck. "I don't understand just how much the change has to do with this new heart or whether God just did his work in you with the furnace of adversity." He paused. "I don't really care. All I know is how I feel toward you."

She kissed him again and grabbed a sheet of paper from a pad on the desk. She wrote 316 in block letters the way she remembered the paper Emily had given her in the memory. She wanted to mark the verse in the Bible so she could reread it later that night. She held it above the open Bible and dropped it, but it skidded off and twirled to the floor. She picked it up again, turning it from upside down to right side up again.

"Wait a minute," she said slowly, drawing out her words. She turned the paper upside down, staring at the paper and repeating, "Wait a minute!"

"What?"

"Phin," she said with excitement. "I think I know where Emily hid the evidence."

42

It was eight o'clock and the day drawing to a close as Christian sat in his car watching the apartment. He had become obsessed with finding and helping Emily and now thought of little else. Maybe it was the challenge of her apparent rejection. Maybe it was the hope for a rekindling of their teenage romance. And maybe it was because she appeared so *lost* and he couldn't stand to think of her that way.

Regardless, he sat watching, sometimes praying, and always wondering what was really going on with this woman who now called herself Dakota.

He saw her a few minutes past the hour. She was carrying a sack of groceries and heading toward the building next door. He jumped out and followed her, thinking this might be his chance to talk to her without others around.

She punched some buttons on a panel to unlock a door. She swung it open. Christian had come up silently behind her and leaped forward just in time to catch the door. He climbed the stairs quietly a flight behind her, following her footfalls. She exited on the fifth floor. He came out of the stairwell and saw her standing next to a door, the sack of groceries on the floor as she fumbled for a key.

"Emily."

She looked up. This time, her expression was softer. She looked down the hall past Christian and then over her shoulder the other way. When she saw no one, she motioned and whispered, "Christian."

He followed her into her apartment. Things appeared to be in disarray. Boxes. Two suitcases by the door. "Are you leaving?"

She nodded.

He continued to scan the room. It was sparsely furnished, a far cry from the luxuries of a girl who drove him to school in a BMW convertible. "What has happened to you? What's going on?"

She looked at him and shook her head. She went to the window and looked out and shut the blinds.

"Are you in some kind of trouble?"

"I'm a cop," she said. "I'm working undercover."

"That's why you denied—"

"Yes, that's why I treated you the way I did." She continued to pace, as if she was looking for something.

"We are in danger," she said. "I've been doing some digging and I've come up with some pretty tough stuff. It involves my own department. I don't know who I can trust. I think someone is trying to set me up to look guilty." She hesitated. "Either that, or they'll just kill me so I can't say anything."

"Can't you go to the FBI or someone outside the department?"

"I'm going to. I had to put the evidence together."

"Evidence?"

She nodded. "A money trail and a trail of drugs that comes right through that clinic I saw you in. That one and a dozen others like it."

"They're collecting narcotics from dead patients. I saw them."

"That's just one strategy. I'll bet they have you writing for large numbers of narcs, don't they?"

"The director told me it was necessary for the palliative patients. They have a big tolerance and need more drugs."

"Yeah, I've heard it all." She went back to the window again and looked out. She stiffened, then cursed. "Oh no. You've got to leave."

"What's happening?"

"A cop is coming up here." She frowned. "If he sees this stuff, he'll know I'm onto them. He'll know I'm planning to run." She pointed. "Help me with these suitcases. Put them under the bed in the back room."

When he came out, she whispered, "Too late. He's at the door."

"We can go out the fire escape."

"No, there's another cop in the alley."

She ripped a piece of paper from a small pad. "I've collected a lot of evidence. If I die, someone needs to take it to the Feds." She wrote something down on the paper, but Christian was nervous and dropped it as she handed it over. "My locker. Memorize it."

He picked up the paper, turning it in his hands.

"Memorize it," she yelled. "It's the proof. I want to make that bastard pay."

He shoved it into his pocket just as the door burst open, evidently kicked in by the bulldog of an officer who now faced them.

He grabbed Emily by the neck and slammed her against the wall. Christian ran toward him, but the man sidestepped and crashed his fist into Christian's nose. The man dragged Emily screaming into the back room.

Christian's world was spinning. He crawled to his feet and started to follow the sound of shouting voices. He heard breaking glass. As he entered, he watched in horror as the man threw Emily against the window. It offered little restraint. Her body tumbled outward, her leg tangling briefly in the window before her shoe flew off and she slipped through the jagged opening.

The uniformed man snarled. "You're next."

Christian held up his hands, but his mind was still cloudy from the first hit he'd taken in the other room.

Strong hands hoisted him up and through the window.

Briefly, he was weightless, flying.

And then nothing.

Tori slept late the next morning, curling herself in the fresh memories she was making and successfully warding off memories of fire, evil men, and abuse. She awoke and thought about the walk she'd taken down the beach with Phin. Hand in hand, enjoying the warmth of the Virginia Beach sand between her toes. The evil still lurked, but she was quickly learning to whisper a prayer. "Deliver us from evil."

After breakfast, they headed back over the Bay Bridge-Tunnel, and soon they were again driving up the long lane to the Greenes' white farmhouse.

Billy and Carolyn met them on the front porch. "We didn't expect to see you so soon."

"I'm so sorry for the confusion yesterday," Tori began. "I found out the truth." She paused. "My heart did come from Baltimore City Hospital the night Emily was admitted. But my heart obviously didn't come from her. It belonged to Christian Mitchell."

Carolyn gasped. "He was such a nice young man. He was a doctor, wasn't he?"

Tori nodded. "A pediatric resident at Johns Hopkins."

Carolyn's eyes glazed. She seemed to be focusing on something on the horizon. "He grew up in Africa. He wanted to return there someday as a Christian missionary."

Tori nodded. *Yes. That feels right.* She looked at Billy.

"You said you wanted to look in her room?"

"Yes."

Phin followed her down the hall to Emily's room. There, she took out the bookmark she'd made by writing the block numbers 316. She turned it over and handed it to Phin. "Read it now."

"Three one—"

"No," she interrupted. "Read it this way. Upside down."

"Ninety-one. E." His eyes widened.

"Exactly," she said. "Christian must have seen the paper upside down. It was never 316. It was 91E." She turned to Carolyn and Billy. "You said Emily came to her room the week before the fire. I think she left something here."

Tori walked to the old high school lockers, the one labeled "91." She reached for the square locker that bordered the larger full-length one. It was labeled "E." Inside was a locked metal box.

She lifted it. "Ever seen this before?"

Carolyn shook her head. "Emily must have brought it in her leather satchel. I remember that's all she carried that day."

"I'm calling Gene Davis. I'm sure he'll want to look at whatever is in here."

Phin smiled. "How did you—"

"I saw it back at the hotel when I dropped the bookmark labeled 316." She pointed her head toward the lockers. "And I remembered seeing this."

She called Gene Davis and told him of their discovery.

"Are you with Mr. Greene now? Could I speak to him?"

She handed the phone to Billy Greene. Tori listened to his half of a several-minute conversation, mostly "uh-huhs" and "yeses."

He handed the phone back to Tori. "Yes?"

"Stay put, Dr. Taylor. We've got a plan, and I think you'll want to watch. We'll be there in a few hours to set up."

"Here? You're coming here?"

"Close. We're coming to the rehab facility to see Officer Greene. Tell Billy to wait an hour before he makes the call. He'll know what you mean."

With that, the called ended.

"Okay," she said, looking at Billy, "what's up?"

He smiled. "A little trap," he said. "He's gonna let Emily nail the coffin of the boys who tried to kill her."

Ellis felt like spitting nails. As soon as Steve Bundrick came into his office, he shut the door to vent. "I can't believe this. Why didn't you check out the doctor's story? How can Emily Greene still be alive?"

Bundrick shrugged. "When the doc said she'd had a heart transplant and Dakota Jones was her donor, I had no reason to believe she was lying."

"She wasn't lying. She was just wrong." Ellis stood and paced his office. "I should have checked. I thought the same thing. I assumed you checked."

"And I thought you did." Bundrick sighed. "I'd talked to Emily's father just a few weeks before, and he said she'd been in a coma so long that they were asking for additional tests to see if Emily still had brain activity. So when that doc came in here telling me she had Emily's heart, I assumed the tests must have shown that Emily was brain-dead."

"Who do you think encouraged him to push for the tests?" Ellis shook his head. "I told Mr. Greene that Emily was so full of life she would never have wanted to live like that. He agreed."

"Still, I should have double checked." Bundrick cursed. "I should have known that if we hadn't been notified of a funeral, something wasn't adding up."

"We should have killed her a long time ago."

"Yeah, well, we didn't."

He pointed his finger at Bundrick's chest. "You're an idiot." He huffed. "And you better be glad your little fire didn't spread to the main house. I thought you were going to dump them in the bay."

"Yeah, I thought about that. But how would it look if the last place they were seen was here and then they disappeared? And I checked it out. The main house was a good thirty yards away. No way the fire could have spread."

"You'd better be glad I have insurance."

"Relax. I knew it would be okay."

"It's not okay. With Emily alive, we still have a loose end."

"She's in a coma. She can't hurt us."

"Oh yeah? Her father called me a few minutes ago with the great news that Emily is waking up. He expects them to take out her trach tube soon so that she can communicate." He stood and paced his little office. "So it looks like we've got another job to do."

"I'll take care of it."

"No," he said, shaking his head. "I'll go myself. I'll need some fentanyl."

"Sure." He sighed. "I feel bad about this."

"Forget it. The sooner we put this behind us, the sooner we can get back on the path of green."

"When do you need the drugs?"

"I'm leaving in an hour. Tell Clara to lay low for a few weeks. Stop pushing the new doctors so hard. Somebody's going to push back if they get suspicious."

Tori and Phin sat with Gene Davis in the back of a large utility truck in the parking lot of the Oyster Point Rehabilitation Center, watching a flat-screen monitor. He moved a small joystick and the image on the screen changed. "See," he said. "We have a full view of Emily's room." He centered the camera over her bed so that they could see Emily clearly.

Tori studied the frail woman on the screen and wiped a tear from the corner of her eye. Her emotions swelled like a wave. She touched her blouse in front of her surgery scar. "Emily," she said, her voice weak.

Phin gripped her hand. "What are you sensing?"

She hesitated and kept her eyes on the screen. "Love."

She took a deep breath, not wanting to fall apart in front of Agent Davis. Instead, she focused on the plan at hand. "What happens if he doesn't use a drug? What if he tries to smother her?"

"Agents Wilson and Chang are across the hall. They can be on him in seconds."

"And if he injects a drug into her IV? What's to stop that from killing her?"

"Her IV is a prop. It goes into a bandage on her forearm, but there's no connection to her blood. If he gives an injection, it will just leak into the bandage."

"Won't he notice the bandage is wet?"

"We'll turn the IV on at a very slow rate just before he comes into the room. The bandage can absorb the drops. Remember, he's going to want to get out of there."

"May I?" Tori reached for the joystick. She moved it so that she could focus in on the IV bag. "What do you know? It's not dripping."

"Not yet."

"You know he's coming?"

"Bugged his office. We know he's coming."

Tori looked at Phin and held his hand. "I feel better every day."

Gene readjusted the camera view to show the doorway. "My boys busted the lock off that metal box. Emily Greene knew how to do her homework. Everything is dated and timed. She's got palliative-care records, scanned prescriptions, photographs, and even Ellis's private financials."

"All that in there?"

"Most of it's on a flash drive."

"Wow."

Thirty minutes later, a late-model Honda Civic pulled into the parking lot. "That's him."

The FBI agent nodded and keyed his radio. "Start the IV drip."

Tori reached for the window control but was stopped by Gene's hand on hers. "Keep the window closed," he cautioned. "I do want to see his reaction when he realizes you're alive, but not just yet."

Tori nodded.

Gene communicated with the agents inside. "Ellis has arrived. He should be in the building in a few minutes."

Ellis was dressed in a blue blazer, a white shirt, and a dark tie. They watched from the truck as he entered the building.

"Ellis is inside," Gene said.

"Okay, we're watching," Chang responded on the radio.

Tori watched the video feed on the flat-screen. Ellis's silhouette filled the doorway. He looked at Emily, who lay with eyes open but unfocused. Her blonde hair had started to grow out, making her roots stand out in contrast to the brunette she had become undercover.

Ellis wasted no time. He shut the door and moved a chair to block it so that if someone entered, the sound of the door bumping the chair would warn him. He glanced at the IV and smiled. He pulled something from his coat pocket.

"He's got a syringe," Tori said.

"Keep watching."

Ellis took the cap from the syringe and shoved it into a side port on the IV. He pushed the plunger of the syringe forward, emptying the clear contents.

Instead of watching, he quickly moved the chair and exited. He didn't want to be anywhere close when Emily's respirations ceased.

The radio sounded. "We're coming out behind him."

"Good. I've got the front door covered."

Gene let Tori step outside the truck so that she could have a full view of the front door.

When Ellis stepped outside the hospital, he picked up speed— until two agents approached from the front with weapons drawn. His face paled as he slowed and stopped. Agents Chang and Wilson slipped up behind him, cuffing him with minimal effort.

A minute later, when the agents escorted Ellis through the parking lot, Tori stepped from behind the truck and called his name. "Oh, Captain," she said. "I wanted to thank you for hosting me at your wonderful island home."

"You!" He wrenched his arms free from the grip of the agents and rushed forward.

Tori jumped away, but the furious Ellis was still able to graze her with his shoulder, throwing her off-balance to the pavement, before he ended up facedown on the parking lot beneath two burly FBI agents. Tori twisted her ankle in her fall, and she felt the fresh wound on her back strain against the sutures.

Phin helped her to her feet. "Are you okay?"

She smiled. "I haven't felt this good in a long time."

43

Two hours later, after a long wait in the Nassawadox General Hospital ER waiting room, a physician finally evaluated Tori for her swollen left ankle.

The physician held the X-ray up to the light. "I'd guess you've had trouble with this ankle for some time."

"It has hurt a bit in the last few weeks. Nothing serious—just an aggravation."

The ER doctor smiled. "Well, the good news is that there is no fracture."

"And the bad news?"

"Did I say there was bad news?"

"When a doctor starts like that, there's always bad news coming."

He chuckled. "That old screw seems to be working its way out," he said. "I'm not surprised it's been bothering you."

"Old screw?" Tori didn't understand.

"It's nothing urgent," he said, reaching for her ankle and turning it to palpate along her medial malleolus, the bony prominence of the inside of the ankle.

Tori shook her head. "I've never had any surgery on that ankle before."

He laughed. "Oh, you jest. Looks like you had a pretty nasty break here at one time." He looked at her and squinted. "Years ago, perhaps."

She looked at Phin, who shrugged.

The doctor continued. "Just call your orthopedic surgeon when you get back home. I suspect they'll want to take that screw back out."

"You must have mixed up the X-rays," she said. "I've never had any surgery on that ankle."

While the doctor moved closer to read the name on the X-ray, an image flashed through Tori's mind. *An evil man. Bad teeth. "You little witch!"*

"Tori?" Phin touched her arm.

"Lay her down," the doctor said, turning back toward her. "I think she's having a vagal response. She's fainting."

The man slapped her, sending her backward against the wall. She stumbled into the stairwell. She reached for the banister and missed, rolling, tumbling, bouncing to the landing below.

"Tori." Phin's voice.

She took a deep breath. "Oh, wow," she said.

The doctor put his hand on her wrist. "You almost fainted." He leaned over her foot and adjusted a gooseneck lamp into position. He twisted the switch and illuminated her ankle. "See," he said, tracing a small scar on her ankle. "You've just forgotten. Here's your surgical scar."

She nodded. "Oh, God," she whispered. "The dreams were mine after all."

Two days later, Tori lay on the leather couch in her suburban Richmond home with her sprained ankle propped on a large rust-colored pillow. Phin, sitting in a chair next to Tori's old friend Charlotte Rains, opened a folder.

Tori felt her jaw slacken. She let her mouth open, all the while knowing how incredulous she would appear. But she didn't care. In fact, she *was* incredulous. "Why didn't you tell me I was adopted?"

Charlotte took a deep breath. "Your parents tried to tell you, but any time they initiated the discussion, they said it upset you. Then, after you started that fire at Disney World, your counselor suggested they wait until you were more mature. They were afraid. Then, the longer they waited, and you finally adjusted, they feared how the news might affect you. Your mom still wanted to tell you, but then your father died, and after that, your mother got ill." Charlotte held out her hand, palms up. Surrender. "When she gave me your birth certificate, she told me that she didn't know how it could ever help you. You'd obviously blocked out your former life."

Phin leaned forward. "They were protecting you." He took her hand. "You suppressed some pretty rough stuff so you could function." He paused. "But when the memories started to resurface, it was easier and less threatening to let them come out because you thought they were someone else's."

Tori sighed. "This is so unbelievable. Some of the memories were Christian's."

Charlotte nodded. "And some were those of a little girl from Richmond, Virginia."

Phin handed her a copy of an old news article. "Gus did some research," he said.

She read the old news article. A fire in a downtown apartment high-rise took the lives of Nadine Benson and Clive Stiller. Tori looked up. "Nadine? Manny's wife?"

Charlotte nodded. "Manny told me you guys were neighbors."

Tori kept reading. Arson was suspected. A third body was found in the burned apartment, the body of an Eva Trexler. Trexler had been dead before the fire started.

Phin handed her a copy of a birth certificate for Victoria Anne Trexler.

She looked up. "Me?"

Charlotte nodded again.

"So Eva Trexler was my mother?"

"And Clive Stiller?"

Phin paged through several documents. "Gus was able to get some old documents from social services. The evidence pointed to arson, and you were their prime suspect." He paused. "The article says you were found hiding outside the burning apartment inside an enclosed playground slide."

Tori understood. *I remember the slide.*

Phin continued. "Clive was an abusive drunk. He abused you and your mother. They think you started the fire to stop him but not before he killed your mother. The district attorney looked at your case but never wanted to prosecute because of your situation."

"I guess I didn't burn my arm on a motorcycle muffler either."

Phin shook his head. "I'm not sure how you came up with that idea. Maybe your adoptive mother suggested it as a way to answer other curious children."

"This means I started the fire that killed Manny's wife." She hesitated with her hand covering her mouth. She began to cry. "That's what he meant when he said he knew what I'd done, but he forgave me."

Tori struggled to her feet and lifted a pair of crutches that leaned against the couch.

"Where are you going?" Charlotte asked.

"Nowhere. I just need to pace." She limped over to stand in front of a glass sliding door that opened to her backyard, shaking her head slowly. "I can't believe Manny knew this all the time. He even put his trust in me and let me operate on his cancer."

Tori felt a hand on her shoulder and turned to see Charlotte. "Manny loved you. He knew you were only a young child."

Tori took a deep breath. "So much of my life has been a lie."

Phin stood up. "Not a lie, Tori. A misunderstanding. You closed up to protect yourself."

She moved away from her friends, trying to process the new information. *I escaped a fire.*

A fire that I started.

She didn't know what to feel. Guilt? Sorrow? Relief? But she hadn't lived with guilt, because she'd locked away the pain. It was difficult to feel immediate sorrow because she'd lived in ignorance of the suffering she'd caused. And although she wanted to know she was forgiven, she hadn't yet processed the guilt.

Mostly, Tori just felt numb.

Phin walked over and put his arms around her. "Are you okay?"

"Time," she said. "I'm just going to need some time."

44

Two weeks later, Tori answered the phone in her study. "Hello."

She recognized the voice as he said her name. "Tori, it's me, Dr. Evans."

"Yes."

She listened as he sighed. "The Board of Visitors met this week. I need you back at work."

"Really?" She paced around her desk. "So soon? Why did they change their minds?"

"I convinced them."

"And what convinced you?"

"Phin MacGrath. His report is rather remarkable. He assures me that you are a different woman."

"You have your doubts."

"We've worked together a long time."

"So what gives? Something must be different. I know you, Dr. Samuel," she said, daring to use the chairman's first name. "Tell me the truth."

"The truth? I need you back. Your patients are asking for you."

"My patients?"

"Well, one in particular. A woman named Kesha has called my office a dozen times this week alone." He imitated her voice. "When is Dr. Taylor coming back? My son won't see anyone else."

Kesha! I should have known.

"Can you start in the morning?"

"Tomorrow?"

"We have a new group of third-year medical students coming in. I need you to give them the orientation lecture."

"Now I see. You hate giving that lecture." Tori tried unsuccessfully to suppress a giggle. "Okay, Dr. Evans, I'll come back."

"Oh, Tori—you should know that Steve Brown isn't working out. The man's got an ego the size of Texas. Our nursing staff is actually asking for you."

She smiled. "I'll see you in the morning."

"The lecture is at eight. Don't be late."

She hung up the phone and sat at her computer. She brought up her lecture notes for the introduction to surgery. She read her opening aloud. "Between the gods and men … are surgeons."

She set the cursor and hit the delete key. *I know better now. The only mediator between God and man is Jesus.*

God, I was arrogant. Help me.

She wrote another opening line. "Surgery can be the most rewarding career in the world."

Sappy. But true.

Her computer emitted a soft note to indicate the presence of a new email.

Happy for the diversion, she clicked on the new letter and began to read.

Dear Dr. Taylor,

I was given your email address by the transplant coordinator at VCU Medical Center. You see, beating within your chest is the heart of a real champion. I should know. It once beat within the chest of a man I loved with all my heart, my son, Christian.

Tori leaned forward and slowly read every word. Inside, she felt her heart quicken.

From the time he was a teen, he possessed a real gift. Christian could sense pain, fear, joy, and sorrow from the subtlest clues. But more than that, he had a remarkable ability to respond with compassion.

Tori lifted her hand to her lips. She let a sob escape her lips. *My heart!*

She continued reading, anxious for a glimpse into the life of her donor.

More than anything, Christian had a love for Jesus. My prayer is that his heart would beat long enough within you until you know the meaning of my words.

She felt her heart thrill. *Jesus.*

Christian Mitchell loved you. Tori laid her hand across her chest as she prayed. *Now I do too.*

I loved him so much and my sorrow is a well that I think will never be quenched.

Sincerely,

Dan Mitchell, MD

Tori wept for the Mitchell family, knowing that their loss was her only chance at life. She wept with tears spilling over and dropping onto her computer keyboard. But her tears were not only those of sorrow. Her tears carried a message of hope, the knowledge that her new heart beat a rhythm of love and joy. A smile interrupted a sob as she brushed the tears from the keyboard.

Tori whispered toward the computer screen, lifting her head so that her tears fell onto her shirt over her heart. "Thank you, Christian."

She paused. The moment seemed alive.

She sat in silence for a minute or two before whispering again. "Thank you, Christian, for your heart of flesh."

... a little more ...

When a delightful concert comes to an end,

the orchestra might offer an encore.

When a fine meal comes to an end,

it's always nice to savor a bit of dessert.

When a great story comes to an end,

we think you may want to linger.

And so, we offer ...

AfterWords—just a little something more after you

have finished a David C Cook novel.

We invite you to stay awhile in the story.

Thanks for reading!

Turn the page for ...

- **Getting to Know Harry**
  - **More from Harry**

GETTING TO KNOW HARRY

If we could sit down together, I'd want to hear your story. Everyone has one.

If you think I get up each morning, fill up my drip coffeemaker, and settle in with my laptop to play with my imaginary friends (my characters, okay? I'm not really crazy), then think again. Oh, I've had days when I wonder what that kind of life would be like, sitting in a wood-paneled office with my fingers busy on the keyboard, uncovering the great American novel, stopping in the afternoon to read email correspondence from adoring readers. But my life is far from the typical novelist: I've spent most of the last decade slugging it out day in and day out with the enemies of surgery in equatorial Africa. Enemies, you ask? Sure. HIV, cancer, bizarre tropical infections, trauma, and tuberculosis, just to name a few. Just this week, I've had to repair a femoral artery severed during a bone-splintering car accident, removed a huge (yes, that's a common word we use to describe the cancers here) abdominal tumor in an elderly woman (I had to remove a portion of her stomach and colon just to get around it), stent open an esophageal cancer, help an old man urinate by removing the bulging prostate gland that had shut off his stream, and carefully excise an overactive thyroid that had caused a young woman's heart to race without an external cause.

The writing part of my life comes at the bookends of days filled with sweat and blood. The sweat is mine; the blood, my patients'. My clinics are filled with people who have long ignored their cancers and have often visited "traditional healers" who only worsened their situations. There is little time during the day to turn my thoughts to the craft of fiction, so that comes when the lights in the clinic are off and the last patient has either been admitted or found a ride up the rutted road toward the highway.

I've been doing more and more work outside Kenya these days, because medicine opens the way into places of political turmoil and trouble, places where Christian missionaries are unwelcome. And surgery provides a practical way to love people desperate with physical needs and hopefully provide a small glimpse into who Christ was and is.

What is it that motivates me, that makes me tick? Why sacrifice my comfortable life in America for this? And why, for that matter, do I spend the hundreds of extra hours it takes to write novels?

It is not my love of writing or a passion for story (although I am passionate about those).

It is not my love of surgery (although that too is a passion of mine).

My greatest passion and motivation is to see Christ treasured in the hearts of all people. That may sound like an impossible goal to get a handle on, but I believe it is helpful to understand the target and how my work may or may not fit.

To this end, I believe medicine (and surgery in particular) is a wonderful field of God-sent opportunities: people come to surgeons when they are in crisis. And these crises create a situation where people finally start asking the right questions about eternity. Many of these people would never seek out a pastor; but, by necessity, they find themselves in my office. And there, with permission, we hope to offer compassion, prayer, and the science and art of healing surgery.

Here in Kenya, I practice in a mission-hospital setting, and many of the patients come face-to-face with the gospel during their hospital stays. It may be a word from a physician, a nurse, the woman who mops the floor, or a chaplain, but my prayer is that everyone has an opportunity to hear the greatest news ever!

This same philosophy guides my writing. A novel is way too long of a project to write simply for entertainment. Don't hear me wrong! I think entertainment is important; if I can't capture and entertain, no reader will hang in there to the end. But in the process, I hope that a small message of hope, faith, or grace is absorbed. My desire is that Kraus fiction will nudge people closer to a life where Jesus is treasured. To that end, I desire my protagonists to be real: people with problems. Not all of my protagonists are Christians; many, like Tori in this book, find faith as a result of the conflicts they face. When I write about a Christian character, it is important to me to show them as real people with real-life issues. Christians struggle with doubt, Christians have pain, Christians are tempted, Christians fall, get angry, and struggle with materialism and lust. So, if you are reading Kraus fiction, expect a transparent look into real life. You won't see a rose-petal-strewn pathway for the Christians in my novels. That's just not reality.

I hope that if we ever have any real face time together, you will see the same kind of transparency in my life. I'm a Christ follower, but I am a ragamuffin. I sin, and I don't like wearing masks that say "I've got it all together." Lots of folks like to put authors, surgeons, and missionaries on pedestals; so you understand, some people have a way of putting me in an elevated place where I don't deserve to stand. When I look down, I'd better be standing on a pedestal of grace, or I'm setting myself up for a fall. I sincerely believe that the world doesn't need more perfect Christians; the world needs transparency! Christians who are willing to say "I haven't got it all together, but I'm holding the hand (actually, I'm engraved on it!) of God, who does."

MORE FROM HARRY

Fiction:

The Six-Liter Club

Salty Like Blood

Perfect

The Claire McCall Series:

    Could I Have This Dance?

    For the Rest of My Life

    All I'll Ever Need

Serenity

The Chairman

The Stain

Lethal Mercy

Fated Genes

Stainless Steal Hearts

Middle School/Young Adult:

A Zebra Tale

Inspirational Nonfiction:

Domesticated Jesus

The Cure: The Divine Prescription for the Body of Christ—
    Life-changing Love

Breathing Grace: What You Need More Than Your Next
    Breath

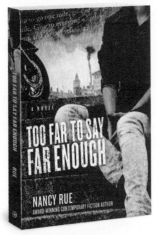

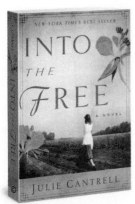
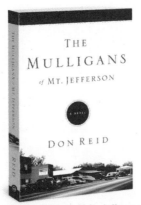